Whispers of the Past

By
Lena Roach

© 2016 Lena Roach

Published by Entrada Publishing.

Printed in the United States of America.

Contents

DEDICATION

To Jeremiah, Jude, Marie, Danny, Cameron, Brandon, Lauren, Jessica, and Matthew who are my inspiration.

Chapter I

Tonight was the night.

Tomorrow it would all be gone.

Heartbeat racing under the lace collar of her emerald gown, Tessa Chandelle glanced at her guests around the refreshment tables that dotted the area she'd cleared in the elegant main showroom of Chandelle's House of Antiques. So far, none of the irate creditors who had threatened to crash her farewell party disrupted the quiet buzz of conversation or the low music from the stereo.

A "Thank God" on her lips, she flipped back her shoulder-length light auburn hair and turned to accept more good-bye hugs at what should have been a traditional springtime gala.

"Jasmine Hills won't be the same without you!" the bittersweet goodbyes flowed around her.

Lifelong friends didn't have to use words to express how they felt. She read their minds in the looks on their faces. Right under her nose, Uncle Lester, her trusted sales manager, had gambled away the family home and business in the two-story mansion that had served Chandelles for more than a century. How could she have let it happen?

"You won't forget to write, to call?" She saw furrowed brows and heard the remark, "Too bad your parents couldn't be here tonight. If ever you needed them, it's now."

"Thank you, I'll be fine." She smiled at the well-meaning comments. "And some day with God's help, Chandelle's will be ours again."

She hadn't seen her folks since her twenty-seventh birthday celebration a few months back. The happy wishes were tainted with grief. That week, Uncle Lester suffered a heart attack and died.

"Leaving Jasmine Hills to conquer the Big Easy, huh, Tess?" Tall and matronly Mrs. Andrews, choir director at Little Grace Chapel, lifted her cup of lemonade in salute. "Soon you'll be the most popular interior designer in New Orleans."

"We'll drink to that!" other guests cheered.

Tessa smiled and made a playful bow. Trust them to put a happy face on the occasion.

Her side glance caught best friend Adrienne in palazzo pants, sunbright color like her spiked hairdo. She pointed to her watch. The gesture said she'd get the patio crowd inside as planned for those who wanted to say early goodbyes.

Tessa nodded, but then she picked up the faint chimes of the doorbell. A latecomer, *or a creditor?*

Determined to keep smiling, she changed courses and headed for the entry hall. As she approached the office set aside for Chandelle's soon-to-be-owner, Magnolia House of Antiques, she overheard the low-key voices of employees who'd begun setting up for business but had promised to stay away tonight:

"Can you believe it? The daughter of missionaries, she gambled away the business right along with her uncle."

"Yeah, blamed it all on him. Even passed off fakes as antiques."

"Now she's applied for a job in New Orleans. Who would want a Chandelle employee on board?"

"No wonder her fiancé broke off their engagement."

Tessa's feet froze, her smile gone. Inside her own store, the words stabbed, sharper than other false rumors she'd heard circulating around town, throughout surrounding parishes, and beyond. Once more, she must ignore them. But tonight, in earshot of anyone passing by?

The doorbell rang again.

She took a deep breath, straightened her shoulders and donned her hostess facade as she hurried across the marble tile to open the heavy, stained-glass door.

The man, a stranger, stood on the well-lit steps, an amiable grin on his face. Not a creditor? Fear nagged.

"Can I help you?" The exuberant welcome she'd given all evening had faded into mere politeness.

"Well, howdy! I'm Brian Le Moyne. Are you our twenty-first century's Miss Scarlett?" The man propped one hand on the door frame and clamped the other to his lean hip. Dark brown hair lay tousled on his forehead as if he'd been driving with the windows down. In comfortably worn jeans and a multi-plaid sport shirt, he would pass as an advocate for proper diet and exercise.

"Sorry, not Scarlett. I'm Tessa Chandelle. Pleased to meet you, Mr. Le Moyne." She rebounded from the unexpected pleasantry with a faint smile. He couldn't know she wore a southern belle's emerald gown as a sentimental tribute to her years in the antique business. That it matched her eyes was a flattering coincidence her dress designer had noticed.

"Are you the owner here?" His voice bordered on a bass.

"Part owner and manager." What else could she say? Until tomorrow?

"Okay if I come in and look around?" Brow lifting, he glanced past her toward the foyer.

"I'm sorry. We're closed."

Cobalt eyes darted to the OPEN, PLEASE RING sign dangling from the antique door handle. "That says you're not."

"Oops." Tessa pressed her lips together and flipped the sign to CLOSED. "You're right. That was careless of me, but I've been awfully busy today."

"Your ad has been in the newspaper and on TV a couple of times this past week. It says you have hard-to-find antiques and you're open Friday nights until ten. Now you tell me the place is closed?" He squinted past her as party chatter drifted out to them.

"The paper's mistake. We canceled that ad a week ago. Tomorrow the business will be under new management, and parts of the floors are roped off. Again, I'm sorry."

The man dug into his shirt pocket and pulled out a card. He grinned and handed it to her. "Proof I'm Brian Le Moyne."

"Nice to meet you, Mr. Le Moyne." She stepped back for better lighting from a lamp on the hall table and glanced at his card. President of Le Moyne Enterprises, which included KPNO television station in New Orleans, his home address in St. Pierre. At the moment, she didn't recall seeing his name on any of her uncle's papers. But dare she trust her memory?

He stepped in past her.

She dropped his card in a Limoges bowl on the desk. "Mr. Le Moyne?"

"You don't mind," he asked, dark brows going up, "if I just look around, do you?"

She hesitated. He obviously wouldn't take no for an answer. But, she reasoned, he seemed harmless.

"I'd really appreciate a few minutes." He turned back to her.

She glimpsed it then, something that stirred in the depths of his dark eyes and reached out to hers. An urgency, tinged with a haunting sadness? Whatever it might be, the fleeting moment jabbed a raw spot inside her that parted her lips in a sudden impulse to please him.

"As you can tell, we're having a party," she said, "but you're welcome to browse around here and meet my guests. Like I said, some sections are roped off."

"I understand, Miss Chandelle." His shoes squeaking on the polished floor, he headed for the showroom close by and stopped.

Tessa saw his awed gaze sweep from the dainty Queen Anne footstool beside the matching evening-blue settee, and on to the Sheraton coffee table with its glossy patina. He nodded in obvious approval toward a set of Chippendale chairs, other settees, serving trays and tables.

Pleased by his obvious reaction, Tessa suspected he must be a connoisseur of quality antiques.

"I'm impressed." He turned and walked back to her. "I should have come by sooner." He pulled a couple of photographs from his breast pocket and held them out to her. "Here's what I'm looking for."

At first glance, Tessa said, "That chair does look familiar." She nibbled her lower lip. "If we have it, the papers on it must be packed." She heard laughter and looked up. The party area was filling up with the patio crowd. "Please, you must excuse me." She handed the prints back to him. "I don't have time to check this out now."

"Sorry I bothered you." He slipped the photographs back into his pocket.

"Oh, no, you didn't."

He hesitated, as if for a final look around.

Over the years, Tessa had seen many customers desperate for a prized piece, but none more intense than this man. He might have waited until the last minute to find that choice gift for his wife or someone else special to him.

"Stay and browse as long as you like," she said. "After the party's over, maybe we can talk further and see if I can find any information about that chair." Besides doing him a favor, she was certain many of the women here wouldn't mind his addition to the party. Already smiling faces turned his way. Unobtrusively as possible, she glanced down at his hand.

No wedding ring.

Her own pleased reaction surprised her. She didn't remember the last time a man had captured her interest. Not since her breakup with Josh half a year ago.

"Thanks." The grin that flitted along the curve of his mouth told her he'd noticed where her gaze strayed.

She blushed. Flustered, she plumped a pillow on a sofa nearby and then adjusted a chair at a different angle. "You're welcome to sample the buffet, Mr. Le Moyne."

"Call me Brian, please." He'd already stooped to examine the cabriole legs of a mahogany coffee table and looked back at her with a smile.

"Okay, Brian. Make yourself at home. Besides, you might find you know some of my guests. Some are from New Orleans and Baton Rouge, as well as from St. Pierre."

"Thanks again, Miss Chandelle."

"It's Tessa." She returned his smile.

The warm glow she'd had when he seemed taken with the appearance of the room returned, but when she saw Adrienne step up to the stereo and turn it off, she remembered what she'd set out to do before the doorbell rang.

She walked up to the piano and paused, her gaze drawn to the family portraits on the wall facing her. They honored three generations of ancestors who'd built and nurtured this store—her great-grandparents,

11

her grandparents, and her parents. What would they tell her at a time like this? That she should finally forgive and forget Lester's betrayal? That she should move on?

Adrienne approached. "Just checked again," she whispered. "Only invited guests. Looks like everybody is in here now."

"Thanks." Tessa struck a few chords on the piano for attention.

"Quiet, everybody!" a male voice commanded from the back of the room. "Listen up!"

Tessa leaned against the cool hardness of the Steinway, her eyelids heavy with the tears she'd fought all day. In the gradual stillness, she folded her hands in front of her and made what she hoped was a bright smile on her face.

"Thank you from the bottom of my heart for planning this party tonight to say good-bye." She tried to put volume in her voice to hide the trembling. "One day we'll be together again."

The place crackled with applause.

"Way to go, Tess!" voices called out.

Her gaze swept over the faces. Young and old, they turned to her in the mellow glow of quiet lamplight. She wanted to absorb every detail of color and shadow in the room, of feelings and images her heart would see later and treasure. With them, Brian Le Moyne, Chandelle's last customer. Arms crossed over his chest, face somber, he looked as if he might empathize in this moment with her.

"Three generations of my family kept the place afloat." She moistened her lips. Words that had piled at the edge of her mind for hours were finally ready to spill out in the palpable silence. "My turn at the helm, and I have to let go of Chandelle's."

Giggles and applause erupted around the room. She didn't know what to make of the commotion until pointing fingers from the guests urged her to turn around. In stocking feet, Adrienne stood on a floral Louis XVI footstool. She held above her head a cardboard sign obviously scrawled in haste with the kind of red marker Tessa used to price sale merchandise: IT'S THE ECONOMY, STUPID!

The crowd cheered and clapped, and Tessa shook her head, now laughing with them. Adrienne was partly right. The economy combined with her uncle's addiction had brought down the store.

"Okay, so it's not original." Adrienne flashed the sign around. "But it fits!"

Tessa thanked her friend with a look she knew she'd understand and then turned back to the guests. "To all of you, my heartfelt gratitude for your support. When I land back on my feet, you'll be the first to hear about it."

"Yeah for Tess!" Again, a roar and wild handclaps.

Adrienne hopped off the stool and stepped into the hallway. In a moment she returned, pushing forward an easel.

"What's this?" Tessa smiled faintly, her hands propped on her hips.

"From your friends, with love." In a grand flourish, Adrienne whipped off the white cloth covering the gift. "Voila!"

Tessa stared at the painting of Chandelle's, the two-story, white colonial structure against a background of cloudless blue sky. The establishment's logo, two magnolia trees in bloom, one at both entrance and exit, graced the curved driveway. Steps like open arms led to a wide veranda. Sunshine slanted onto a porch swing, and an early-American bench flanked by rocking chairs offered a relaxed setting before an expanse of floor-to-ceiling windows.

In the waiting stillness, Tessa stepped up to the painting and touched trembling fingertips to the silver plate in the left corner, "Chandelle's House of Antiques, est. 1904." Turning, she hugged Adrienne and then blew random kisses to the audience as they broke out again in applause. Her fleeting gaze caught Brian, his attention fixed on the masterpiece.

"On behalf of my family, thank you. We will always treasure your friendship and support, the most precious gifts of all. No matter where we might go, we'll never forget you. Now, my heartfelt thanks for the grandest party ever." Glad she hadn't broken down, she let her voice ring out, "Let's enjoy it to the end!"

While some of the guests stepped up for a closer look at the painting and a few others said their early good-byes, Tessa saw Brian hesitate and then meander toward her.

"And who is this handsome young man?" Mrs. Andrews stopped him, hand extended in welcome. The two joined in the gradual movement toward the patio and the keyboard strains of "I've Got Those Jasmine Hills Blues."

Just like Mrs. Andrews, Tessa thought, to make sure no visitor went unnoticed. She indulged a lingering look at the painting. A deep sigh, she brushed off a tear, turned and headed off to check on the excitement outside. On newcomer Brian.

A full moon brightened the backyard along with electric light stands beaming here and there about the wide, newly-trimmed grassy lawn. *The last party.* The three words that formed a banner headline wherever she looked dimmed when she spotted Brian absorbed in conversation with a group of young men. She would get to him later, but now she wandered from table to table to chat with players at a chess game or with dominoes. Other guests, devoted friends from her childhood, relaxed in lawn chairs as they chatted, some misty-eyed when she paused to reminisce with them about past gatherings at Chandelle's.

Her gaze finally wandered back to Brian in a group near the bandstand. Judging from the laughter there, elderly "Uncle Dud" had just finished one of his still-popular, old alligator tales.

"I'd forgotten what fun crashing a party can be." Brian grinned as she walked up to him. "Besides, now I know how a 'gator proposes to a 'gatorette."

Their looks met and held. The dash of mischief in his tone and manner, unlike his demeanor earlier, startled her. She stopped short of saying she was glad he happened by.

"Did you have these parties often?" He gave her a raised-brow look.

"Every April and any other time the mood struck." Tessa liked the start of this relaxed conversation as they ambled toward other guests.

"We'll miss you, Tess," youthful voices called out from a gazebo in a corner of the yard.

Tessa waved and bit a tremor in her lower lip, forcing a smile, or at least what she hoped would pass for a smile from that distance.

"I think I know how you feel tonight," Brian said as they stopped by the patio. "Good-byes are never easy when you really care."

Taken aback, Tessa waited for him to continue.

He didn't.

"Moonlight at Chandelle's." She looked up at the full moon. "I'd like to scoop it up and hold on to it forever."

"Moonlight?" Brian rubbed the side of his neck. "It's like happiness. Nothing but a dream. You wake up in the morning, and it's gone."

"Not always." Tessa glanced at him and caught his averted gaze. "Happiness comes from within and stays there if you let it, don't you think?"

Before he could answer, she noticed guests coming out of the gazebo, others packing up their instruments or tabletop paraphernalia, ready to leave.

"The party's breaking up," she said, a sudden catch in her voice. "Talk to you in a few minutes?"

He nodded. "I'll be here."

She hurried away and caught up with Adrienne near the bandstand.

Adrienne glanced back. "Who's the hunk? You aren't keeping secrets from me, are you?"

"A would-be customer," Tessa said lightly. "I thought Mrs. Andrews would introduce him to just about everybody. Perfect stranger, a would-be customer. Probably married."

"Sure, and he's hunting antiques on a weekend night without his wife? Moon-gazing with another woman?" Adrienne shook her head. "Happens, I guess." Her tone said she didn't believe it.

Tessa dismissed her with a shrug as other guests joined them to say goodbyes.

An overflow of hugs and tears followed her inside. At last, with a soft thud, she closed the door on Mrs. Andrews and the end of the party, grateful no demanding creditor had shown up to spoil the evening.

Now she faced Brian. He leaned against the wall separating the foyer from the main showroom. The thought that she might help Chandelle's last customer locate a treasure became the perfect antidote to the feeling of loss washing over her. Besides, after their talk on the patio, she was intrigued and wanted to know him better.

"You stayed. I'm glad." She pointed left to a small showroom. "Let's sit in there."

She led the way past the now empty office where employees from Magnolia Antiques had been working on their office setup. Faint sounds of clattering dishes, banter among the catering crew, and Adrienne's occasional laughter drifted from the kitchen. Tessa walked into the designated room and snapped on the ceiling light. She motioned Brian to the Regency settee and sat opposite him in a matching chair beside a small table and lamp. Facing him squarely now, she noticed for the first time a pale scar, perhaps an inch long, fading into his left temple.

"You probably need another good look at these." Eagerness shone in his eyes as his tanned fingers whipped out the two glossy photographs from his shirt pocket and handed them to her.

Tessa leaned sideways and switched on the lamp to bright. She studied first one print and then the other. No doubt about it, they were the front and back views of an elaborately embellished chair, unmistakably Spanish in design, a work of art with a lively sense of strength and beauty. Masculinity showed in the overlay moldings and carvings and in the leaf-scroll sculpturing around the gold-and-red upholstered back. She wasn't surprised Brian seemed desperate to find that antique.

"It's a King Alphonse." She handed the photographs back to him.

"That's right." A triumphant smile played along the curve of his mouth. "Then you have it?"

"Let me check." She got up and went to a corner desk, opened the top drawer, and withdrew a sheaf of papers. From the corner of her eye, she could tell Brian was focused on her every move. Her nerves taut, she shuffled through the sheets until she found the one labeled Rarest Valuables. Slowly she ran her finger down the list. "It's not on here."

"Which means you don't have it?"

"It looks so familiar." Tessa hesitated. "I was almost certain it was in the warehouse." A memory flashed. She snapped her fingers. "Just a minute." Turning, she pulled open the bottom drawer and took out a file. "Like I said, I placed most of our papers in storage. But I should have another list in here—somewhere—on pieces I sold with dates. Not names, mind you, only dates. Let's see, I think maybe it was . . ." She pulled out one sheet, shook her head, and rummaged through the other pages. "Oh, here," she paused, her eyes scanning the record.

"You found it?" Brian's tone rose, guardedly cheerful. "You do have it?"

"I'm sorry, Mr. Le Moyne—Brian." She took a deep breath and turned back to him. "It was here at one time, but we sold it. More than four years ago. So rare, that's why I remember it now. I was hoping it was still one of the pieces my uncle moved to a warehouse." *Or so he said,* she thought, still upset over the fact she'd discovered half of that special inventory was missing.

Now his look sharpened on hers. "Who bought it?"

"I have no idea. I'm so sorry."

He stood, one eyebrow hiked in disbelief. "An antique like that and you don't remember the buyer's name?"

"We've handled many rare antiques through the years for customers all over the world. I can't possibly remember on a moment's notice who bought what and when. Especially something that sold so long ago."

"Surely you have that information somewhere in your files?"

"Believe me, I wish I could help you right now," Tessa said, "but the shop is changing hands tomorrow. As I told you, our other records are locked up in a warehouse on the other side of town. There are so many things I have to do before I sign the final papers in the morning. Then I'll be on my way to New Orleans for a job interview. Please, just give me a little more time."

"How about your business partner? Or an employee? Maybe one of them would remember?"

"I'm afraid not. Our employees, two couples, just retired and left on a cruise. My parents and I share ownership. They're out of the country too."

"Now what?" His chest lifted in a deep sigh.

"Check back with me in three weeks or so." Tessa would have given him her new business card, but she hadn't yet picked up her order from

17

the printer. She tore off a piece of paper and found a pen in a drawer to scribble the new owners' phone number and address. "Write or call here," she said, handing him the information. "The new staff will know how to reach me. First chance, I'll be sure to come back and check our records for you."

He tucked the note inside his shirt pocket. "I guess it was too much to expect . . . that I'd find the other chair here." He rubbed his neck, the way he'd done earlier on the patio when he compared happiness to moonlight. "It was a gift."

Tessa waited for him to go on.

A sudden closed look on his face, he turned aside.

"Don't give up," she said softly. "It's out there somewhere. Too bad I'm so pressed for time right now, but please try to be patient a little longer."

He took a deep breath, as if suddenly weary. "Well, thanks for your time." Head lowered, he started for the door. "I'm sorry I bothered you."

"Oh, no. You didn't."

"Goodnight, Tessa." Hand on the doorknob, he paused and looked back at her. "And best of luck on that interview."

"And to you—" The door closed behind him before she could finish. She rushed forward to open it, to say she wasn't sure what, and then hesitated. But she couldn't forget the sad squint of his eyes and the disappointment in his lowered voice as he'd walked off. *Dear God,* she breathed the words, *please be with Brian. I think he needs Your help more than anyone else here tonight, even myself.*

Brow knitted, her thoughts raced. She knew what she would do, had to do. Tomorrow she'd go through those files in storage. No matter how long it took, before she left for New Orleans she'd find out who bought the Alphonse.

Energized as she hadn't been in a long time, for the moment she forgot about Adrienne and the kitchen help. She forgot about creditors and this being her last night here. She forgot about everything except her determination to help Chandelle's last customer, the man who had crashed into her life, Brian Le Moyne.

Chapter II

The morning of the third day since the party, Tessa stepped into the downstairs office at Chandelle's as the Seth Thomas clock struck four. The new owners had hired Adrienne to be sole caretaker of the business for the next week and then a member of the office staff. She and Tessa spent their nights in the old home place, the time together laced with tears and laughter.

Now Adrienne propped her hands on her hips and frowned. "Changing your mind about leaving a couple of days ago, for what? To find out who bought a chair, as if that was an emergency?" She gave a disbelieving shake of her head. "You should already be in New Orleans, asleep in your La Louisian' hotel room, not on the highway in fog thick as pea soup."

"Relax, Adrienne." Tessa waved off her friend's concern. "I couldn't miss a chance to make new contacts." She slipped her free hand inside the pocket of her jeans and felt the hard edges of Brian's business card stapled to another with the Alphonse buyer's name and address. Besides, she'd programmed the information on her cell phone.

Adrienne's eyebrows shot up. "So you already gave this Le Moyne guy the good news?"

"I'll call him later in New Orleans." Tessa paused by the hallway mirror and tucked a strand of hair behind her ear.

"So it's that way, huh? A perfect excuse for him to ask you out to dinner." A teasing grin lit up Adrienne's eyes.

"Quit dreaming. After Josh, it'll be a long time before I can trust a man again."

"Oh, Tess, someone is out there waiting for you. He'll be nothing like that guy you finally broke up with."

Tessa shook her head. "From now on, it's all work and no play for me."

"But that will make Tessa—'"

"Debt free and the owner of a new Chandelle's. The family reputation tops again. Nothing dull about that." Tessa slipped her bag to the other shoulder and shook her head. "I did give you my new business card?"

"Yes, and info committed to memory." Adrienne tapped her forehead. "Now about driving off in all that fog, you'll never change, will you? Impulsive, didn't your folks always say?"

"Oh, Adrienne, stop it. You have more than enough to worry about here. I'll be fine."

"Okay, I give up." Adrienne threw her arms around Tessa. "Drive carefully and ace that interview. Call me first chance."

"Promise," Tessa murmured against her friend's mussed hair. "Now quit worrying and go back to bed. You know I hate good-byes."

"You and me both!" Adrienne's voice broke. She gave Tessa a gentle shove and dashed off as if she couldn't get away fast enough.

Tessa stepped up to the leaded glass door and reached for the knob. With a final determined twist, she pulled the door open and hesitated. Her gaze lingered on the aged magnolia trees that stood like fuzzy guards in the hanging dampness, while the wooden tub of multi-colored blooms near the flagstone walk lay shrouded in misty haze.

Head lowered, she closed the door behind her with a soft thud. She hurried down the walk that curved to her car in the driveway and climbed inside the cranky old model she had packed earlier with her belongings. From her pocket, she took out her cell phone and slipped it along with her handbag on the passenger's side beside the small overnighter with a change of clothes for her interview. A quick glance at the back seat, she checked the position of two large suitcases. Between them nestled a gift from her parents on a long-ago buying trip, the Zuni Indian jar with its hearty plant, a dwarf jasmine. Like herself, somehow it must survive.

She turned on the ignition, the wipers, and the headlights. A last look toward the shadowed yard sign, CHANDELLE'S HOUSE OF ANTIQUES, and tears started. She didn't try to stop them. Gone was life as she had known it, dreamed it would be. All because of Uncle Lester. Well, maybe not all because of him. There was Josh— She gave a dismissing shake of her head. No way could she blame all her problems on either of them. *Accept responsibility for yourself,* her parents had taught her.

She bowed her head. "Dear Lord," she whispered, "please hold my hand and never let go. Give me the strength to follow wherever you lead. And please help me to forgive Uncle Lester and Josh as you forgive me."

She reached for a tissue in the glove compartment and dried her eyes. A quivery sigh, and it was past time to adjust her seat belt and put the car in reverse. Slowly she backed out onto the street. Her foot touched the brakes, and she took one last look around. Then, with a long sigh, she slipped away from the early morning quiet of the old neighborhood.

She drove eastward into open country with alternating walls of somber mist and wispy threads suspended like aimless puffs of smoke. She turned on the car radio and listened to newscasts, then to favorite musical tapes. Windshield wipers squeaked. Minutes ticked into an hour, then two. She judged she must be near the St. Pierre road sign, Brian's hometown.

Thinking again of the store's last customer brought the start of a smile. She did believe he was single. Why was that antique chair a gift so important to him? When she told him the good news about it, maybe he wouldn't just say, "Thanks." Like Adrienne teased, he might want to see her again and ask for her cell phone number, her email address?

She tapped her forehead. She'd forgotten her computer in the office at Chandelle's. It might have answers to job applications, some she'd want to pursue if Mirbeau's interview didn't work out as she hoped, besides news from her parents in Ireland.

No time to think about that now. Between the fog and the increasing traffic she'd likely encounter as she neared New Orleans, she must concentrate on arriving for her interview on schedule. She'd have to stop at Delacroix's Gas 'n' Groceries on the outskirts of the city. Faye Delacroix, the co-owner, had an obsession about cleanliness, and Tessa had no qualms about changing clothes in that well-kept ladies room.

She squinted to check the odometer to see how far she'd driven. On the instant, the car sputtered, and then jerked with a ratta-tat. Her hands froze on the wheel. Engine trouble? She leaned forward, ear inclined.

The noises stopped as suddenly as they had started. Daring a sigh of relief, she decided the car had probably run over something on the highway and then spun it off. Yet when a St. Pierre road marker appeared, she slowed, her eyes straining for an exit sign to a twenty-four hour service station. She'd feel better if someone took a quick look under the hood.

But if a place nestled along the highway, the foggy dark hid it well. She bore down on the accelerator and then slowed, testing the engine while she listened and watched the road with a prayer the old wheels wouldn't fail her.

Another noise, this time a jarring clickety-clack. The car lurched. Frowning, she slowed to a crawl, pulled off to the side of the road and turned on the flashers. What to do? Call 911 for help? Or Brian, since she planned to see him today? She glanced at her watch—ten minutes past seven o'clock. She grabbed the cell phone from her purse, pressed the button for Brian's home number and waited, gaze narrowed ahead on mounting pockets of fog. No answer. The motor sputtered so loudly she couldn't have heard him anyway. She switched it off and tried his cell. It rang only once before she heard a click.

"Le Moyne speaking." The deep baritone voice drifted across the line with surprising wide-awake geniality.

"Brian, this is Tessa Chandelle." She cleared her throat to try to stop the quiver in her voice. "I'm sorry to call you so early."

"No problem. Your timing is perfect."

"I've got a job interview in New Orleans at nine o'clock. Just now I passed the St. Pierre road sign. My car is jerky, and it's making strange noises."

"Don't worry. Here's what you do." His instant take-charge attitude flowed out to her. "Slow down and park off to the side of the highway on neutral ground."

"I've done that."

"Lock your doors. Don't dare open them for anyone. I'll meet you in no time at all. You got the flashers on?"

"First thing I did—"

Behind Tessa, an engine growled. Her gaze flew to the rearview mirror. Those beams of ragged light, did they aim straight for her? She sucked in her breath, dropped the phone and clamped both hands to the wheel. A blinding instant, and the monster struck.

Metal smashed metal. Pain exploded in her head. Lights flared with the sounds of shattering glass. A thunderous roar mixed with someone's scream. Hers? She gasped for breath, glazed eyes focused on the explosion of colors that swirled in the maelstrom and then faded off.

"Tessa? Tessa!" That voice calling her name from the phone beside her—Brian? Blinking, she realized she still sat in the car. Left and right, metal and glass popped like time bombs, fragmenting against her arms, her shoulders, and down to her legs.

She struggled to move and groaned at the sharp ache in her head. Again, that sound in the distance, calling her? A thin glimmer of light floated by, then another. Peering through the hole in the windshield, she realized her car rested in a slant toward the ditch. That smell? Gasoline?

Fingers wobbly, she worked to loosen her seat belt and then groped for the door latch. The handle creaked. It gave way when she pushed. She crawled out and steadied herself. After a moment's pause, she inched forward to cross the ditch and climb the embankment. Her foot slipped on wet grass. She fell. Down on her back, she called up every ounce of energy she possessed. Finally she got up to a sitting position. *Of all times for an accident,* the thought whirled. Now she would be late for her interview, maybe not even make it.

A high-pitched wail pierced the air. Then, abrupt silence. The distant slam of car doors, a jumble of voices. ". . . skid marks here . . . another car? . . . the fog . . . not the other guy's fault. . . yeah, but hit and run, it's gotta be . . ."

She squinted at flashes of red and blue lights. Radio chatter echoed from what had to be police cars nearby. *Praise God. Someone is here.*

She tried to get up as faces neared. One, two, or more? Arms reached out to her, and gentle hands forced her down on a board. "Sorry, Miss. We will have to examine you . . ." Figures in police uniform conferred with each other. She glimpsed forms rushing back and forth. To someone who was in the car that hit hers?

"Hang in there, girl," came from a soft, female tone.

She felt pressure on her arm, and then it relaxed. She blinked as lights flashed from one eye to the other. Straps zipped across her chest, her thighs, pinning her to a board.

"Here's the officer . . ." Sounds dulled around her.

She was lifted, carried. Vague moments, and the sound as of doors squeaking open. She felt herself being slipped inside what had to be an ambulance.

"Just a minute, guys," a fuzzy voice said. "I'm the one who called you."

A lean figure in a blur of gray bent over her, the warm strength of his hand covering hers. "Tessa, it's me, Brian."

"Br-ian?" She winced as the door behind her slammed shut.

"Yes. Relax now." He stroked her hair back from her forehead. "I called 911. We're taking you to the hospital. You'll be fine."

"The chair." Her eyelids fluttered open. "I found it. The name—in my pocket . . ." Her head swam, and her eyes closed. "My appointment with Mirbeau's. I'll . . . never . . . never make it . . ." She drifted off, lost in the tearful warmth of remembered goodbye hugs at Chandelle's last party, promises to write, to call...

Later, she was conscious of being in a hospital bed, muffled footsteps around her. Fingers roamed her body as they pressed deep into her flesh or tapped as if in play. Subdued voices urged her to turn over and slide onto another bed. Probing lights flashed into her eyes, threatening like those in the fog and made her cry, "No, no," but she couldn't hear a sound pass her lips.

What were they doing to her?

Someone murmured, "This might sting a little, honey, but you'll feel better soon," and pricked her arm with a needle. A chlorinated smell made her nose twitch while hazy forms lingered and then drifted off like celestial beings into gauzy swirls of fog.

How long she slept, she had no idea, but she awakened to voices in the hall just outside the partially open door to her room:

"I'm sorry. Miss Chandelle can't have visitors. Doctor's orders."

"But I'm Simone Duvall, with television—"

"I know. You're a New Orleans TV reporter."

"If Brian Le Moyne can visit the poor girl—"

"Please, Miss Duvall."

Tessa's door closed with a sudden, swishy thump. She lay awake, the conversation she'd overheard faintly replaying in her brain. A reporter wanted to talk to her, and she'd mentioned Brian's name. She was ready to fluff her pillow and go back to sleep when she saw her door open again. In walked a woman, long yellow hair trailing her shoulders.

"Tessa, I'm Simone Duvall, Brian's friend," she whispered as she approached the bed. "He told me about your accident. How do you feel?"

"Sleepy." Tessa rubbed her forehead.

"If there's anything we can do, Brian and I will be here for you. Now, I'd like to ask if you remember anything about that car, the one that struck yours—"

"Miss Duvall," a voice ordered from the doorway, "out this minute."

"Rest now, and get well soon," Simone said and then walked off. "I was just trying to get information about the accident—" Their voices faded.

The next time Tessa woke up, she lay on her left side facing a wall. She eased up on an elbow and turned to look around the room, memories unreeling like the replay of a movie in slow motion. The fog. Adrienne begging her not to get on the road. Car trouble on her way to her appointment with Mirbeau's, and then the crash. The ambulance. A strong hand holding hers. Brian Le Moyne had been there for her. Last night he'd told her about finding her phone and Adrienne's worried calls, which he'd returned, assuring her Tessa was in St. Anthony's Hospital and doing "just fine."

Even now, her face started a slow flush. Brian had seen her in a hospital gown, no makeup. She'd been embarrassed, afraid her heartbeat would land her in the intensive care unit. She took a deep breath and stretched, on her lips a whispery, *Thank you, Lord, for your loving care.* She must call Adrienne. But first, she needed to talk to a doctor or nurse about her condition.

Brow furrowed, she sat up to check her arms and legs for bruises. Scratches here and there looked like they were minor, even beginning to heal. Where was this hospital, and what time was it?

She glanced at her wrist. No watch. On the wall hung a television set. She got the remote from the bedside table. The instant she pressed Power, the screen came alive with a car logo. After other ads, the time, "7:03 a.m.," appeared on the left top corner of the screen, followed by the weather report "from Magnolia Pass, Tuesday, April twenty-first . . ."

So close to New Orleans, and yet she'd missed her interview yesterday with Mirbeau's. She tried for an aggressive shake of her head. Surely the manager there would give her another chance when she explained why she missed her appointment. If her face didn't have scratches and bruises like the rest of her did, maybe she could still make a good impression.

Slowly she sat on the side of the bed, testing her balance. That's when she looked down and saw the plain, straw bedroom slippers there on the floor as if in place for her. She worked her feet inside them and stood, holding onto the bedside table.

A moment and she let go with cautious steps, each surer than the one before toward the open bathroom door. She entered and stopped before the mirror that hung above the lavatory. A pale scratch, maybe a half inch, angled on her lower left cheek. Mid forehead was a dark blue knot, like a small shirt button.

Hard to believe, she reflected in a surge of gratitude, that her injuries looked minor. She could hear her father's warning when she acted on a foolish impulse, this time driving in foggy dark: "Before you listen to your heart, Tess, get a second opinion from your head."

Promise I'll try from now on, Dad. A deep sigh and she walked back into the bedroom to call the nurse's station.

A light tap at the door as it opened stopped her.

In walked a tall, auburn-haired woman. She wore a sky-blue uniform and carried a breakfast tray. "Ah, the patient is awake." Her cheery voice matched the sparkle in her eyes. "How do you feel, dear?"

"Fine, but I need to talk to a nurse."

"They're awfully busy right now. So how about breakfast? I'm Jen, one of the 'Friendly Ladies' here at St. Anthony's."

Food was the last thing on Tessa's mind, but she took off the slippers and sat back in bed. Jen placed the tray on a roll-away table and eased it toward her. As soon as she lifted the cover on the plate, Tessa was tempted by the scrambled eggs, toast, a small container of butter and another of what looked like blueberry jam. Beside it was a glass of orange juice, a small coffee server and cup. She looked up. "This looks good."

"Earlier this morning, someone at the nurse's station was asking about you." Jen's smile teased. "Brian Le Moyne."

"Oh?" Tessa didn't know what else to say. She picked up the glass of orange juice and took a sip. Then she tried the eggs and the toast.

"The guy is a hunk and a gentleman besides." Jen's grin deepened. "He's been our worrier-in-residence from the moment you were admitted. Every girl should be so lucky to have an admirer like him. Old friends of my family, the Le Moynes. Finest folks anywhere."

"Is he here now?"

"I'd be surprised if he weren't."

"He's been very kind." Tessa decided this cheerful Jen exaggerated those remarks about Brian's concern for her to boost her morale. After all, they'd only met a few days ago. But, as she said, "a hunk and a gentleman," that's who he appeared to be.

"It was Brian who insisted Dr. Arceneaux take care of you. He's the Le Moyne family physician. Honey, you're getting the royal treatment."

"God sent him my way, I know it." After a few more bites, Tessa picked up the paper napkin and touched it to her lips. Her appetite gone, she sat up and pushed the tray aside.

"Are you sure you've had enough?" Jen stepped forward.

"Yes, thank you. Would you know where my bags are, my purse? And if my car—?"

"You poor dear." Jen's forehead creased in a frown. She swiveled away the tray table toward the foot of the bed. "People say I talk too much, but why should everybody know your business but you?" She glanced toward the door and then back to Tessa. "Honey, I'm so sorry. Her voice lowered. "I heard your car was hit again. It was totaled."

Tessa scarcely breathed, her gaze riveted on Jen's face. "So I got out just in time."

"Your purse should be in that drawer." Jen pointed to the night stand by the bed. "The patient's bags are usually turned in to security but, like I said, this is the Le Moyne wing." She nodded toward the closet. "Your suitcases and make-up kit are in there."

Tessa got up and pulled open the night stand drawer. As if untouched by other hands, there lay her purse. Butterflies quieted at the pit of her stomach. She pulled out her bag and unzipped it. Fumbling the contents, she found her wristwatch. Inside a zippered pocket was the wallet with her driver's license and credit card, as well as the paid phone card and check book. The money she'd cashed for trip expenses? Gone. She eased back on the bed, hands numb on the purse.

"Something missing?" Jen stepped closer.

"Every dollar bill. Every penny. But thank God, nothing else is missing. A miracle, really."

"I hear travelers on the road stopped to snoop around your car even before Brian showed up—"

The door to the room swished open with a simultaneous knock. Wearing a white medical coat, a thin, elderly man entered. Dark-rimmed glasses framed his soft gray eyes, and a stethoscope hung around his neck. Beside him, a slender, dark-haired nurse carried a folder. The tag on her white uniform identified her as Edith Soileau.

"Good luck." Jen winked at Tessa. She picked up the breakfast tray and slipped out.

"I'm Dr. Arceneaux. How do you feel, young lady?" He stepped up to her side of the bed. "Had a good breakfast?"

"Yes, thank you. I feel fine, Doctor. When can I be discharged?"

He let out a little "Uhmm, let's see," and put a stethoscope to her chest, asking her to take deep breaths. He repeated the test on her back.

The nurse handed him the folder. While he made notations and studied it, she wrapped a cuff around Tessa's arm and then slipped a thermometer into her mouth. Short moments later, she showed the results to the doctor.

"Excellent." He gave an emphatic shake of his head. "Now, young lady, will you get up and walk around the room?"

Tessa eased off the bed and smoothed her gown as she stood. She rounded the bed, stepped toward the closet and back, only a slight, momentary ache she could ignore in her left ankle.

Dr. Arceneaux held up a hand. "Very good. You have only a mild concussion and several contusions, so it's the medication that caused your extended sleep. X-rays show no fractures or internal bleeding. This morning you ate a good breakfast, and now I can discharge you. You're in excellent health and a very lucky young lady. But don't run off as if nothing happened. Take it easy for a while. The nurse will give you pain pills in case you need them."

"Thank you, Doctor." Tessa couldn't stop a smile as he lifted a hand in good-bye.

Edith held out the bottle of pills. "You might not need more than a couple of these. Call the desk when you're ready to check out. Stay well."

As she walked off, the phone on the bedside table rang.

Tessa picked up the receiver. "Hello?"

"Dr. Arceneaux just gave me the good news, Tessa," Brian said. "Before you call Adrienne or anyone else, I'd like to come up to your room. We need to talk. Okay?"

"How about in a half hour or so? I have to get ready to leave."

"No rush. Take your time."

Tessa wondered what Brian had to say before she called a cab to get her out of there and checked into a local hotel. After a quick shower, she got one of her bags from the closet and noticed that all three had been only slightly dented in the crash, another miracle for which she was thankful. She took out her make-up kit, along with a light blue pantsuit.

Soon dressed, she stood before the mirror in the bathroom. She brushed her hair in a casual fall on her shoulders and coaxed her bangs to cover the knot on her forehead. Lip gloss and a blusher completed the makeup ritual.

Back in the room, she sat on the side of the bed. She'd need to call a cab later and had just pulled out the phone book from the table drawer when she heard a tap at her door. Brian, she thought, and called out, "Come in."

He entered and then paused, an admiring glint in his eyes. "I hope you feel as great as you look."

"Thanks. I'm fine."

"I like the sound of that."

She wanted to say she liked the deep, husky sound of his voice and the way his head tilted with a chuckle. "Thanks again for your help yesterday. You might have saved my life."

"None of that hero stuff." He held up a hand. "I heard the crash. The least I could do was call for help."

"You also took care of my car and my luggage."

"Please, enough with the thanks. Your wheels are in the junk yard now. The runaway drunk who ran into you was in a stolen car. He had another accident and died on the scene."

Tessa stared at him, a sudden shiver rippling down her back. "Oh, no. I'm so sorry for him—for all that happened."

"You delayed leaving for your interview," Brian went on, "just to get the information about the Alphonse. I didn't realize the pressure I'd put you through."

"Don't tell me you feel guilty about my accident?"

He shrugged.

"Professional ego," she went on, "had a lot to do with why I put off leaving Jasmine Hills. One last time I had to try to help a Chandelle customer."

"Well, it was wasted effort on your part. The guy who bought the chair just moved out of the country. Address unknown."

Tessa's hand went limp on the phone book. "I'm sorry. But that's the way it goes in the business. We'll just have to keep trying. It doesn't matter where I end up working, I'll follow up every lead I get."

"Don't worry about it now. You have other problems to deal with."

"Yes, like getting out of here." She looked down at the phone book on her lap. "Excuse me a minute, will you? I have to find the number and call a cab. Then I need to check out of here."

"About a cab, please wait." Hand extended, he took a step closer to her. "You feel well enough to go on to New Orleans?"

"Yes. The sooner, the better."

"Ride with me. I have business in the city too."

"Thanks, but I can't go on taking advantage of your kindness."

"So let me take advantage of yours. Do me a favor. I'd like your company. I'm absolutely ready, willing, and have the time to take you wherever you'd like to go. My pleasure, believe it." He touched her shoulder. "I forgot your cell at my office. On our way out, you can use mine to call Adrienne, Mirbeau's, or anyone else."

"Brian, thank you, but— "

"There's something you should know. After you were admitted here, I called Mirbeau's and left a message to explain why you couldn't keep your appointment."

"You thought of everything, didn't you?" Tessa laid the phone book on the bed and stood, close to tears of gratitude. "Now ride with you? Impose again?"

"Impose? You've got to be kidding." He motioned toward the closet. "If you're ready to leave, I can grab your bags right now and take them to the car. Okay?"

Tessa took a deep, relenting breath. "Well, thanks again, Brian."

As he headed for her luggage, she took out her phone card for a quick call to Adrienne's cell. She must let her know she was being discharged and would go on to New Orleans with Brian. No answer. She left a brief message. That settled, she dialed the nurses' station to say she was ready to check out.

She had just swallowed a pain pill to ward off any possible start of an ache when she heard a clickety-squishy sound. A nurse pushed a wheelchair into the room.

"Oh, no," Tessa moaned.

"Hospital policy." The nurse glanced at Brian and smiled. "Right, Mr. Le Moyne?"

"If you say so." Arms loaded with luggage, he elbowed the closet shut.

"Meet you out front, Tessa."

Heaving a sigh, Tessa collapsed obediently onto the chair, purse in her lap. A squeak of the wheels and they were off into the hallway to join a crowd by the elevator. Hurrying past them, Brian sprinted toward a downward staircase.

Tessa listened to the echoing thud of his footsteps. She wondered who, really, was this guy taking center stage in her life? She straightened in the wheelchair, her eyes wide on the opening doors of the elevator.

Chapter III

Outside and on her feet again, Tessa squinted in a dazzling burst of sunshine. She thanked the nurse and turned to Brian there waiting for her.

"Feel good to be outside?" He took her hand.

"Guess." She smiled up at him.

He led her to his car parked at the head of the vehicles lining the curved driveway for patient pickup. He opened the passenger door.

"Careful," he warned before touching her head to guard against a possible bump as she slid into the soft embrace of the seat.

She fastened her seat belt and then glanced up at Brian to murmur her thanks. The tender look in his eyes brought a lump to her throat, and the best she could offer was a nod. She had never known such gentle concern from a man.

He eased the door shut and walked around to the other side of the car to slide behind the wheel. They pulled out of the parking lot, carefully merging onto the street and away from the sights and sounds of the hospital.

Slowly, Tessa worked her shoulders, dazed by the fast changes taking place in her life.

His eyes on the traffic ahead, Brian pulled a phone from his shirt pocket and held it out to her. "Want to call Mirbeau's now? I programmed the number."

"Oh, Brian, talk about an answer to prayer. That's you." An excited quiver in the pit of her stomach, she took the cell, pressed the number, and held the receiver to her ear.

"Nilas speaking." A pleasant but business-like voice answered.

"This is Tessa Chandelle, Mr. Nilas."

"Ah, Miss Chandelle, how are you?"

"Just fine, thank you." She swallowed to steady her tone. "I'm sorry I missed our appointment. But I'm out of the hospital and on my way to

New Orleans as we speak. Could we please reschedule the interview?"

"I'm glad to hear you recovered so quickly." He paused.

The silence that fell started a slow burn in Tessa's cheeks.

"About your interview, I'm sorry." The words came, slow and deliberate. "A friend of yours called and said you'd been in a terrible accident. He had no idea when you'd be available."

Tessa glanced at Brian and frowned.

"I was out of town," the owner of the antique company explained. "Someone here took the message and didn't get the caller's name. I hate to tell you, but we already filled the position."

Tessa's hand went limp on the phone.

"If it's any comfort," Nilas added in the strained moment, "I'm as disappointed as you are. We'll keep your application on file. Who knows, we might have another opening soon. Check back with us from time to time."

"I'll do that. Thank you, Mr. Nilas." Tessa pressed END. Eyes lowered, she handed the cell back to Brian.

"So?" Brian's voice dropped, guarded. "What did he say?"

"Someone else got the job." Tessa couldn't look at him. "He said you told them it might be a long time before I got over the accident. Did you really think I was that bad off?"

"Hold it. I said nothing of the sort."

"Well, if you didn't, then who did?" Tessa sat back, trying to process what she'd just heard from Mr. Nilas.

"*If* I didn't?" Brian glanced at her, brows raised.

Tessa clutched her hands tightly in her lap. What could she say? She was grateful he had tried to help her, yet she wished he hadn't become involved.

Brian fixed his gaze on the traffic ahead. "Look, I thought you'd want Nilas to know why you didn't keep your appointment. He wasn't in. So I left a message about your accident with somebody who said he'd inform his boss. I told him you were in the hospital, mainly suffering from shock, the doctor said. He was running tests to be on the safe side. I assured the guy you looked forward to the interview and would probably call in a day or so."

Tessa blinked hard, mulling over what he'd explained in a matter-of-fact tone. "Well, maybe the person at Mirbeau's misunderstood?"

"No way any sane person could have." Brian's fingers tightened on the wheel.

Tessa turned aside. An uneasy silence simmered between them. She tensed at the creeping fear that somebody at Mirbeau's, maybe even Mr. Nilas himself, had heard about her problems at Chandelle's and didn't want her on staff. No matter where she applied for work, she'd known that could happen. As for Brian, he'd been there for her throughout the accident and even now.

"I'm sorry, Brian. What Mr. Nilas said shocked me. You deserve thanks for calling Mirbeau's, not blame." She turned to look at him. "I overreacted and took it out on you. Please forgive me."

"There's nothing to forgive." Brian shrugged. "Whoever answered that phone wanted someone else for the job. And he succeeded. But maybe not." He reached for his cell. "I'm going to straighten out Nilas right now."

"No, please don't." Tessa touched his arm. "I know you feel bad for me."

"You bet I do." Brian hesitated, finger poised on the phone.

"Let's leave the man alone." Tessa could have told him she suspected Mirbeau's had decided not to take a chance on Lester Chandelle's niece. Too well she remembered the conversation she'd overheard among the employees of Magnolia Antiques the night of her last party at Chandelle's. To spare her feelings, Mirbeau's had likely concocted the story about what Brian said over the phone. This was not the time for her to blurt out private matters to him. Besides, what could either of them do about it? "The last thing I want," she said, "is to stir up trouble in that house."

"Looks like somebody already did. But it's your decision." Brian slipped the cell onto the dashboard. "Haven't you learned to fight for what you want?"

"I'm not sure the job at Mirbeau's is worth fighting for. I want to enjoy my work, not endure it. I'm overreacting. "

Brian's cell rang. Brow furrowed, he reached to give it a quick look. He turned it off and placed it face down on the dash.

Tessa had no doubt she interfered again with his work. Guilt and those suspicious thoughts about the job at Mirbeau's caused her stomach to knot and become queasy. She must relax and accept what had happened. Only then could she decide what to do next. Brian had been kind, but she'd imposed on his time long enough.

"We can't always control what happens. We just have to move on." She looked back at the road ahead. "Things will work out. They always do."

"Sure. One way or the other."

She'd heard the bitterness that laced his lowered tone and glanced at him.

"Could we talk?" His hands eased on the wheel.

"About what?" Tessa matched his now calm demeanor.

"Tell you over lunch?" Brian stopped for a light and shot her a quick look. "We could try Mignon's Café. It's just around the corner. Her café au lait and beignets are as good as those at Café du Monde in New Orleans. She has great lunches too."

Tessa shifted in her seat. She wasn't hungry, but just what was on his mind? Whatever, she must deal with it. "Fine with me."

They drove the couple of blocks to Mignon's in silence. Brian slid the car into a parking space, got out, and came around to open the door for her. He held her hand a moment and grinned. She couldn't deny the thrill of his touch, smooth but strong, and returned his smile.

Mignon's didn't seem to be very busy. From a jukebox in a corner came the wailing sadness of the Cajun classic, "Jolie Blonde." A few people sat at tables covered with scalloped red oilcloth and centered with unlit glass and bronze hurricane lamps. A group of khaki-clad men, likely on coffee break, looked up as Tessa and Brian entered.

He returned their nods and friendly French helloes with a jovial

"Bonjour, mes amies."

A tall, bulky woman hurried forward to greet them. The name "Mignon" was stitched in red on the top pocket of her white apron. Inky-black hair, short and teased, matched the lively dark eyes peeking out between lashes thick with mascara.

"Brian Le Moyne, how you doin'?" Lips curved in a broad smile, she placed a finger on the cheek she turned to him. "Right here."

"Ah, ma chere Mignon." Brian gave her the expected peck.

"Every few minutes that phone, it'll be ringin' for you," the woman said in a low tone Tessa barely heard. "Uh . . . say you don't pick up yours . . . maybe you're headed this way."

Tessa stepped aside to give them privacy, but the distance couldn't shut out Brian's reply, "If she calls again, take a message. I don't want to be disturbed."

"Gotcha," Mignon said. "Your usual table is ready."

Judging from the amount of time he'd devoted to her since the accident, Tessa didn't think the "she" was a wife. Secretary? Business associate? Perhaps the reporter, Simone Duvall, her visitor at the hospital? The incident renewed that guilty feeling for taking up his time.

Brian took her arm and led her toward a secluded corner table. After he'd helped her settle on her chair, he took the one opposite her, picked up a couple of menus from the table and handed her one.

"I heard you had breakfast, but I haven't," he said. "That's what I'm going to order."

"The truth is, I hardly touched the food. I was too anxious to get away."

"Then you'll enjoy breakfast here. It's an experience you won't regret."

"I'll give your 'experience' a try." Tessa smiled. "Order for me?"

"You won't be sorry." Brian turned as Mignon walked up. "The usual, but two this time, please."

Seeing him in the chair opposite her, Tessa recalled times past when she sat like this with Josh. Since those days, she hadn't felt such a strong attraction to a man. Dates had been pleasant companionships with friends. Something drew her to Brian, something she couldn't put into words, or was afraid to put into words. She couldn't deny a certain thrill when his eyes met and held hers. His nearness, his smile, or just the sound of his voice sent her into a kind of happiness unlike anything she had ever experienced even with Josh. It was more than all that, more than the strong, clean planes and angles of his face that stayed with her from the moment she saw him standing on Chandelle's doorsteps. She had to admit his love for antiques was a plus in their relationship. And how about the way he cared for her, a stranger, enough to see her safely to the hospital and now to her destination? That struck her as unusual for any man in today's busy world. A least, none she'd known.

"Do you have any family? Brothers? Sisters? Someone else?" she asked.

"I have a sister–"

"Well, Brian Le Moyne, eh? Hello, mon ami?" A paunchy, balding man in jeans and red-striped shirt greeted him in a hoarse voice.

"If it isn't Willis Doucette." Brian smiled cordially as they shook hands. "Working hard these days?"

"Yeah. That latest tornado whipped us up something awful around here. Everybody needs a new roof like yesterday."

"I'd like you to meet Tessa Chandelle." Brian nodded to Tessa.

"Chandelle?" The man's brows went up, forming deep lines on his forehead. Brown-black eyes fixed on Tessa. "Kin to Lester Chandelle?"

"My uncle." Tessa's steady look ignored the scorn in his voice.

"Had to sell your business, did you?" Willis didn't wait for her answer but turned to Brian. "I hear creditors were ready to hang that old scoundrel. He sold fakes as antiques."

Tessa wadded the napkin in her lap. Heat rose in her face, her look on Brian for his reaction to what he'd just heard.

He leaned sideways and looked toward a far table. "Oh, you brought a guest, Willis. She's waving."

"Ah, yes. That's Lisette, my latest amour. Well, it was good to see you again, Brian." He glanced at Tessa, then back toward Brian as if to say more but shrugged and walked away.

"That guy's a jerk," Brian said.

Tessa blinked off in an overflow of gratitude toward him. She'd pushed the thought aside, but she would have been surprised if he hadn't heard about Uncle Lester the night of that last party at Chandelle's. Out of respect for her feelings, he hadn't mentioned it. Now he wanted to get rid of Willis to spare her embarrassment. He couldn't see her fingers knotted tightly in her lap to keep from reaching across the table to squeeze his.

"You knew, didn't you?" she said softly and looked back at him.

"About your uncle?" He shrugged. "Rumors, yes. But that's nobody's business but yours. Let's not spoil our first meal together. We have other things to talk about."

Again overcome with his caring, Tessa pressed her lips together to stop the tremor.

Mignon approached with a loaded tray.

"Bon appetit." She settled the tray to one side of their table and then placed before them white mugs of steaming black coffee and plates loaded with buttery grits, fluffy scrambled eggs, sliced ham, and brown, flaky biscuits with individual tubs of whipped butter. Assorted preserves, too, and the sugar-powdered beignets Brian had promised.

"Y'all enjoy now." She winked and walked off with her empty tray.

Tessa stared at her plate. "I can't believe all this food."

"The taste is even harder to believe," Brian said. "Try it. Even the AMA says it's okay to indulge once in a while."

Tessa looked down for a moment's silent prayer. She couldn't tell if Brian also returned thanks. His obvious enthusiasm for the ham and eggs with the beignets before him caught on, and she found herself joining him more heartily than she had expected.

"You won't have any trouble getting back into the business of antiques." Brian curled a finger around the handle of his coffee cup. "You're very good at what you do. I saw that right off at Chandelle's."

"Breakfast like this and flattery besides. You're too generous." Tessa picked up her knife and cut gingerly into the ham. "Before we were interrupted, you were going to tell me about your sister."

"Darrie lives in New Orleans with her husband Kyle and is one of the reporters for our Le Moyne-Duvall TV station." He paused, picked up his fork and scooped up a bit of fig preserves on a piece of toast.

Tessa waited for him to go on. She bit into a beignet, careful to avoid a sugary mustache.

"When I'm not traveling, I commute from the family estate, that's Le Moyne House in St. Pierre. A tornado whipped by a couple of years ago and caused a lot of damage. The next day the place caught on fire. My father died from smoke inhalation."

"I'm sorry to hear that," Tessa said.

"Our house survived." Brian's tone lightened. "A colonial-style home. Practically every stick of furniture dated back many generations, most from the best antique dealers in the world. We lost a small fortune in that fire."

"I don't doubt it." Tessa put down her fork and gave him a long look. "Now I know why you'd like to replace that Alphonse. You said it was a gift. From your mom to your dad?"

"No."

Tessa heard that closed-book sound in his voice and regretted the question. For whatever reason, he didn't want to talk about the gift aspect of the chair. She looked down and reached for her water glass.

"Mom wanted to refurnish the house," Brian went on after a moment's silence. "She had problems with the decorator and gave up. I was out of the country at the time."

"Maybe she'll try again?"

"She's traveling abroad with friends and will probably be back the end of August." He paused and looked at her plate. "How's your second breakfast?"

"A real treat, thanks." Tessa dabbed the napkin to her mouth and wondered when he'd get to the point of their need to talk.

"Mom deserves to be happy again. That's my primary concern right now." He curled an index finger around the handle of his coffee cup. "She'd like nothing better than to have the house back like it was before the fire."

"I should think so." Tessa met his eyes intent on hers, a vein prominent on his forehead just above the left brow. She noticed again the scar that disappeared into the temple hairs.

"Maybe you and I can help each other," he said.

"Help each other?"

"You need a job, and my family needs to replace those antiques we lost."

"Oh, no. So that's why this talk." Tessa dropped the knife with a clink on her plate. "You won't pull that one on me."

"Pull what on you?"

"Offer me work out of guilt."

"Not that again. Didn't you understand what I've been saying?"

"Perfectly." She started slicing butter out of the bowl. Before she realized it, she'd deposited four squares on her plate, enough to make an entire bread pudding.

"You've got it all wrong. Guilt has nothing to do with it."

"You expect me to believe that?" Tessa gave a little laugh.

"Please look at me, Tessa."

She wouldn't at first, but something in his tone finally forced her attention from the mess on her plate to the pleading in his eyes.

"You're an expert in antiques and a professional decorator. You're the very person I need."

Tessa heard the words, music to her ears. Working for one person. Bringing a house back to its former glory. What an ego booster that would be. She'd lost so much lately—her fiancé, her business reputation with some folks, and the old family enterprise. Now creditors en masse on her back. But she hadn't lost her pride. Her eyes lowered to her plate again. "I need a job, not a handout."

"Is that really what you think of my offer?" Brian frowned. "You didn't listen to a word I said."

"About wanting the house redone, yes." Tessa rubbed her napkin at coffee stains on the table. The job might be just what it seemed on the surface, an answer to prayer, but she thanked God she wasn't ready to accept charity.

"So?" Brian waited.

"Let me remind you, it isn't always easy to replace antiques." She sat forward, her gaze holding his. "The Alphonse you want is a perfect example. Besides, the market is flooded with clever imitations."

"You're right. My mother doesn't want fake. She wants the real thing."

The set of his jaw and the determined gleam in his eyes said more than she could understand. He seemed desperate to find something other than furniture. Was it material, or spiritual?

"That's why I need you, Tessa Chandelle. You're a seasoned professional." He straightened as if he might be at a board meeting about to pitch a plan he had no doubt could benefit all concerned. "I'd expect nothing from you except what your reputation says."

"My reputation?" The question flew out of Tessa's mouth. She stared at him. Besides the gossip about Uncle Lester, what did he know or had heard about her?

"Not your uncle's reputation," he said, as if reading her mind, "yours. You're known to be a hard worker who knows her stuff. Your credentials are tops. Besides, I want a decorator who will really care about the house and even live there for however long it takes to get the place back in shape."

"*Live* there?" Her mouth hung open.

"Why not? You'd have all the conveniences of home besides the use of an office and a car. You'd have a better feel for the place and get the job done quicker than if you had to commute."

"You're asking me to move in with you?"

"Well, I wasn't going to put it that way." He stroked his chin, and a teasing sparkle lit up his eyes.

"Forget it." Tessa drew back. *Shades of Josh.* "I'm not that desperate for work."

"Seriously, I live in the guesthouse when I'm home." The silliness left his face. "We'd be neighbors. You could choose your bedroom in the mansion. Ada, our housekeeper, and her husband Cede have an apartment on second floor. If a big bad wolf knocked on your door, no way would either of them let him come in."

Tessa managed a faint smile at his attempted humor. She just wasn't very good in the "judging men" department. Josh, too, seemed oh-so-proper and trustworthy until he asked for a honeymoon before the marriage she found out he didn't want.

"This is so sudden, Brian."

"Earlier you said things have a way of working out." His tone and a raised brow challenged. "The job could be the perfect opportunity for you to show your talent and make new contacts."

"Not so fast. I'd have to know what all is involved in the job. Is there a time limit, like before your mom comes home maybe? What is included and excluded in your offer? What type of references or records would you expect me to keep for you? There's so much to consider."

"I'm sorry. I'm rushing you, and you just got out of the hospital." He shook his head in apology. "Take all the time you need or want to decide. If you do take the job, you can write up a contract so we're both straight."

Tessa leaned back, her hand absently stroking a spot on the place mat. He tempted her. And yet?

"Neither of us is in a hurry to get to New Orleans. Why don't we drive over to the house right now?" Brian pushed back his plate. "You can meet Ada and Cede. Instead of going to a hotel, you could spend the night with them. No questions about the job. Just a relaxing visit. After all you've just been through, you deserve some TLC. Ada would enjoy fussing over you."

"But shouldn't you check with her before you barge in with a guest?"

"Don't worry about her. She's like my mother. Always loves and welcomes company."

"Earlier you said you have to be in New Orleans this afternoon."

"One call, and business can wait. Right now, your well-being is top priority." He glanced at his watch and then took out his wallet, extracted a bill and dropped it beside his empty plate. "What do you say? We can leave for St. Pierre this minute."

"Just remember I haven't made up my mind about the job." Tessa reached for her purse.

"Understood. Even after we're on the road, if you decide you'd rather go on to New Orleans and stay in a hotel, just say the word. I'll change course and take you there. Shake on it?" On his feet at once, he got to her side of the table and pulled back her chair as she got up.

His strong fingers swallowed hers and held. Firm, not limp like Josh's were all too often. A tender stroke of his thumb along the back of her hand sent a surge of excitement coursing through her veins. She couldn't deny the moment transported her to a dreamlike moment she had not expected.

Mignon's "Y'all come back now," startled them apart.

"As always, ma chère," Brian raised a hand in playful salute, "tell the cook merci beaucoup for a meal fit for a governor though not for the waistline."

"You got nothin' there to worry about, mon ami." Mignon threw back her head in a rich, deep laugh. "You jus' come on back and bring this here pretty girl with you, promise?"

"I intend to." Brian took Tessa's arm, and they walked out to his car.

They headed for St. Pierre.

"Perfect weather for jogging." At the wheel, Brian's gaze flitted about the countryside.

"Or just for a long walk, one of my favorite pastimes." Beside him, Tessa smiled at the sunshine illuminating a field of sugarcane, the tall green stalks reminding her of corn without ears.

Brian pointed to a steel-gray mansion on a knoll in the distance. "That's Ardoin's plantation, once a real showplace. It sits between a bayou and the widest swamp around here. It's hard to get there unless you take a boat or a plane."

"Interesting." Tessa sat up taller for a better look.

"That bayou is dangerous. Besides, the old recluse in that house is still nursing a broken heart. When he was young, someone stole his fiancée. Word is he never got over it. Now he's senile. He's even been seen standing at a window with a shotgun." Brian shrugged. "Anyway, that's the gossip. The smart thing to do is to stay away from his place."

"Don't worry about me." Tessa laughed and leaned back in her seat, trying to imagine some ghostly madman firing at random or ranting in the halls of a mansion not far from the one where she just might live for a while. "I don't know the first thing about piloting either boats or planes. Besides, if I work for you, I won't have time to waste."

"I like to keep my employees happy." Brian grinned. "I don't consider doing that wasted time on their part or mine."

"All you'd need to do is agree to my terms, and I'd be happy." Tessa tried for a playful tone to match his and stared off into the distance, the handshake at Mignon's still too vivid a memory. She pointed to a lane that led to a two-storied pink-blush mansion and an approaching sign that read, Entrance—Duvall Property. "Duvall—as in Simone Duvall?"

"One and the same." Brian shot her a quick glance. "Do you know her?"

"She came by the hospital to see me. The nurse stopped her, but a little later she sneaked into my room."

"Sneaked in?" Brian laughed out. "Sounds like her. Determined to get her way. That's Simone."

"She said you told her about my accident. Is that where she lives?"

"It's her parents' place. We've been friends forever. And business partners."

Tessa wondered if they were more than he admitted. Simone sounded single. Tessa knew the type. They had shopped at Chandelle's many times. Socialites flitted from one house to another, wanting to decorate each in a whimsical choice of antiques.

"She's a top-notch reporter," Brian said. "Great business head and a real asset to our joint enterprises." He made a turn, then a sharp left that sent the car nosing down an oak-lined alley. Slowing his approach, he said, "Well, there it is."

Tessa's breath caught, and she forgot about Simone.

An imposing white, three-story mansion boasted two wings, one on the east and another on the west. It lay partially hidden by massive oak trees. Their branches were low-slung or trimmed high up the trunks, perhaps due to the tornado Brian had mentioned. The grounds were landscaped with palm and magnolia trees, here and there banks of flowers in varied gold, blue, and crimson.

"What a showplace!" Tessa said. "Talk about 'out of this world'!"

"I hope not. I like it here."

Tessa couldn't play word games with him. Her gaze darted to the front porch. Large, square columns reached the top of the third-story balcony and continued on both sides toward the back.

"We hired the best carpenters in the state to get the house back in shape." Brian brought the car to a stop in the curved driveway. "The fire was worst on first floor. Some of the rooms are empty."

They were barely out of the car when an engine purred. The compact white sports car slammed to an abrupt stop behind them.

A petite young woman emerged, her dark hairdo tousled. She wore a canary yellow dress with a wide belt that accented her slender waist. Breathless, she rushed toward Brian and clutched his arm, her eyes shiny with excitement. "I've been calling and looking all over for you!"

"What's going on, Darrie?"

Tessa stood aside and studied Brian. Hands in his pockets, he looked at his sister, a questioning grin on his face. His calm demeanor said he might often witness this kind of outburst from her.

"Have I got good news! Simone and I found a buyer for the house!"

"You what?" Now Brian's eyes narrowed, his cheeks going into a flush.

"Forget tradition, Bro." Darrie sighed and waved a hand, tossing aside his anger. "It's time you let go of the past. All of it." Her gaze zoomed to Tessa as if she'd just noticed her. Turning back to Brian, she asked, "Who is she? What's going on here?" A mix of hurt and reproach in her eyes, she reminded Tessa of a little girl who fretted she'd been left out of a secret.

"Darrie Landry, meet Tessa—"

"Is she another one of your girls?"

Tessa's jaw dropped.

"Watch your manners, Darrie." Brian pointed a finger at her. "You need to engage your brain before you engage that tongue of yours. Tessa's here on business. I just offered her a job."

"Oh, at the studio." Darrie brought a hand to her lips, as if in apology, relief flooding her face.

"No. To replace the antiques we lost."

Darrie frowned. "That'll never happen. Haven't you learned when to give up?"

"Excuse us a minute, will you, Tessa?" Brian took Darrie's arm and started toward the shade of an oak tree beyond the driveway. "What made you think our house was for sale? Is it your husband? Has he run you out of money again? Talk to me."

Tessa turned her back on their fading voices. Plainly they disagreed about what should be done with the house. Besides, Darrie said Brian should forget the past, "all of it." What secrets hid behind the closed doors of Le Moyne House?

Her brain and heart at odds, Tessa didn't know if she should see this to a conclusion or interrupt and ask Brian to take her on to New Orleans. "Your will, Lord," she prayed and slanted a look toward the two siblings. The hostility between them seemed to worsen with loud voices and hands waving in each other's face.

"Chandelle? Is that her last name?" now Darrie cried. "You're telling me she's *Lester Chandelle's niece?*"

"So what?" Brian shot back.

Darrie gripped his arm. "Ada was away taking care of her sick mother, and you were out of the country when it happened. Tessa's uncle is the guy that got Mom all upset with a bunch of fake antiques! That's why she gave up on the house!"

Tessa's hands flew to her lips. *Their mother, one of Uncle Lester's victims.* On the instant, she started toward them, words of apology for his betrayal whirling around in her head. As with Mirbeau's, the Lord had spoken. Gone was the offer of a job here. Tears threatened, but she held them back.

Her prayer was answered. She must leave for New Orleans as soon as possible.

Chapter IV

She had barely taken a couple of steps forward when Brian turned her way. He lifted a hand to stop her.

"Wait until Mom hears what you plan to do!" Darrie shook a finger at him.

"Nothing is settled. Don't you dare say a word to her—!"

Darrie backed away from him. She ran toward her car and climbed inside. Slamming the door shut, a moment and she whizzed off in a squeal of brakes without a backward look.

Arms swinging at his sides, Brian strode toward Tessa.

She met him halfway. "I heard what she said about Uncle Lester and your mom. Believe me, I had no idea—"

"Brian?" A short, plump woman in a tan, short-sleeved housedress and a white apron stood in the open doorway of the mansion.

Brian lifted a restraining hand toward her and turned back to Tessa. "Please, we'll talk later," his tone lowered. "For now, let's go on with our plans."

"I can't do that." Tessa shifted her purse from shoulder to hand, squirming under the softening blue of his eyes, a magnet that wouldn't let hers go. "Your sister doesn't want me here and neither would your mom."

"That's my problem, not yours. Trust me. I'll handle it—" His voice faded in a helicopter's drone.

The aircraft rose from the left of the house lawns and drifted into wispy white clouds. The pilot's hand lifted toward them.

"One of our employees." Brian waved back and then turned to Tessa. His fingers, gently urgent, touched her arm. "Please, let me introduce you to Ada."

"Well..." She frowned. After what she'd just heard, how could she even consider stepping inside the house? But being here and now that Darrie was gone, could she refuse to meet the housekeeper and see his home? She slanted a quick glance at her watch. Almost one o'clock. She had plenty of time before she headed for New Orleans. Another, "Well," and she added, "if you insist."

They walked up the porch steps. The woman waiting there turned questioning, hazel-flecked eyes toward Brian.

"Expecting someone, Ada?" he asked.

"Surely not you, Brian Le Moyne. Not before tonight." Now her mouth twisted in a fond grin his way. She raised a square, stubby hand to flick short strands of moss-gray hair from her forehead and turned back to Tessa.

The woman's welcoming aura, a contrast to Darrie's hostility, made Tessa smile. She felt an easing of tension, almost like in the presence of an old friend.

"Ada, meet Tessa Chandelle. She was the one in that car accident. Tessa, Ada Guidry is our housekeeper." He chuckled. "Acting CEO."

Ada ignored his playful remark and reached to clasp Tessa's hand. "Are you all right now, young lady?"

"Yes, thank you," Tessa said.

"You know the Chandelle missionaries?'

"My parents."

Brian's phone shrilled. He pulled it out of his pocket and glanced at it. Then, "Ada, aren't you going to let us in? I'll have to leave in a half hour or so. Business right here in town. But it shouldn't take long. Tessa is here to look the house over."

"Oh, excuse my manners, Tessa. Do come in. Look the house over, did you say, Brian? I'm surprised. Your mother called me this morning and said nothing about that. In fact, she hasn't mentioned refurnishing the house in a long time. We talk at least once a week."

"It's my idea, my gift to her," Brian said.

"Oh? You're sure you shouldn't discuss that first with her?" Her brows went up as she pushed the door wide open.

"Please, no. I want to surprise her. I don't want anyone in the family to mention that to her. Tessa is an antiques expert, a first-class decorator," Brian went on. "If anyone can put this place back the way it was, she can.

I know Mother would be delighted."

"Well, I hope you know what you're doing," Ada said with a shake of her head.

"I do, Ada." Brian turned to Tessa. "I hope you'll spend the night here like we talked about earlier?"

Tessa felt undecided. "Well..." Tessa hesitated. He was rushing her decision. Besides, it might not be a good time for Ada to have an overnight guest. What would Darrie say if she walked in at that very moment? And how about their mother who surely wouldn't welcome another Chandelle in her home? But since neither was around, maybe just this once, and tomorrow she'd be gone? Brian had given her his total support when she needed it most. Shouldn't she try to please him, at least for tonight? She looked at Ada. "It might not be convenient for you."

"Honey, it's for you and Brian to decide. As far as I'm concerned, you'd be more than welcome."

Tessa hesitated. She turned to Brian. The look on his face reminded her of the kind of desperation she'd seen that night at Chandelle's when he wanted a look inside for the Alphonse chair. She took a deep, relenting breath. "Then, yes. Thank you."

Again, the ring of Brian's phone. He pulled it out of his pocket, his gaze flicking over a message. "Sorry. Excuse me a minute." He stepped back on the porch and leaned against one of its square columns, his voice low.

Ada put out a hand to welcome Tessa inside.

They started through the doorway. The squeaky rumble of wheels sounded behind them. They both turned. Shuffling up the walkway, a slightly stooped man, tall and wiry in blue overalls, pushed a red wheelbarrow loaded with dirt. He stopped on the side of the walkway and shoved his straw hat to the back of his head, exposing a fringe of cotton-white hair. His sunburned face was thin, his nose a broad diagonal that gave him a sturdy look.

"My husband, Cede." Ada waved him over. He thumped slowly up the steps. "Cede, this is Tessa Chandelle. She's the daughter of those two missionaries. And a decorator, too."

"Mr. Guidry." Tessa smiled and offered her hand.

"You'll have to 'scuse me." He held his hands close to his sides, palms turned out to show the stains. "They need a good washin' on account of the weedin' I've been doin'. But it's real nice to meet you, Miss."

"Just Tessa, please."

"Well, well, the daughter of the Chandelles." He slanted a glance toward Brian, now walking back to join them. "You never know, never ever know."

Never know what? Tessa waited for him to go on. When he didn't, she thought he might be surprised Brian would try to have the house refurnished while his mother was away. *Or, had he been around here when Uncle Lester, a Chandelle, was the hired decorator?*

"Cede, please get the luggage out of the back seat of the car and bring it in." Brian slipped the phone back into his pocket and held out a ring of car keys to Cede. "Ada, since Tessa just got out of the hospital, she needs to rest. After a quick look on first floor, would you show her to a room upstairs?"

"My dear, I have the very one for you." Ada touched Tessa's arm.

Tessa glanced back at Brian. She noticed the tightness around his brows and thought he looked nothing like the man she was beginning to know, strong and confident. Had disturbing phone calls changed his mood? Maybe he'd found out Darrie had already made contact with their mother about his plan to hire another Chandelle?

As they stepped farther into the entry hall, a babble of voices rose with the clink of cooking utensils. Savory smells of freshly baked breads, spicy meats, and apple cobbler filled the house, reminders of happy times at Chandelle's.

"We're having dinner guests tonight." A sparkle lit up Ada's face. "I enjoy the commotion when something's going on, like gabbing with the help while we prepare the food. But we don't entertain often now. Not since Felice or . . ." She broke off as a perky young woman in a white apron bustled by toward a table, hands tight around a pan loaded with silverware.

Tessa gave her a smiling "Hi" and turned to Ada. "It looks like I'm intruding. Brian didn't tell me you'd be so busy."

"This is when she's her happiest." Brian gave Ada a teasing glance.

"He's right," Ada said. "Tonight's dinner is just a small affair for us, more fun than work. I've got plenty of help. Besides, it's to celebrate a fund-raiser. Brian organized it for those folks in New Orleans hit with the latest tornado."

"And now you do all the work." Brian led the way into a large, airy room. "The parlor." He motioned to the walls. "We had those redone. Some paintings and portraits that hung there were badly damaged. Probably nothing can be done to get them back in shape, but they're in storage."

"Uh, 'scuse me, Brian." Cede came up from behind them. "A foreman from the south cane field over past the lake is outside. He's waitin' to talk to you."

"I'll be right there." Brian turned to Ada. "Please show Tessa around, but just down here, okay? She can see the other part of the house later when she's rested." He looked at Tessa. "Back soon as I can."

Tessa watched him walk away looking more confident and carefree than he'd been earlier, but she was disappointed he had to leave. She wanted to see his reaction to the rooms, emotions that might let her better understand what this home meant to him.

"Always busy, that man. Pushes himself like crazy." Ada led Tessa through an archway and another room. "Here's the family's most popular gathering place."

Tessa paused in the large area with its high ceiling and an expanse of windows facing west. A black marble mantel and a fireplace centered the opposite wall.

"All the grand old pieces burned to the ground." Ada frowned as if she relived a distressing scene. "These days we entertain dinner guests in the kitchen when it's just a few friends. For the large group we expect tonight, we'll open up this area and set up folding tables and chairs." She glanced toward the door Brian had just exited. "I want to hear about your dear parents when we can be alone."

Tessa gave her a quick look. "You know them?"

"I met them once." Now Ada's tone was surprisingly dismissive of any comment about the Chandelles as she led Tessa into another room. "This one, Felice's favorite place in the whole house, I do believe. She had just redecorated it. She was scared to death fire would leap up in here too. But it didn't. We loved having meetings of church folks in here. Now I got orders, no more of that in this house. Not ever."

Tessa waited for her to explain about forbidden church meetings.

But again, changing the subject, she turned aside and pointed upward. "Ever see anything like that?"

Tessa looked at the ceiling with its medallion in the shape of elongated flower petals. The pastel colors blended with the stained-glass windows, depicting a slice of life in genteel eighteenth-century gardens.

"Beautiful," she said.

Ada nodded. "An artist, that's Felice."

Tessa's gaze flitted on to the south wall with its off-white marble fireplace. Above it hung the portrait of a young woman in a soft, blue-toned gown. The eyes, a dreamy shade of gray, looked on serenely under arched brows. Blonde curls, wind-blown, kissed tiny clusters of pearls centered on the ear lobes. A ray of sunlight from the windows touched the delicate features and the illusory ruffles that caressed her slender neck. The tapered fingers resting in her lap might paint, Tessa reflected, or play the piano to entertain guests or accompany a church choir. She wondered if this classic model of femininity might be Brian's mother in her youth.

"Now over here—" Ada began.

"That lady in the portrait," Tessa interrupted, "is she Brian's mother?"

Ada's look sobered. Before she could answer, Brian returned, Cede behind him with Tessa's luggage in hand.

"If you'll tell him where that goes, Ada, I'll take over with Tessa," Brian said.

"You know the room. It's your mother's favorite one for guests. Need me," she added as she walked away, "I'll be in the kitchen."

Brian waved her off and hurried into another large, vacant area. "The dining room."

Tessa let go of her curiosity about the portrait and followed him.

"Now the library. Both empty, as you can see. Over here," he continued, "these two rooms open into one another. Great for parties."

Tessa heard the nostalgia in his voice, his gaze scanning the emptiness that begged for attention. She saw the areas as a canvas that waited for some capable hand to revive the past and create a present with the promise of a future. She sighed. Because of Uncle Lester's betrayal here, no way could she be the one to try to make that miracle happen.

"Most bedrooms are on second floor, as well as the sunroom and other sitting areas. You'll see them all later." Brian glanced at his watch. "I'm sorry, but one of my phone calls was from a couple of guys with our sister station in New York. They got our schedules mixed up. I must meet them downtown here sooner than we'd planned."

"You're the consummate business man." Tessa smiled. "Please go on, and don't worry about me. I shouldn't even be here now."

"The timing for your visit is perfect. Unless," he hesitated, his tone going soft with concern, "maybe this is too much for you so soon out of the hospital?"

"Not at all. I feel fine."

"Then you'll join us for dinner?"

The words lingered, like his gaze on hers with an urgency she hadn't expected. "Thanks. I'd like to, but—"

"You haven't changed your mind about spending the night, have you?"

She hesitated. "I'm having second thoughts. Before dinner, maybe you or Cede could drive me to a hotel in town? Or, I'll get a cab. Darrie would be upset if she saw me here at dinner."

"Forget my sister. She won't be back. She's on duty tonight at the studio. Besides, I'm in charge of this event. You'd be my special guest."

Tessa clasped a hand to her throat, embracing the thrill of an unguarded moment. She leaned against a door frame and tried for a casual, "Well, thanks again, if you're sure—"

"I am. Promise you'll get some rest while I'm gone?"

"Promise."

"I'll ask Ada to show you to your room." Matter-of-factness now in his manner, he lifted a hand and walked off, calling, "Ada?"

A moment and, her face still bright with that welcoming glow, Ada was back. "This way," she said and headed for the stairs.

Tessa's fingers glided on the rail of the polished pine balustrade as she followed her up to the second floor. She paused in the hallway to ease the faint start of an ache in her left knee and came face to face with a portrait of Darrie that hung on the wall. She drew back and held a hand to her forehead. No matter what Brian said, what was she doing in this house when his sister had declared her persona non grata? When his mother was one of Uncle Lester's victims?

"Our most popular bedrooms are on this floor. Cede and I have an apartment farther down." Ada stepped up to the first door on her right. She pushed it open. "Felice's guests love this room. Brian slept here for a while after he gave up the apartment on third floor. Now he prefers the guesthouse." She looked back at Tessa. "Honey, are you all right?"

"Oh, yes. Nice picture of Darrie hanging back there on the wall." She hurried to follow Ada into the bedroom.

At once, she paused, her attention caught by the rosy blush of the crocheted bedspread and matching pillow shams that softened the four-poster bed in dark walnut. On the floor beside it lay an oval rug decorated with spring flowers splashed in a pale, cream-colored background. She was quick to notice it brought out the stain of highly polished wooden floors, a reminder of Chandelle's.

"Like downstairs," she said, "this does look like the work of an artist."

"Felice redecorated it after Brian moved out." Ada pointed to a mirrored armoire in a corner. "You're welcome to hang your clothes there. Also, it has shelves on one side."

"Thanks." Tessa could have told her she'd never be unpacking her luggage here. She was tempted to confide in the woman what she herself had just learned about her uncle's deceit here and how she felt about being in Le Moyne House at that very moment. But break her promise to Brian?

Ada pattered to the rear of the room, opened a door and peeked inside. "The bathroom is clean. Make yourself at home. I'll be right back."

"Please don't worry about me," Tessa said.

"Goes both ways." Giving that careless flip of her hand again, Ada hurried out.

Tessa dropped her handbag on a small marble top table and kicked off her low-heeled pumps. She snapped open the overnight bag Cede had placed on a rack at the foot of the bed with her other luggage. She took out her slippers and put them on.

Waiting for Ada to return, she relaxed on the pale Victorian fainting couch below the bay window opposite the bed and let her gaze wander about the room's romantic, restful air.

A silky blush of wallpaper flecked with artistic swirls of tiny flower petals in subtle shades of pink covered the walls. The effect melted into generous folds of satin framing the window behind the couch.

Her gaze landed on the miniature photograph. It sat in a gilded frame on the bedside table. *The woman in the portrait downstairs.* She got up for a closer look. Hearing a tap on the door, she turned and said, "Come in."

The door opened. Ada stood there, holding out the Zuni jar with the jasmine plant slightly askew over the rim.

Tessa muffled a cry of joy. "I can't believe it!"

"Brian rescued it for you."

Tessa rushed to clasp her "security blanket." She rubbed a finger over the rim. "It's a miracle it didn't break to pieces."

"Well, part of it did. Brian picked up even the tiniest bits and brought them to me. I glued them back together the best I could. The jasmine's a little puny. But it's alive."

"What a great job you did on both, Ada." Tessa carefully eased her treasure to the marble coffee table. "You and Brian—how can I ever thank you two."

Ada plunged a hand into the pocket of her apron. She pulled out a cellular phone with its charger and set it beside the plant. "It's ready for you."

Tessa stared at the instrument. She recalled blinding lights piercing the fog that morning on the highway. Eyes growing moist, she blinked and reached for the cell. Another miracle.

"Brian planned to take it back to you this morning, along with the plant. He left in such a hurry, he forgot."

"Talk about being at a loss for words, Ada. I don't know how to thank you and Brian."

"God is good, Tessa." Ada started for the door, then paused and looked back at her. "As for the job here, don't go feeling obligated. Felice wouldn't want it any other way, and neither would Brian, that dear man. No matter what we do to this house, it'll never be the same again. Not until—" She stopped and shook her head.

"Until what, Ada?"

"Until it returns to the Lord." She stroked her forehead and looked off.

"I'm sorry. I didn't mean to pry. And you're right," Tessa added slowly. "I mustn't rush into a commitment to work here, for Brian's sake as well as mine." Before she could stop herself, the words were out, "You probably guessed I'm Lester Chandelle's niece. I just found out Brian's mother hired him to have the house refurnished with antiques. She was one of his victims."

Ada stepped up and put a hand on her shoulder. "The kitchen help told me about that. I was away taking care of my sick mother when it all happened. Don't you worry one minute. You're not your uncle. Some of the folks downstairs had nothing but praise for you and your parents. They know your work firsthand."

"You're very kind, Ada. I just can't decide what to do—"

"About taking the job here?" Ada's hand waved off her indecision. "Don't worry about it. Just pray for God's will. The right answer will come to you."

"I'm worried about Brian's mom and how she'd feel if she knew I was in her home—" Her glance fell on the silver-framed miniature photo on the table. "Is that the lady in her youth maybe? I saw the large portrait on the mantel downstairs."

"Honey," Ada's voice lowered to a whisper, "that's Maureen, Brian's wife."

"His wife?" Tessa stared at her.

"She's dead. A year ago last Friday." Ada blinked, her tone wavering. "She was murdered."

"Murdered?" Tessa's mouth hung open. "A year ago last Friday? That's the day he showed up at Chandelle's looking for an Alphonse chair."

Ada sighed. "A fine Christian, that Maureen. So sad. I loved her like she was my own daughter."

"Where, and how did it happen?" Tessa asked softly and dropped to the edge of the bed.

Ada hesitated. "They were on a trip. A stray bullet. It was such a shock. You never expect that." She shook her head, as if tossing off the horrific memories. "I have to run, and Tessa, you ought to rest. Dinner, about eight o'clock." She managed a faint smile and hurried out.

Alone, Tessa felt the quietness press around her. Her brain spun with images of pain she'd seen on Brian's face and heard in his voice almost from the moment they met. She sat still, unable to keep her eyes from growing moist. A storm had taken the life of his father. His wife was murdered. Upset and depressed more than ever because of Uncle Lester's deceit, his mother had left town. He and his sister were at each other's throat. No wonder Ada wept for the family.

Shoulders hunched, she wondered why God had led her to this house of sorrows. She needed to talk to someone.

To Adrienne. She reached for her cell phone and pulled back the crocheted bedspread. A deep sigh and she sat on the bed. She leaned against the headboard and pressed the familiar numbers.

"Tess! What's happening? I've been waiting for your call," Adrienne exclaimed.

"I'm fine now and out of the hospital." Tessa paused for a deep breath. "Go ahead and say, 'I told you so.'"

"Where are you?" Adrienne's voice soared with concern. "Can I come get you? Bring you home with me?"

"Not to worry." Tessa put a smile in her voice. "You ought to see me.

I'm sitting on a bed with satin sheets, in a turn-of-the-century mansion, even grander than Chandelle's."

"Now that doesn't sound like Hotel Louisian'?"

"Le Moyne House."

"As in Brian Le Moyne's house? That Le Moyne? Are you kidding me?"

"Relax, Adrienne. Since I missed my interview with Mirbeau's, someone else got the job. Brian wants to hire me to redecorate his family home."

"Brian wants to hire you?" A pause, then, "Tess." Adrienne's inflection took on a "be sensible" note. "Tell me you're not spending the night in the man's home."

"Adrienne." Tessa echoed her tone. "Don't be silly. Yes, I am. He lives in the family guesthouse, but most of the time he stays in New Orleans. The housekeeper and her husband have an apartment on this floor, not far from me. They know my parents. His mother is off on a cruise."

"Okay, so what are you doing there now?"

Tessa hesitated. "Brian and the housekeeper convinced me to stay here instead of going to a hotel." She went on to explain about the fire, the death of Brian's father, his mother's grief and what the colonial-style home meant to her. About his wife who was murdered, she'd wait and tell her that in person. "He's devoted to his mother and wants her happy again."

"He does sound like an okay guy," Adrienne said slowly. "Not like Josh."

"The opposite, it seems." Tessa thought back to what Ada had said about this house, that it would never be the same until it returned to the Lord. She didn't know if she'd been talking about Darrie or Brian—or about the entire family. "As for his sister . . ."

"What about her?"

"She doesn't want the house refurnished. Brian says he can handle her. I'm not so sure. Working here would have pros and cons." She paused. For now, Uncle Lester's legacy as a decorator hired by Brian's mother was something else she wasn't ready to bring up over the phone.

"Is Brian one of those pluses?"

Tessa looked toward the jasmine in the Zuni jar. "How do you mean?"

"As a man, what else? Are you interested in him?"

Tessa stroked the satiny sheet. "He's been great to me. I owe him so much, Adrienne. He might have saved my life on the highway. And he never left my side."

"And the minuses?"

"He's—well, there's something about him I don't understand. He's got a past."

"Want some advice?" Adrienne's voice lowered. "Run out of there fast before you fall for the guy."

Fall for the guy! Tessa's hand tightened on the phone. "Are you serious? *After Josh?* I'm not about to let myself even *think* of a man until I know we share the same values." She shifted on the bed thinking, *except feelings sometimes don't line up with what you believe is right.* "I'll say it again. I have to concentrate on getting a job, not a man." But for a second, she wasn't sure she was trying to convince Adrienne or herself of that.

"Say the word, and I'll be right over to bring you back home. Or, I can take you to New Orleans if that's what you want. I could leave here in five minutes."

The caring in Adrienne's voice lingered. Tessa hesitated, conflicted as to what she should do. "Let me pray about it. I'll call you tomorrow, if not before."

She punched the End button and held the phone to her chest. She swallowed at the lump in her throat and looked around the room, her gaze on the beautiful young woman who watched her now from the miniature on the bedside table. Why hadn't Brian mentioned her? Not that he should have, but he told her about his father's death, his mother's grief, and his sister Darrie. His mood seemed to have held a confiding tone, as if they might be friends.

But then, she had to admit, she hadn't told him about Josh, news she considered irrelevant between them. He'd found out about Uncle Lester from the guy at lunch and, earlier, surely from talk he'd heard among guests the night of that last party at Chandelle's. Perhaps, like herself, he didn't see the need to share hurtful parts of his private life or pry into hers.

She took a deep, quivery breath. This place had more than its share of heartaches. Besides, no doubt matters would get worse for Brian with his sister when they found out Tessa Chandelle had been here.

Her gaze settled on the armoire that held her bags. Maybe she should do as Adrienne suggested, leave now. Wasn't that her plan when she agreed to come inside the house and meet Ada? Her temples throbbed. *Heavenly Father,* her heart cried, *I'm so into making snap decisions. I need Your help. I have this feeling You led me here. Or was it a diversion from where You really want me to go? Tell me what I should do.*

She fluffed a pillow, lay down and closed her eyes. As she finally drifted off to sleep, Brian's doleful words resounded in her ears: "Happiness is like moonlight. You wake up in the morning, and it's gone."

Chapter V

Bathed in a stream of light, Tessa strolled along a wooded pathway. Ahead, a man ran toward an incline. Winds whipped at his back, chasing him in hurricane-like waves of black fury. He staggered and turned, cobalt eyes fixed on hers. "Tessa!" he cried and catapulted toward the cliff. A noiseless scream rose in her throat. "Brian, no! Come back!" Arms flailing, he teetered.

The ground crumbled from under him, his despairing "Help me!" snatched away in the howling wind.

Gasping for breath, Tessa woke up. Her hands reached out to someone who wasn't there. For the man she'd just dreamed about. *For Brian . . .*

That jingle? What was it? *The phone!*

Pulse battering her temples, she sat up and fumbled to grab her cell from the bedside table. The nightmare's sights and sounds replaying in her brain, she barely made out her accountant's name on the caller ID, Gregory Faulk, CPA.

"Greg?"

"Sorry to disturb you, Tessa. But business calls."

"Business?" Her glance flitted to the open windows. It was still daylight. She saw Brian on the grounds. He leaned against the trunk of an oak tree. Before him was a man whose back was turned to her.

Her hand went limp on the phone.

"Tessa, what's going on? I haven't heard from you since you left town."

"I think I'll accept the job here." The words glided off her tongue as if she'd lost power over them.

"Which is?"

"Today Brian Le Moyne asked me to redecorate the family home."

"Where your uncle worked for a while and was fired?"

"Yes."

"That's a surprise." A moment's silence. "But it could be in your best interest."

"In my best interest?" Tessa rubbed her eyes and straightened. Fully roused now, she stiffened at the unexpected comment.

"You'll have a chance to make matters right with that family." He paused. "I wish I didn't have to tell you this. A couple of guys just showed up here. They have new claims against Chandelle's."

New creditors? Tessa's fingers tightened on the phone. "Did they—I mean, are they legit? Do they have proof?"

Greg hesitated. "I'm afraid so. It's your uncle's signature on a promissory note."

"Do whatever you can to satisfy them." Tessa scooted up against the headboard. "I'll get more funds to you as soon as possible."

"I'm sorry about all this pressure on you right now. But hang in there. This nightmare will end."

"Thank you, Greg."

She slipped the phone back to the bedside table. New creditors showing up to harass her and create a second nightmare, just when would it end? And what had she just told her accountant—that she'd accept the job here? All because of that terrifying dream? What coincidence that his call came at the very moment Brian screamed for help.

A thought, like a revelation, flashed. She hardly breathed. Could that nightmare be God's way of answering her prayers about the job here? At breakfast, hadn't Brian said they needed each other?

Her thoughts raced, colliding with pros and cons. What could she do for him other than try to restore the house for his mother? She remembered the pained look on his face when he asked about the Alphonse. Something troubled him. He needed help. As for herself, she must redeem the family name and pay back creditors.

Yes, Dad, she wanted to say, *this time God had a hand in my spur of the moment decision.* As soon as possible, she'd find Brian and tell him she couldn't wait to sign a contract with him.

"If's" came up, but she dismissed them for now and studied her watch. More than an hour before dinner. She got up and worked her feet into her slippers. After several deep breaths, she stretched her muscles and walked about the room. At the window she stopped and looked for Brian. He and the other man strolled about the grounds, heads shaking as they talked. He had seemed to be on a tight schedule. Maybe she could talk to him before the party.

Now in a hurry to try to carry out a sudden plan, excitement soared. She opened one of her bags and chose a silky, tawny dress, the flared skirt mid-calf. She hurried into the bathroom to wash her face. When she applied her makeup, she was careful again to make sure wispy strands of hair hid the knot on her forehead.

Finally dressed and mirror-approved, she got a handful of new business cards from her briefcase and tucked them inside her small hand bag. When folks tonight found out what kind of work she did, some might ask for her services. And, in case Brian did want a look at her usual contract, she took out a copy from her packed portfolio and slipped it alongside the cards.

Ready for business, she walked out into the long hallway. Her gaze took in the polished look of wooden floors and freshly painted walls. Straight ahead, double doors were open. Resisting the urge to find out where those led and if the area there needed furniture, she stepped down a staircase to her left.

After a couple of wrong turns, she reached the back stairs and walked out onto a patio. She looked around but saw neither Brian nor his companion. Nearby was a swimming pool. She smiled at the shape, a silhouette of Louisiana, and wondered if Brian or his father had designed it. The area enticed with its shady cabana and tables with umbrellas. Here and there were mounds of blooming white irises, blood-red zinnias, and dwarf-pink azaleas. She heard horses neigh in the distance, but no animals roamed in sight. Past the lawn lay a barn, rusty red in the honeyed haze of setting sun.

"Look this way, s'il vous plait?"

Startled by the masculine voice in a Cajun accent, Tessa turned. A man stood only a few feet from where she had stopped. Above the camera leveled at her loomed a head of thick, sandy hair and a high forehead. The camera clicked and then lowered. Tessa met dark eyes and a strong nose in a lean face with perhaps a day's growth of beard. The overall twenty-something look appeared more rugged than handsome.

"Whatcha doin' here, girl? I heard you've been 'dissed' by those relatives inside." Mischief flickered in his laughing eyes.

A puzzled half-smile on her face, Tessa stared at him.

"Glad to see there weren't no truth in it. Miz Le Moyne wouldn't want none uh that." His grin widened as he adjusted the camera case slung over one shoulder.

Tessa let out a sudden hearty laugh. "Wrong girl. I'm Tessa Chandelle from Jasmine Hills. You wasted your film."

"Me and my big Cajun mouth. Sorry about that." He hung a hand on his hip and shook his head. "I was sure you were that niece come to visit from east of our border. Mississippi, that is. I hear she likes our lingo down here. About the film, definitely not wasted," he corrected. "I liked the way you looked walking around, pretty and belonging."

"And I like your self-styled dialect. Merci beaucoup for the laugh. I needed that."

He rubbed the fuzzy beard on his chin. "I'm Gene Dupre, degree in journalism from LSU, would you believe, and a born-again Cajun. Also, photographer/writer for Le Moyne Enterprises."

"I'm a house decorator, from Jasmine Hills." Tessa felt a light breeze ruffle her hair and reached to smooth her bangs. "I might work for Brian too. He wants me to replace those antiques his family lost in the fire."

Gene slapped his forehead. "Now I know. You're the one Ada told me was in that car accident. The way you look, I never would have guessed it. I suppose you'll be living close by while you work?"

Tessa nodded toward the house. "Brian thinks I'd finish quicker if I stayed here than if I commuted. Nothing is settled yet about the job."

"Moi, I live in a trailer." He flipped his thumb in an easterly direction. "Near the marshes back there, at the edge of Le Moyne property. Hey, maybe I'd be able to help you. Brian had me photograph every stick of furniture in the place. The family always kept careful records. You'll have original photos, of course, but if you need duplicates, I'm not far."

"Thanks. Right now I'm looking for Brian."

"You'll probably find him in the sunroom. That's on second floor, in case you don't already know. I was talking to him earlier, trying to stay in good with the boss-man."

"Thanks again, Gene." Tessa gave him another smile. "Nice meeting you."

"Pleasure's mine. I'm working City Hall tonight, or I'd be at the party. See you around, Tessa. Don't forget, if you need help, I'm at your service."

"Au revoir." Nice guy, Tessa thought. She waggled her fingers in goodbye and then hurried off toward the side entrance she had exited earlier.

She climbed a staircase and came upon the threshold of a large, L-shaped room, the one Gene might have mentioned. The door was open. She knocked softly, her gaze taking in pale lighting from lamps on end tables, a white wicker settee and, facing it, matching chairs with cool, green cushions.

The muffled sound of footsteps broke her concentration.

"Tessa?"

Brian stepped from behind a floor-to-ceiling walnut cabinet. He wore gray trousers and a white open-neck shirt. A grin lit up his eyes, the greeting, "Tessa," surprised and low.

Tessa let go the memory of that pleading figure in a nightmare. Coming face to face with this Brian Le Moyne sent her into an upward spin, time and place forgotten. But reality promptly replaced the moment for her. Most likely, Maureen's image appeared between them, making anyone else a trespasser on his memories of other times when his wife might have walked in, dressed for a party.

"Is this a good time to talk?" she asked, her tone hesitant.

"Sure. Come in. The sun room is our temporary family den on this floor." Brian strode forward, one hand encompassing the area in a wide sweep.

"Nice and private. That is," Tessa entered and smiled, "unless some house guest has the nerve to invade it."

"I'm glad this one did." Brian touched her arm and nodded her toward the settee. "By the way, how's your room?"

"Perfect, thanks." Tessa backed onto the edge of the couch.

Brian sat on a wicker armchair opposite her and leaned forward, hands capping his knees. "I thought I'd come here to watch the news before dinner." He motioned to the TV set in a corner. "But now I'd rather visit with you."

Tessa looked around. "A lovely room."

"What little damage there was here after the fire, we fixed it up right away." He pointed to a well-stacked cabinet. "Lucky that survived. It holds DVDs of every piece of furniture in the house before the fire. Each is identified with a complete legend of acquisition. After the party, maybe we could come back here? Look at a few shoots?"

Tessa hesitated. That face and those eyes oozing charm and kindness reached out to her. Spend an evening alone with him? *Watch it, Tessa. Not so fast. Don't put blind trust in this man like you did in Josh.*

"On second thought, we'd better not rush it," he said before she could answer. "You've had a long day."

Tessa nodded. "I've been thinking about your job offer."

"Still interested, I hope." He leaned forward. "Forget what you heard Darrie say about your uncle. That's history."

Tessa glanced toward the windows and the deepening twilight. A long moment, and she faced him again. "But how about your mother? What would she say if you hired Lester Chandelle's niece to work in her home? Doesn't that worry you?"

"Worry me? Absolutely not. She was always for giving second chances. You want to win back the Chandelle reputation. What better place to start than right here? She'd applaud you for that. Not a doubt in my mind."

"But shouldn't you call her, ask her permission?"

"No. I already know her answer. Besides, I want to surprise her with the house back like it was in her 'good old days' before the fire. As for Darrie, she's my problem, not yours." Easing back in his chair, he linked his hands behind his head. "Getting this place refurnished is what matters. When Dad died, it was left in a trust for my sister and me. It allows Mom to stay here for the rest of her life or until she decides to sell.

She gave me power of attorney while she's away. Take the job, and you'll answer to me, no one else." He held a forefinger to his chest. "Whatever comes up, I'll handle it."

"About my living in this house, wouldn't that be a problem?"

"Not at all. Our mom would see it as a plus. If you lived here, you'd be free to work day or night, at your discretion. You'd finish the work sooner than if you commuted."

Tessa held a hand to her forehead, another reality taking over. How could she commute when she didn't have a car? As for buying or renting one right now, what about those creditors hounding her accountant almost daily?

A stillness between them, and their gazes locked. Tessa could hear it again, his cry for help in that nightmare. "Well, then," she smiled off a sudden tremor in her voice, "I accept your offer. I'll do my best not to disappoint you or your mom."

Brian lowered his arms to the sides of his chair. "Are you sure you're ready to make that commitment?"

"Yes. You're willing to give a Chandelle another chance. I'd like to take it." She watched his features relax in a mix of gratitude and relief she hadn't put on a client's face in a long time. She had missed that look. "About the Alphonse," she added, "don't think I've given up on it."

"It was from my wife." Brian's face sobered, his words low. "Maureen's last birthday present to me before she died."

"I'm sorry." Tessa's sympathy hung in the quietness of the moment. So now she knew why he seemed desperate to find the chair on that particular day.

He drew a long breath. "We'll draw up a contract." His tone lifted, seemingly eager to change the subject. "Whatever your terms, I'll meet them." He stood. "Shake on it?"

Tessa stared at him. Was it really happening, a job about to be sealed with a man she had come to trust? A man who returned that trust to the Chandelle name? She gave him a tremulous smile and got up, hand reaching out to meet his.

"You can change your mind at any time." His fingers tightened around hers, emphasizing he meant what he said. "Even after you start, if you're not happy with the way things are going, say the word. No questions asked."

"You'll have the same option."

"Not a chance I'll take it." An extra squeeze of her hand, and then he let go. "It's early yet. Let me show you Mom's office. It'll be yours with everything you'll need at your fingertips."

Sidestepping the couch and chairs, he led her toward the back of the room and a paneled door. She stood aside while he fumbled with a set of keys from his pocket, chose one, and inserted it into the lock. He pushed the door open and reached inside to switch on a ceiling light. A playful wave of his hand, and he urged her inside.

Tessa took in the decor that reminded her of Chandelle's hideaway working space, especially with the Louis XIV walnut writing desk.

"We'll replace the manual typewriter there with a computer for you," Brian said. "Mom likes that antique and can still make those keys fly."

"Good for her." Tessa smiled. "I forgot my laptop at Chandelle's, and I'm lost without it."

Her gaze shifted to a western expanse of windows covered with cerulean draperies in a light, free-flowing fabric. Brian pulled them open, exposing flowerpots on the wide sill—begonias, violets, and gloxinias. The opposite wall, lined with filing cabinets, gleamed stark-white. A lounge chair beside the other wall matched the purplish blue of the draperies.

"Are you sure," Tessa asked, "your mom won't mind if I take over her private office?"

"Positive. Especially when she walks back here one day and finds the house like it was before the fire. You'll need all furniture records at your fingertips." Brian unlocked the top drawer of the desk and opened it. He took out a thick album. "This contains another pictorial record of every room in the house." Eyes downcast, he placed the volume on the desktop and, as if transported to another time on the instant, he stroked the leather cover back and forth.

Tessa recalled tense encounters at Chandelle's when, desperate for Josh's comfort, he said, "Good riddance, this place. You'll forget about it in no time." Brian's grief, his wife's tragic death, and the loss of his father surely ran deeper than her sadness over losing Chandelle's and the life she'd planned with Josh.

From the expression on his face, Tessa thought Brian might want to talk about the past. Maybe about Maureen.

But he tapped a forefinger on the desk and then looked at her. "So there, all yours. In a couple of days or so, you'll have a charge card for purchases and incidental expenses. Now about contract terms, let's talk." He pulled out the swivel chair for her and anchored his long frame on a corner of the desk.

She'd always have a car at her disposal, he assured her. If she couldn't find certified antiques, she'd use her discretion in choosing replacements. Should she question what she thought might be more than he'd want to spend at any time, she'd consult him. But if it came to a decision between contacting him first and missing an important acquisition in the process, she was to go ahead and trust her judgment. As for living in Le Moyne House, no charge because, at his request, she would be available both day and night to hasten the work.

"Along with your fee," he went on, "jot down anything else you want to stipulate and give me a copy."

"Here's my usual contract." She pulled it out of her purse and handed it to him.

He did a quick read. "Perfect. I'll have my secretary type one up, and you can check it out. You're free to get on with the project here whenever you like."

A job at last. An answer to her prayer. Her mouth opened but, for a moment, she lost words. "I'll do my best," she finally managed.

"I know you will, but I don't expect miracles." He slid off the desk, pulled a business card from his pocket and handed it to her. "An extra one. I'm in and out of home or office without notice. Ada can be a big help to you, even better than I can. Especially," he went on, "when it comes to picking out furniture replacement she knows my mother would like. But never hesitate to call me whenever you want to talk." He grinned. "And it doesn't have to be about antiques."

Tessa smiled back. "But to interrupt you in a business conference?"

"And make my day? Nothing wrong with that." His grin widened, and then he grew serious again. "Ada will give you a set of house keys. This one," he said, pulling another from his key ring, "is yours, a duplicate, for the office. If there's anything we can do to make you feel at home here, just ask. Until we sign, another proof of agreement?"

Tessa dropped the key inside her purse and stood for a second handshake.

He chuckled. "I'm really liking this."

She had to force a smile. The day's emotions threatened an overload, and only the warm pressure of his hand stopped the trembling in hers and the start of a tear. "You can't know what this work means to me."

"You're doing the favor—"

"Brian?"

The moment shattered.

They drew apart and looked toward the doorway.

Darrie. Her mouth in an instant's party-mood smile, she reminded Tessa of the "after" picture in a commercial, a distant likeness to the "before" picture she'd met earlier. Eye-catching in a slinky, low-cut black dress, the smile fled her face when she looked squarely at Tessa.

"What are you doing here, Darrie?" Brian asked. "You're supposed to be on duty at the studio."

"I got a sub." Darrie's smile was gone. "Soon guests will be ringing the doorbell. Ada told me you invited our New York friends too. You should be downstairs to greet them when they arrive – and everybody else who was so generous with their donations."

Tessa stepped back. "Please excuse me, you two."

"Party's at eight," Brian said. "I'll see you then?"

"Yes." Tessa smiled, her hand lifting in a friendly, "You too, Darrie."

Darrie nodded and looked back at Brian.

Tessa turned and walked out. Without a doubt, her thoughts fled, the woman could be a troublemaker. Was already. She might even persuade

Brian to rethink their unsigned contract.

A few minutes after eight, Tessa went downstairs and entered the party room. Off to one side, white-clothed tables glowed with candlelight. A small refreshment bar offered appetizers and cold drinks. Next to it was a long table. The kitchen help, including Cede, loaded it with platters of what was doubtless a gourmet feast. In the background, Ada pattered around in a deep-blue dress with white frilly collar and apron. Her face flushed, she smiled toward Tessa.

Guests, perhaps forty or more, Tessa decided, mingled in a background of soft symphonic music from the stereo. On a far side of the room, as if they had expected her to walk in that very moment, Tessa saw Brian and Simone look her way. Brian said something to those around them, mainly the television guests, she assumed. The next moment, he and Simone headed in her direction.

"Remember me, Tessa?" Simone dashed forward. A sparkling jeweled pin rested on the deep V of her pale lavender dress. Long-lashed grey eyes lit up her smile, the diamond-ringed fingers cool but firm as they circled Tessa's hand.

"Oh, yes, Simone," Tessa said. "It's nice to see you again."

Other guests gathered around them.

A plump young woman with short-cropped hair, shiny brown and wavy, was quick to offer a greeting. "Hi, Tessa. I'm Estelle Arceneaux. I've already heard so much about you from Ada and Brian. All complimentary. How nice to meet you."

"And here is Estelle's husband, Martin, our Dr. Arceneaux' renegade son." Brian nodded to a tall, wiry man with thick, dark-rimmed glasses. "This guy actually ran away from med school to become one of my business partners in television."

"Dad said you'd made a remarkable recovery." Martin reached to shake Tessa's hand.

"But did he have to be so protective? Not let her have visitors?" Simone's shadowy pout changed into a sympathetic smile toward Tessa.

"That's my father." Martin laughed. "Super cautious."

From somewhere in the group, Darrie appeared. "Simone, do you know that Tessa is an expert in antiques?"

Tessa felt the stares of a battery of eyes, making her the center of attention. Just the kind of advertisement she needed, *but from Darrie?*

"An expert? What luck! I bought a foyer table, early Louis XV period, some time ago. It's a gift for Brian's mother." Simone motioned to the back of the room. "It's over there. Would you be so kind as to take a look, Tessa, and tell me if you agree it is the real thing?"

"This is a party, Simone." Brian frowned. "Please, drop it."

Her hands flew to her hips. "But this is as good a time as any. You doubt it's an antique, and I say it is. Why not let Tessa tell us who's right?"

"She just got out of the hospital." Brian lowered his voice. "This is asking too much of her right now."

"Let her decide." Darrie stepped forward and looked around at the guests. "Tessa hit hard times and had to sell her business, Chandelle's House of Antiques. But, hey, everybody needs a new start."

"Darrie—" Brian began.

"And guess what, my dear brother here," Darrie's motioned to him, "just offered her a contract to redecorate this house." She smiled toward Tessa. "You're desperate for work, aren't you? I would think you'd appreciate the chance to show off your expertise. Let's see how you go about telling the real thing from the fake."

"Give it up, Darrie." Brian gave her a hard look. "This isn't the time or the place for that."

Tessa's hands knotted at her sides. Just what did Darrie have in mind?

"Well, Tessa?" her smile challenged.

"You don't have to do this, Tessa," Brian said.

"Of course you don't." Simone touched her arm. "It was just a sudden thought. If you'd rather not, I'll understand."

Tessa fought a burst of pros and cons on her tongue. Was Darrie ready to mention that some rumors accused her of being her Uncle Lester's partner in passing off fakes as antiques? No doubt she had just argued with Brian about that proposed contract. Besides, folks here who knew or had heard of her uncle might not trust her to give an honest opinion and want to question her judgment.

She glanced around at expectant faces turned her way. Darrie had pushed her into a deep hole. She must try to climb out of it. "Okay. Let's take a look."

Guests broke into applause.

She flashed a quick glance toward Ada. The woman nodded lightly up and down.

Boosted by the subtle affirmation, Tessa turned at once to follow Simone and the guests toward the back of the room.

"There it is." Simone nudged Brian. "You'll eat your words, I guarantee it."

"Don't be too sure," he said.

Quiet fell while Tessa gave the table top a concentrated look and then ran both hands slowly over the surface, back and forth. She looked at Brian. "I need to check underneath."

One of the male guests stepped forward to help him turn the table over as Simone cautioned, "Careful!"

Tessa tried to forget watchful eyes. She went on with the standard appraisal her parents had taught her and always used in the business to determine the authenticity of any supposed antique.

She managed a little laugh when she got down on her knees. "It's the only way to examine the joints." She ran her fingers over the spots she indicated and explained, "The hammer marks should look old, not new. And the nails in an antique are generally wood, not metal." Squinting at the texture of the grain, her gaze probed. "Indentations, however slight, might indicate recent moisture." She rubbed at residue on the sides of the drawers. "The glue should be aged. The drawers should be a little hard to pull—" But she slid them right out. "That likely means a recent application . . . of something."

In the expectant hush, she drew a long breath to delay her verdict: not an antique, but a phony. She was sure of it. Now to expose Simone as one easily fooled?

She asked Brian and his helper to turn the table upright so she could examine the top again. Brow furrowed, she stroked the surface. "If the texture is smooth, the sheen too bright, that denotes an absence of age . . ."

"The dealer I bought it from said he was positive it's an antique," Simone said. "I believe he's right."

Tessa took a deep breath, conscious all ears waited for her reply. Forefinger to her lips, she stood back, her gaze fixed on the table. Words circled round and round in her head for a tactful way to tell Simone the truth. She looked up at her. "I can see why you—why anyone might think—"

"I asked for your opinion." Simone placed a slender, red-nailed hand on the table top. "Please, be honest. You won't hurt my feelings if you say I made a bad bargain."

"I think it's a fake," Tessa said.

"You think," Simone repeated, voice modulated, controlled, as if she might be conducting an impersonal television interview. "You're saying you're not sure, that you could be wrong?"

"I'm sorry, Simone." Tessa shook her head. "It's nothing but a clever copy. If I were you, I'd return it and ask for a refund."

"The score is one-to-one, folks," Simone's performance voice sang out, laced with frivolity. "We need a deciding vote."

"Then I cast it. I agree with Tessa," Brian said. "Too bad you lost, but Mom would appreciate the effort."

Simone's face blossomed into a smile. "Thank you, Tessa. I know that wasn't easy." She faced her audience. "Everybody, let's give Le Moyne House's new decorator a big hand."

The crowd applauded. Tessa managed a playful bow. She caught Brian's grin and two fingers raised in a V for victory. From Ada on the fringes, a smile and a nod. Darrie stood aside, arms crossed over her chest. The grim look in her eyes held a threat rather than a compliment.

Folks gathered in little groups, the conversation in a buzz about antiques. Tessa felt a tug on her arm.

Simone pulled her aside. "We need to talk." Her whisper held a secretive ring, her smile gone.

"What about?" Tessa matched her lowered tone.

"Something you ought to know before you make a big mistake."

A rice buyer approached. "Miss Duvall, I wonder if . . ."

"Later. I'll call you." Simone let go of Tessa's arm.

Tessa stared at her as the two walked off.

But she had no time to dwell on Simone's warning. Guests approached her for advice about locating certain antiques. While no one mentioned Uncle Lester's name, some asked if she was the daughter of the Chandelle missionaries. Her reply brought a slight lift of the brow or a surprised inflection in the tone, "You are?" followed by, "And Brian hired you?" She wondered if the questions had anything to do with Simone's comment earlier that they needed to talk. While a couple of people asked for her business card, their attitude seemed casual.

She glimpsed Ada, tinkling bell in hand as she approached Brian. He moved to the middle of the room. Chatter droned off, attentive faces turned toward him.

"Welcome, everyone." His gaze circled the guests "Thank you for your generous donations to help our unfortunate friends in New Orleans. Be assured that your thoughtfulness is deeply appreciated by everyone there who has suffered loss from hurricanes, tornadoes, and other disasters. Tonight we honor you for your love and concern which helped many to put a roof over their heads and food on their tables."

A burst of applause.

When the sounds died off, Brian continued, "Our own Ada and her helpers have prepared a feast for us. So now, dinner is served, folks! Find your place at one of the tables. *Bon appetit* to all!"

Estelle rushed over to Tessa. "Sit with me."

Tessa followed her to a round table set for five guests. She saw Brian and Martin who, along with Simone, head toward the other side of the room with the two New York visitors. Close by, Darrie settled down with a younger group.

"The three hosts will table-hop and might join us for a late cup of coffee," Estelle said. "Those extra seats here are for them."

Tessa bowed her head in a moment of silent prayer and then looked up to see Estelle's head lift as if she too had just returned thanks. Small talk between them praised the elegant table service with its Wedgwood china and Waterford crystal. Later when Ada stopped by their table, they raved about the veal cutlets with the creamy sauce and the carrot soufflé.

Sipping coffee after red velvet cake for dessert, Tessa saw Brian, accompanied by Simone and Martin, escort the two visitors toward the hallway. The hosts returned shortly and, as Estelle predicted, they went from table to table to visit with the other guests. Tessa overheard them explain that the two out-of-town guests had to catch an early flight the next morning.

Brian finally sank into an empty chair at the table across from her. A questioning look in his eyes on hers, and she thought he wondered if the evening's activities were too much for her.

"I'm really enjoying tonight," she said and smiled toward him.

"Now what about your mom's usual summer party, Brian?" Estelle asked. "Since she's away, Martin and I would be glad to host it in our home."

"How lovely of you, Estelle!" Simone walked up and pulled out the chair next to Brian.

Tessa went on alert. Maybe Simone would find a way to clue her in as to why they needed to talk.

"I appreciate the offer, Estelle." Brian reached for the cup of coffee Ada set before him. "But I'll handle it here. It'll be for her, a homecoming affair. Maybe you'd be one of the hostesses?"

The conversation took off in a hum of excitement. Simone recalled Felice's traditional parties. Guest lists, she went on, included governors and other dignitaries, favorite food and refreshments, musicians, and "the most beautiful floral decorations you ever saw throughout the house. Everyone loved those affairs!"

"We entertain in the large activity room on third floor." Brian looked at Tessa. "It's still in great shape. You probably already know it needs a new piano."

"What's with those rumors, Brian?" Martin appeared, brows

going up with a jovial grin. "You're planning a big splash for a special announcement?"

Brian shrugged. "Announcement?"

"Oh, you know what I mean." Martin slanted a glance toward Simone.

"No idea." Brian sipped his coffee.

Tessa's gaze flitted to Simone. The supposed fiancée sat quietly, a faint smile on her face. She wore several rings. The one on her third finger, left hand, looked more like an heirloom than a traditional diamond setting. Clearly Martin had hinted at an engagement party for her and Brian.

Tessa tried for an amused grin to hide an inward jolt. So that was what Simone meant when she said there was something she should know before she accepted the job with Brian? And, could it be she didn't want her living in Le Moyne house, afraid she'd be too close to her fiancé? But if they were engaged, reason countered, why did Brian act as if he didn't know what the rumor might be?

"Sorry, y'all." Now Darrie rushed to their table, a shake of her head as if she was upset about something. "Kyle just texted from the driveway. He's in a hurry. I've gotta run."

Brian started to get up. "I'll walk you out."

"No, that's okay. 'Bye, all. See you later."

Darrie's exit signaled the other guests the party was over. Soon only the Arceneaux couple and Simone lingered with Brian and Tessa for second cups of coffee at a table on the patio. While the two men talked in low voices about an impending strike at Acadian Oil, the women discussed the latest fashions.

"It's not too early to start looking for a new gown for Brian's party," Estelle said.

The engagement party, Tessa wondered, and looked at Simone to get her reaction. Again, only a smile.

"New gown? Did I hear right?" Martin mockingly held a finger to his ear. "Our cue to stop that kind of talk and say good-night."

Everyone stood and laughed.

"*Men.*" Estelle hugged Simone and Tessa, leaving Brian for last and applauded him for "finding a jewel like Tessa" to redecorate the mansion. She and Martin sauntered off, hands lifted in goodbyes.

Simone checked her watch. "My, the time! We should go, Brian. I'll get my purse." Not waiting for his answer, she hurried back inside the house.

Brian turned to Tessa. "About Simone's table, you handled the whole thing like the pro you are."

"I had to be honest."

"That's why I want you to decorate this house. No one else."

Tessa hesitated. *Something she ought to know,* Simone had said. "Are you sure you haven't changed your mind?"

Brian's brow furrowed. "Now why would you ask that?"

Heels clicked toward them. Simone appeared and looked at Tessa. "I'll call you soon."

Tessa nodded. "Goodnight, you two."

"Get some rest," Brian said, a long look meeting hers. "Talk to you tomorrow."

Tessa smiled and waved them off. She put her worries on hold and reverted to an old playful custom with Adrienne, her eyes on a star. Not the first of the night, her friend would remind her. Too late to make a wish. It wouldn't come true. Like all those she'd made for herself and Josh, wasted, even though she'd poured out her heart on first stars again and again.

A deep breath and her arms folded. Now her gaze lowered to the floor. Brian's job offer, had she been too quick to accept it? She could see her dad shake his finger at her and say, "You did it again, Tess. Acted on impulse."

Chapter VI

A week later, no signed contract.

Hurried calls from Brian the next few days. "Something came up. I can't get away." Or, "Be sure to get plenty of rest. Take your time going over the house files with Ada. I'll call back soon."

Energized as she had not been in a long time, with Ada often at her side with remarks as to what was in view or suggestions for replacements if needed, Tessa spent hours watching videos and began a notebook list of every antique needed to return the house to its former grandeur. Experience had taught her some of those pieces could only come from prominent, well-known dealers out of state or in another country, like France, with whom she and her parents had often dealt. But, pen poised in reflection, before she went further with her work, she needed a signed contract and the promised credit card from Brian.

Now she felt his lack of obvious enthusiasm to finalize their oral agreement was a letdown.

"He changed his mind, Ada," she said. "I just know it. Maybe it's because he and Simone are engaged and she doesn't want to live here. At the dinner here the other night, she told me we need to talk."

"You worry he changed his mind about having his mother's house refurnished? Because of Simone, that they'll marry and she doesn't want to live here?" Ada shook her head from side to side. "I'll have to hear that from him to believe it. Be patient. Brian wants this house redone as much, maybe even more than Felice does."

Later, trying to hold on to those words and dressed in pajamas, robe and slippers, Tessa sat on the side of her bed, her brain in a whirl. Tomorrow she would attend a private sale of antiques in New Orleans. Although she'd been to scores of those through the years, she dreaded this one. It was the first since Uncle Lester had brought down the Chandelle name. She might run into someone who had been swindled by him. No matter where she went, she'd known that might happen.

"I need to calm down," she murmured in the quietness. She got up. Pacing, she eyed her cell, picked it up, and asked the room out loud,

"Wonder if Adrienne would like a talkfest."

No, she told herself. Too late.

She dropped the phone into her side pocket and ambled toward the bedroom door. Casually she opened it and stared down the dimly lit hallway that led to the sunroom. Since she still wasn't sleepy, now would be a good time to check out other DVDs as she'd been doing the past few days.

A moment's hesitation, and then she stepped out, quietly closing the door behind her. She tiptoed down the hall, past Ada and Cede's apartment. Excitement grew as she entered the room and switched on a table lamp. From the cabinet, she picked a random DVD and inserted it into the television set's player. Then, controls in hand, she perched on the lounge chair and lost herself in the charm of antiques that graced Le Moyne House before the fire.

A second disc, a third, and finally her finger hit the pause button on the controls. She stared at the armoire, the pair of 1870s French fireside chairs, and the rosewood bookcase, a 1770s treasure with hand-carved maiden figures on each side. Those antiques waited at Chandelle's. For the clocks and the French tapestry, she could contact old reliable dealers in France.

"Tessa?" Ada leaned in the doorway. "I can't sleep. I thought I'd get a glass of milk from the kitchen. Then I saw the light—"

"You're just in time. Take a look." Tessa pointed to the screen. "We can get some of those rare pieces at Chandelle's."

Ada's brows went up. She stepped forward to inspect the antiques Tessa clicked on and indicated which ones should be available. "Oh, my." She eased back and sat on the edge of the settee, her gaze never leaving the screen. "At Chandelle's, just waiting for us. Who would have guessed it?"

"First thing in the morning, I'll contact the new owners. They just opened up for business a couple of days ago. Surely most or all of what we want hasn't sold yet." She glanced at her watch and pulled the phone from her pocket. "It's late, but I've got to call Brian with the good news."

"Right after that, you go to bed." Ada stood and shook a finger at her.

Tessa gave her a teasing smirk. "Look who's talking."

"Well, unlike you, I nap in the daytime. Goodnight, honey." Walking off, Ada glanced back at Tessa over her shoulder. "And some people say God doesn't answer prayer."

Tessa punched in Brian's number. Phone to her ear, her thoughts raced. If the news didn't excite him, she'd know without a doubt he was having second thoughts about the project.

"Tessa?"

"I couldn't wait to tell you, Brian. I've been looking at DVDs. Chandelle's has several antiques we need."

Silence, except for vague background noises. Her grip tightened on the cell. "Brian?"

"Great news, Tessa."

"Should I put in a purchase order?"

"Of course." His tone sounded preoccupied.

"Did I disturb you? I'm sorry—"

"No problem. I'll be in touch soon."

"Thanks . . ." He'd already turned her off.

The thrill of her unexpected success dimmed to a flicker. She put away the discs and turned off the light. Head lowered, she ambled back to her room. Something *had* gone wrong, and did it have to do with Simone? Tomorrow she'd demand a clear yes or no answer to their verbal agreement.

In a see-saw mood next morning after a quick shower, she slipped into jeans and a cotton blouse, applied lip gloss, and pulled her hair back with a clip. If Brian didn't phone by lunchtime, she'd call him. She'd know then if she should go to that sale of antiques in New Orleans. Meanwhile, to be sure the pieces she'd seen last night were still available if needed, she decided to contact Chandelle's new owners before they opened up for business. She hoped they'd answer when they saw she was the caller. She glanced past Maureen's picture on the table and reached for her cell.

Adrienne picked up at first ring.

"Lucky you!" she exclaimed when Tessa told her why she called and indicated where she had last seen the needed antiques on display. "Everything you want is still here. Besides, we've had a cancellation and can deliver late this afternoon."

"Just in case, Adrienne, if for any reason we decide to return the furniture—"

"Same courtesy you offered your customers. You'll have thirty days, guaranteed. And, know what? Unless business really picks up, I might hitch a ride with the delivery guys."

"You'd better," Tessa said with mock seriousness, "or we'll refuse the order. And, oh, Adrienne, my laptop—"

"I won't forget!"

"One more thing. I'll have to charge the furniture for now. Okay?"

"Your name and that of the Le Moynes, good as gold. You should know that."

Fun chit-chat, giggly good-byes, and Tessa eased the phone into her side pocket to be sure she didn't miss a call, especially one from Brian.

A hurried trek downstairs and her gaze caught the sparkle of sunlight on the hallway's leaded glass doors. Memories of mornings at Chandelle's flashed. She couldn't ignore the urge to step outside for a breath of fresh air.

Just past the threshold, she stopped. A white van with a Landry Realty insignia stamped on the door was parked under an oak tree. Beside it sat a silver sports car. Dressed in dark pants and a red blouse, Simone ambled farther out on the grounds, accompanied by two men. One, youthful in a blue shirt and jeans, carried a notebook under his arm. The other, short and paunchy, wore khakis. Hands gesturing, they talked, now and then glancing back toward the house.

"I can't believe it."

Tessa turned.

Ada stood in the doorway. Back and forth, she rubbed the short, thick fingers of one hand on the side of her white apron.

"What's going on?" Tessa asked.

"Simone and Darrie have their heads in the same bonnet, that's what. And there's Kyle, Darrie's husband, the man in jeans. He owns Landry Realty. He and Darrie are dying to put the house up for sale and make a big commission. They're always broke." She shook her head. "Now Simone? She wants to move on to New York and climb higher in the business world. On Brian's coattails, of course." Ada gave a wave of her hand as if to order them away. "I wish he could see this."

"And you think—?"

"That Felice will agree to sell?" Ada shrugged. "She could change her mind, I suppose. Same goes for Brian. But I don't see them doing it. They both love this place too much."

"But maybe," Tessa hesitated, "if Simone and Brian—?"

"Are engaged? All I know is they're business partners." She gave a dismissive shake of her hand. "I can't stand to look at that woman with Kyle and the other guy one more minute. Anyway, this is none of my business. I should keep my mouth shut." Her hands relaxed at her sides. "How about breakfast? Cede and I had ours. I've got to run an errand downtown." She glanced at her watch.

"You go on. I'll get breakfast later." Tessa looked back at the visitors who still walked around, hands on hips or gesturing as they talked. She took out her phone. "I've waited long enough. Simone said there was something I should know before I sign a contract with Brian. It's time I find out what that is."

"Now, honey, I'd check with him first," Ada said.

"That's who I'm calling." Tessa punched in his number. Seconds, and only a call-back message. She turned off the phone. "No choice, Ada. I've got to talk to Simone now, face to face."

Tessa dashed down the steps and turned off the walk. She hurried across the lawn toward a moss-draped oak tree where they stood, the men with hands moving as if in deep talk. Simone stood back, camera lifted on their surroundings. She wore sunglasses, her hair pulled back from her face in a smooth coif. Full, red lips matched the color of her blouse.

"Hi, Simone." Tessa approached them.

"Oh, Tessa. I was going to call you." She smiled and lowered her camera. "Meet my friends." She nodded to the younger man. "This is Kyle Landry, Darrie's husband."

"It's a pleasure, Tessa." He grinned, deep brown eyes lively as he pumped Tessa's hand and then added as he turned to the man next to him, "Please meet my business partner, Gary Marino."

Gary's handshake, politely firm, matched his with a smiling, "Nice to meet you, Tessa."

"Well, Gary and I gotta run," Kyle said. "We'll let you two ladies get better acquainted. See you soon. Have a great day now." He nodded to Simone. "Call me." Broad smiles from both men, and they walked away.

"I had to go out of town on business and just got home yesterday." Simone stepped closer to Tessa, her tone lowered. "Sorry to keep you waiting. Like I said, we need to talk."

"Please, I have to know now." Tessa couldn't stop the words. "Is this place for sale? Is that what you wanted to tell me?"

Simone touched her arm. "What I have to say is confidential. Will you promise to keep it that way?"

"Of course, if that's what you want."

"Then let's go for walk."

They started down a concrete path bordered by bright yellow lilies and orange-red zinnias. Any other time, Tessa would have indulged in the refreshing sights and aroma of the landscape. Now she wanted nothing more than to hear what Simone thought she needed to know before she signed a contract with Brian.

"First, let's talk about you." Simone smiled, her tone lilting on the instant. "After that display of talent the other night, I'm convinced you're a great decorator."

"Thank you. I've had good teachers. My parents were in the business for years."

Simone kicked at a pebble in her way. "How would you like a glamorous, fun job that paid you what you're worth?"

"Oh?" Tessa's brows went up. "Like what?"

"A TV show about antiques. You'd be perfect for it."

Tessa stared at her. Had she pegged Simone wrong? She hadn't expected an offer like that from her or anyone else. "I appreciate the offer, and yes, it sounds like something I'd really enjoy. Maybe we could talk about it after I finish the work for Brian? We're signing a contract any day now."

"So he says. Yet he keeps putting you off, right?"

Tessa whisked back a strand of hair from her forehead. "He's been awfully busy."

"Or, maybe he's having second thoughts. Has that occurred to you?"

Tessa shrugged. "Sure. It's happened before with clients. Things come up. People change their minds."

"He saw how easily fooled I was with that table for his mother." Simone smiled. "Maybe it convinced him his dream for the 'original' Le Moyne House is just that, a dream. An impossible one."

"Oh, but it is possible," Tessa said. "Just last night, I located a few of the pieces we need. They're at Chandelle's."

"At Chandelle's." Simone hesitated and touched a finger to her lips. "Excuse me for being blunt, but can you be sure they're real antiques? Your uncle did get into a lot of trouble selling fakes."

The dreaded mention of that family member and business partner sent Tessa's face into a quick burn. "Yes, he failed to live up to Chandelle's standards. No telling how long I'll be paying for that. The antiques I found last night come with certificates of authenticity, as did all of those we carried."

"Well," Simone began slowly, "I'll take your word for that. But, when you called him last night, was Brian excited about your news? I don't think so. I was with him."

Tessa blinked, trying to dim the surprise of those simple words, *I was with him.* "I'll admit he didn't whoop and clap. I shouldn't have phoned so late." She cleared her throat. "What's really on your mind? What is it you think I should know? Is Le Moyne House up for sale?"

Simone slowed and placed a hand on Tessa's arm. "It should be. Look, Tessa, I like you. You're a beautiful, talented person. And yes, I saw right off, you're kind and caring," her words rushed. "The last thing I want to do is hurt your feelings. But I have to be honest with you."

"Please do. I'm confused."

"You don't know it, but you're making things worse for Brian by being here. He really doesn't want the house refurnished. He's using the excuse it would make his mother happy. The truth is, he can't let go of the past. It means letting go of Le Moyne House. Deep down, he wants to do that, get away from here and the memories. He just can't admit it. If—" She hesitated.

"If what? Out with it, please."

Simone flicked back her hair, her gaze averted. "If he'd hear it from you—that there's no way the place can be like it was before—he'd believe it and give up the crazy notion."

Tessa stared at her. "You want me to lie to him?"

Simone took a deep breath and shifted her bag to the other shoulder. "You're encouraging him in his daydream, don't you see? It's time to quit this tiresome charade before it goes any further. You Christians are supposed to be above that, aren't you?"

"Charade? Are you saying—?"

Simone raised a hand to stop her. "You have to tell him you want out of the bargain. He has to hear from you there's no way the house can be like it was before the fire. He'll pretend to be upset, but deep down, he'll be relieved. I know him."

"I can't do that."

"Okay, I didn't want to tell you, but you leave me no choice." Simone assumed a patient tone. "Brian feels he owes you. He blames himself for your accident. That's why he offered you the job. He feels guilty."

Tessa stared at her. "Did he say that?"

"Of course not. He's too much of a gentleman to admit it. So hear me out. Go on and let him feel obligated." Simone's steps slowed as her words quickened. "You couldn't make him stop anyway. Just don't punish him for being a man of principle. Deep down, he'll thank you. That's when Darrie and I will suggest a job for you at our station in Baton Rouge. All you have to do is tell him that after checking out the house, you're convinced it can't be restored."

"I understand your concern, and I appreciate your offer of a TV job." Tessa tried hard for a patient tone. "But right now—"

"Maybe you're thinking of the bad publicity about your Uncle Lester and doubt the TV job would attract viewers. But I can assure you the publicity we'd give you would work to your advantage big time along with your professionalism on the screen. Talk about a perfect chance to rebuild your family's reputation. That's the alternative to giving Brian false hope."

"It does sound like an answer to prayer. Your offer, I mean. You're very kind, but I won't lie to him."

"Oh, come now." Simone's voice lowered, her brows puckered in a show of disbelief. "You want him to keep feeling guilty about your accident? To feel indebted to you?"

Now they stood in the middle of the walkway, staring at each other.

"I asked him point-blank if that was how he felt," Tessa said. "He denied it. You talk to him. You're very close, aren't you?" Tessa hoped she'd finally spill the truth about their relationship.

"Haven't you heard anything I said?" Simone threw up her hands. "He needs your help. Brian must move on. Bigger and better business connections are waiting for him—for us—all over the country."

"Look, you get him to change his mind, and I'm gone. No hurt feelings, no strings attached."

Simone raised a brow. "If I have to spell it out for you, I will."

"Spell what out?"

"Your parents are missionaries, right?"

"Yes."

"In Northern Ireland?"

"Yes. They're also helping with a program called Volunteers for Peace."

"Oh, really?" Now Simone's tone mocked. "You've got to know all about the religious fighting that still happens there, people even killing one another. Doesn't sound like anybody is listening to them, does it?"

They stopped and stood face to face.

"My parents are part of a mission to help heal wounds," Tessa said. "They're trying to spread the love of God for everyone. Relations are getting better."

"Go tell that to Brian. Every time he looks at you, he remembers—" Simone blinked, her satiny cheeks flushed.

"Remembers what?" Tessa frowned.

"His wife was killed there. A missionary fired the shot."

Tessa stumbled back, one foot slipping off the walkway. She righted herself. "What did you say?"

"I didn't want to tell you," Simone rushed on, "but I thought you should know. You'd want to know."

"Murdered by a missionary?" Tessa blinked in disbelief.

"A little over a year ago. People of different religions—" Simone paused, her breath coming in short gasps. "They met and started fighting—"

"Not my parents." Tessa shook her head from side to side. "They'd never be involved in something like that. Besides, they weren't there then."

"Why do you think Brian's staying away from home?" Simone's voice lowered, her tone breathless. "Every time he sees you he thinks about how Maureen died and who killed her. Finally he sees Christianity for what it is."

"But he can't—surely he can't," Tessa stammered, "he doesn't blame my parents. Or all Christians?"

"Now you know why I had to talk to you." Simone's breath came in short gasps. "You shouldn't even be here."

"He—he almost begged me—" Tessa backed away from her.

"Like I said, he feels he owes you. You have to understand that, put yourself in his place." Simone shook a finger at her. "You Christians—"

"Stop, please." Tessa gave a dismissive wave of her hand. Head lowered, she stumbled back and then turned and hurried away, Simone's words clamoring in her ears. What to do now? Where to get answers? Unaware which way she headed, she came upon the gazebo.

Eyes blurry, she stumbled inside and collapsed on a bench, her head shaking from side to side. It couldn't be true, what Simone had said. A missionary like her parents killed Brian's wife. He couldn't cope with having a Christian in his home. He felt guilty for her car accident. That was why he'd offered her a job. Now he regretted the impulse.

Her phone rang. She ignored it, her fingers flicking at tears. How could she talk to anyone, especially if that was Brian on the phone, and make sense?

Chapter VII

She got up and paced the concrete floor.

If only she could talk to her parents. Their last call said they'd be on mission tours in designated areas of the country for another week. No way would she disturb them with the kind of news resonating in her head. When she phoned them about Brian's offer of a job and mentioned his full name, they never indicated they knew or had heard of the Le Moynes.

Should she try to get answers from Ada? Her hand strayed to the phone tucked in her back pocket. She pulled it out. No, Ada was off on business in town. Besides, the woman was right. She needed to hear from Brian himself. But when and where? She'd promised Simone to keep their talk confidential. Could she do that now?

She wandered out of the gazebo. How much later, she didn't know, but she found herself on the highway off Le Moyne property. The steeple of the church she'd visited with Ada and Cede loomed close. *"God, where are you?"* she mouthed the words.

Clouds dimmed the sun as she turned and started down the path toward the place she knew her parents would tell her to turn for answers. Reproach welled inside her: *God, I know Your Word says all things work for good to those who love You, but right now I find it hard to believe that.*

The name, Living Word Bethel, swirled in an arc above the church entrance. No sign of life on the premises. Nearby, but set farther back, sat a modest white frame house surrounded by shrubbery. Ada had pointed it out to her. Attached to the porch banister, a board in large, black print said: PARSONAGE, DR. JOHN DEROUEN. Maureen's death, Tessa's thoughts fled, a tragedy hitting so close to home, most assuredly made headlines, especially in St. Pierre. The pastor would know the details whether or not he'd been there when Brian and Maureen were members of the church.

She walked up to the house and rang the doorbell. No answer. That's when she remembered Ada had said the pastor would be out of town until tomorrow.

Her gaze strayed toward the church. Maybe an assistant pastor or a deacon would be there to substitute for him. She headed for the front entrance, her sandals a hurried swish on the paved walkway.

On prior visits, she'd seen the simple sign on the front door, *Come in.* Ada had said the church was never locked. At first turn of the knob, the door opened. She entered and looked around.

Quiet everywhere. No one in sight.

As on her first visit, she gave in to a peaceful aura that reached out like a friendly arm around the shoulders. On either side of the aqua carpeted aisle, narrow pews with padded cushions invited rest. Ahead, an arrangement of white calla lilies still graced the altar. Behind the choir loft was a plain large cross, almost touching the ceiling. High, stained-glass windows on each side reflected the splendor of mid-morning light.

She slipped into a back pew, absorbed yet deeper into the sanctuary's calmness. Better that she was alone. *Dear Lord,* her words pleaded in silence, *please watch over everyone who works to spread Your love and peace around the world. May they be spared the kind of death Maureen suffered and the agony that haunts Brian. Please, let him find again in You the comfort and peace he deserves.*

Her unspoken request centered so vividly on Brian that at the faint swoosh of the entry door opening, she turned, half expecting to see him.

"Hi," Gene whispered. He wore brown trousers and a light tan, open-neck shirt. His grey eyes held an apology. "Sorry to disturb you. Earlier I saw you head this way. I figured I'd find you here."

Tessa rose slowly, hand tentative on the smooth, hard coolness of the back of the pew. "I just needed some quiet time." She waited, wondering if he'd seen her with Simone and would ask questions she didn't want to answer.

He stepped forward and looked around the sanctuary. "I'm a member here. Small church, but nice. Built with Le Moyne money, folks will tell you. Hard to believe Brian never sets foot in the place anymore."

Oh, please, Tessa held back the words, *let's not talk about Brian's reaction to the church. Not now.* "This sanctuary reminds me of Little Grace Chapel back home."

"Really? I don't attend services here often as I should. Too bad the outside world is in such a hurry." He glanced at his watch. "Case in point. I was just leaving for work when I got a call from Brian. Earlier Ada told him you were probably wandering around the grounds. He's been trying to track you down."

"Oh?" Tessa's nerves jolted into panic mode, shattering the peace she'd found. She remembered the couple of phone rings she'd ignored when she was in the gazebo.

"Brian said he was going back into a meeting, or he would have called you again. He wants to talk about your contract."

"Then I should get in touch right away." *He's finally decided to do it, tell me he's changed his mind.* Tessa stepped out into the aisle and slanted a final glance toward the altar in the soft-hued stillness. Then, head lowered, she turned and hurried toward the front door.

Keeping step with her, Gene said, "Probably Brian wants an excuse to take you out to lunch, the lucky guy."

Tessa didn't answer.

"Don't go committing all your dinner dates to our boss. Simone wouldn't like that, and neither would I." He chuckled as they walked out into the sunshine. "Leave time for a gourmet feast at my place one evening. Okay?"

Simone, Simone. She wished she didn't have to think about her now. "Oh, Gene, there's no telling what's on Brian's mind besides that contract."

"But I can guess," Gene bantered.

I doubt that, Tessa wanted to say.

"Whatever it is, I'm sure it couldn't match a romantic moonlight ride with me in my boat on the bayou." Gene lifted an eyebrow, his grin teasing her. "We could even get lucky and bog down in water hyacinths. No rescue till morning."

Tessa forced a smile at his attempted humor. "Thanks for chasing me down. You're already a special friend."

"Give you a lift back?"

"Nice of you, but I need the exercise. See you later, Gene."

She headed for the house and pulled the phone out of her pocket. No matter what Brian had to say, she kept telling herself, she must control her emotions.

She punched in his number.

"Tessa? Hello!"

"Hi, Brian." She imagined a smile that went with the light-hearted sound of his bass tone. She had no doubt he'd want their parting to be as friends.

"Glad you called," he said. "How about lunch today? We need to talk about our contract."

"Okay." She swallowed at the sudden hoarseness in her throat. "What time? Where?"

"One o'clock? Antoine's sound good to you?"

"Yes. I'll be there." Her pulse started a gallop she wouldn't have been surprised he heard over the wires.

"Traffic in town at noon can be a mess," he cautioned. "Take it easy. I'll wait, no matter how long."

"Thanks. See you." She flicked the phone shut and almost ran for Le Moyne House. Words came and went in her brain. Just what would she say to Brian? About Maureen? *About her talk with Simone, if she must?*

She took a back entrance and climbed up to her room. She changed from jeans to her favorite dark blue pantsuit with a peacock-colored blouse. Fingers clumsy, she fussed with the closure of a single strand of pearls around her neck. She let her hair down in a casual flow about her shoulders and renewed the lip gloss.

Straw purse in hand, she rushed off, down the hallway and stairs, empty like those secret places inside her. She went out the front door, glad she didn't have to face either Ada or Cede and add to their worries.

On the outskirts of Magnolia Pass, raindrops splattered the windshield and turned into a downpour that continued into New Orleans. The city lay in a watery blur beneath mushrooming clouds. Stopped for a street light, she started up again when it turned green. She braked just in time to avoid hitting a man who darted in front of her to make it to the sidewalk.

She sat forward and gasped. *Kyle!* Strange that she should see him again today, and in the city. Two police cars with lights flashing approached on the lane opposite her. Could Kyle be in some kind of trouble with the law? She remembered Brian had asked Darrie if he'd run them out of money the day she arrived at Le Moyne House.

She had no time to think further about him. Soon she'd be facing Brian. A couple of missed turns and a long wait behind a traffic jam made her worry she'd be so late that Brian might have little time for her.

Frustrating minutes later, she entered a mist-shrouded Antoine's parking lot. After a slow drive around the crowded area, she finally saw an empty spot. She parked and got out of the car. A scatter of raindrops pelted her hair and shoulders as she rushed into the restaurant.

The place, elegant as she knew, throbbed with the subdued excitement of diners. Waiters bustled about with trays of food or empty dishes. She'd hoped to sneak into the restroom for a quick check of her appearance before she met Brian. A glance at the mirrors in the entry hall showed him a few steps behind her in a tan business suit and striped brown tie.

The prospect of a touch-up gone, she turned to face him.

"Hi." His grin widened. "Glad you made it okay."

"But a bit late." She returned his smile. "You were right about the traffic."

He took her hand. The admiring look in the cobalt eyes almost made her forget where they were. But that unrelenting voice inside her warned she should remember what Simone had said and try to ease away from his touch.

A waiter approached. "This way, Mr. Le Moyne."

With every footstep toward their table, Tessa reminded herself this luncheon would doubtless turn into a red-letter event like her farewell party at Chandelle's. But finally seated across from him, she must pretend a moment's carefree laughter to match his. Too soon reality zoomed back to twist and burn that tender spot at the pit of her stomach.

"Your pleasure?" Brian asked.

Not food, Tessa wanted to say. "Thanks." She reached for one of the menu booklets. "Anything really light this time," she said, turning the pages. "Oh, here is what I'd like, the half chicken vegetable salad and iced tea."

Brian lowered his gaze to study the day's offerings.

Now hands clutched in her lap, Tessa tried to concentrate on other diners. But, blotting out faces and voices, Simone's words reechoed in her brain: *Every time Brian looks at you, he thinks about how Maureen died.*

The waiter appeared and took their order.

Brian sat back, hands relaxed on the table. "I'm glad you didn't change your mind about the contract."

"Changed my mind?" She looked down at her silverware. "That depends, Brian."

"Depends? On what?"

She had wanted to talk. Now words she'd arranged in her head scrambled out of order like scattered pages of a script she'd dropped on the floor.

Brian rubbed his chin. "Out with it."

The waiter appeared with their drinks.

Dear God, take charge, Tessa cried out in silence.

"Can't start? Then I will." The waiter walked off, and Brian leaned forward. "Gene tells me Simone and Kyle came by the house today. They probably gave you the impression the place is for sale. It is not. He said you and Simone went for a walk. Right so far?"

Tessa gripped the glass of tea the waiter had just placed beside her. The way her hand shook, she'd spill the liquid all over herself if she tried to take a sip.

"Simone told you about Maureen—" Brian stopped, picked up his fork, laid it down again. "How she died?"

"We talked in confidence," Tessa admitted.

"That part of my life," he said quietly, "has nothing to do with you."

She wanted to cry, *But it does.*

"I've learned never to do business with anyone without a background check." He went on in the same controlled tone. "Sure, I knew your parents are missionaries. That night at Chandelle's, I heard people talk."

"I expected that. And you were shocked?"

"Surprised," he corrected. "Maybe shocked when I found out where they are. Maureen—and our—" He stopped, looked off, and then faced her again.

Tessa shifted in her seat. "I'm so sorry. We don't have to talk about it. Not now."

"The way my wife died," he went on, like one talking to himself, "you can't understand unless you were there—saw what happened." He shook his head and pressed a finger to his lips as if to stop the pain of words. "*How it happened.*"

No matter what she might say, Tessa wasn't sure he'd hear her. He seemed to be back in that world he'd tried to forget. Here, voices laughed, waiters came and went. "Stop, Brian," she whispered. "We'll talk about it later."

"An anniversary gift from me, a trip there to research her roots. Visit family. We were all decked out." Eyes lowered, he gave a hollow laugh, sinking deeper into another time and place. "Her—in a new dress."

Tessa wanted to get up and wrap an arm around his shoulders. "I'm so sorry," she said again, her voice soft. "Please don't do this to yourself now. Later, when we're alone…."

He gripped his hands together. His gaze hardened on the table, then shifted to the silverware by his plate, on to the other diners, then back to her. "It was a terrorist attack, Tessa. And Christians were part of it. We were going up to the door of a church." A flush ignited his face, redness edging the scar at his temple. "For a Sunday night service." He cleared his throat, fussed with his napkin, folding it and unfolding it beside his plate.

Silence fell between them, like a heavy curtain Tessa didn't know how to lift. Or even if she should try.

He glanced up at her. "How do you forget? You don't."

"Brian, please, later."

"When it started, those guns aimed toward us, hatred in eyes that stared, mocked." His jaws tightened. "It was war, Tessa. *People professing to be Christians* also taking up arms at the church door—"

"Maybe they were afraid for their lives?" On the instant, she couldn't hold back, her voice scarcely above a whisper. "Or the lives of their children?"

"Christians there with guns." Brian went on as if he hadn't heard her. "You'd have to see them to believe—"

"Oh, Brian, I can't tell you how sorry I am. But we Christians aren't perfect. We're only human."

"You're pleading their cause?" He frowned, his gaze holding hers. "Defending them?"

"No, no. Oh, no." Tessa wanted to take back words she'd spilled out at the wrong time. "It's hard to forgive someone who has wronged you. In your case, the taking of a life, and one so dear to you. I can only imagine—"

"You can't. No one can, unless it happened to them. *I was there. I saw it all with my own eyes.* People filled with hatred *in the name of God*, they said. It's one thing to read about it, hear about it. But when you—you see them point a gun at you, at your family and others—" The flush deepened on his face. "Then it's different. You cry out to a God you worship, a God who promised to be with you—and He's not. When someone you love is shot, dies in your arms, only then can you understand—" He looked down, his head shaking from side to side.

"Later, Brian," Tessa pleaded.

"And to think I planned the trip for that very time . . ." Now his voice was so low she could hardly hear his next words, "If only I'd listened to her, hadn't put business first."

"You've convinced yourself it's your fault too?" *Like you blame yourself for my accident,* she wanted to say. "Believe it, Brian. You're not responsible for what those people did."

"Well, now you know." He touched his fork, moved it aside, and then slid it back closer to his plate. "That's the way it happened, and there's nothing I can do about it."

"And nothing you could have done about it. Remember that."

His eyes, windows of unresolved pain, lifted back to hers. "I wish I'd told you myself about Maureen. It didn't seem urgent. But if I had, we'd be past this now. You wouldn't have to worry about how I feel—about our contract, or anything else, for that matter."

"I didn't tell you my life story either. We can't go around talking about personal matters right off to everyone we meet."

"I know that. But you're living in the family home right now. Sooner or later, you'd hear about it—how Maureen died. You should understand why I don't want anything to do with religion." The gloom in his face, in his voice was back. "Why would God let her die—*like that? If there is a God.*" He looked off, brow creased. "You might as well believe in the tooth fairy."

"You don't mean that." Tessa's tone was soft, gentle.

"Yes. I do mean it." His gaze swerved back to hers. "I'll never darken a church door again. Religious affairs in Le Moyne House? Not as long as I'm in charge."

"So how do you feel about having *me* there?" Now Tessa couldn't hold back. "Do I remind you of what happened to your wife? Is that torture for you? Is that really why you've been staying away?"

"Slow down. Of course not. I'm here, there, and everywhere with my work. That's the story of my life. My absence now has nothing to do with you. I'd like to come to the old home place every night and sit at Ada's table with you there across from me. You want the truth, you got it."

Tessa's look wavered on his. He'd like to see more of her on a *personal level*? Was that what he'd just said? She moistened her lips. "I didn't mean to pry into your—your personal life."

"Of course you didn't." Tone lowered, his gaze probed hers. "What happened to Maureen has nothing to do with you or your parents."

"It's not your fault either. You have to accept that."

He stopped her with a flip of his hand. "Your folks weren't there when my wife—when she was killed." He glanced down and then looked back at her. "No way were they involved," he stressed. "I know that. I also know they're leaders there now in a peace movement among people of different religions." He paused, looked off, then back at her. "You're a compassionate, honest person. I saw that right off when we met at

Chandelle's. You make me want to believe there's goodness left on our planet."

Tessa glanced at her fingers knuckle-white around her water glass. "I'm not sure I deserve the kind words, but thanks." She looked back at him. "I must ask again. Did you offer me a job because you blame yourself for my car accident? Please be honest."

He frowned. "No. Absolutely not. How many times do I have to tell you that? Yes, I did and still do feel some responsibility because you changed your plans to try to help me. But I didn't have to offer you the remodeling job at Le Moyne House. I could have suggested something else in one of my businesses out of town. Or even recommended you to a friend or an associate."

"I'm glad to hear that," Tessa said, "but something else bothers me. You heard I had to sell Chandelle's because of my Uncle Lester's gambling debts. That he sold fakes as antiques. Did you offer me a job because you feel sorry for me? That you don't think I should be punished for what he did?"

"I did hear something about your uncle. Oh, sure, some hinted they couldn't understand why you didn't know what he was up to and try to stop him. But your reputation in the business is tops with people who really know your work and ethics. As for a business going bust, that happens every day, for whatever reason. I don't doubt your honesty for one minute. Besides, you're a top decorator, the best to refurnish my family's home." He tapped a finger on the table for emphasis. "Rest assured I didn't offer you a contract out of pity."

Tessa eased back in her chair. "I needed to hear you say that."

"Well, I'm glad we understand each other. Anything else bothering you?"

She held back the words, *Yes. You've lost a loving relationship with the Lord, and I wish I could help you get it back.* "That's it for now," she said slowly. "What about you?"

"Nothing you should be concerned about. No matter what you hear or who says it, I'm committed to our contract. Speaking of which . . ." He pulled out a couple of envelopes from his coat pocket and handed them to her. "Here are two copies, yours and mine. I've already signed them. Will you look them over now? Sign both if you're still with me."

"Oh, Brian." Relief swelled inside her. She reached for the coveted document in duplicate and slipped out the one from the envelope with her name on it. At once she unfolded the paper and began a careful scrutiny of every word.

Finally she looked up at him. "Perfect."

"Need this?" Brian grinned.

She matched his smile and reached for the gold pen he offered. She signed the copies and returned his along with the pen. As she slid her copy back inside the envelope, she noticed a check.

She pulled it out and frowned. "What's this?"

"An advance." Brian shrugged. "Need more later, let me know. Now dig deeper into the envelope."

She did and found the credit card he'd promised for purchases. Her heartfelt "thank you" whispery, she slipped the contract and the card with the unexpected advance into her purse. She had no doubt he wanted to help her pacify creditors.

The waiter appeared to refill their glasses and chat about the rain that had mercifully cleared the city and headed toward Baton Rouge. Tessa only half-listened to them, her conversation with Brian replaying in her head. Her prayer was that somehow she, and her parents later, might help him find the kind of help he needed to regain his faith. She thanked God he knew they weren't involved in Maureen's death. She would wait and tell them about the tragedy when they could talk face to face. As for Simone, how little she really understood the man she no doubt wanted to marry.

The waiter walked off, and Brian's fingertips reached to connect with hers beside her glass. "The moment I saw you at Chandelle's, I wanted you—your—" He stopped, cleared the huskiness in his tone and started over, "I knew I wanted you to redecorate Mom's house."

Tessa heard the simple words, accented with that gentle touch. "I'm sorry I caused you to bring all this up about the—the past."

"Don't be. I'm the one who should apologize. This talk was overdue." He pulled back his hand. "Don't ever hesitate to come to me when something bothers you."

"One more question."

"I'm listening."

"It's about Simone. You said I should answer only to you about my work."

His brows wrinkled. "Why would you bring up her name? She has nothing to do with the house." A tap of his fingertip on the tablecloth emphasized, "You don't answer to anyone but me. Not even to Darrie. Understood?"

"Understood." She straightened in her chair. The last bit of tension that had plagued her since that talk with Simone faded away.

The waiter was back with their order.

"So now, let's celebrate." Brian straightened in his chair.

She saw it in his face, heard it in his voice, the attempt at an upbeat mood almost like the day they discussed their verbal contract. She looked down for a prayerful moment, more in gratitude for the result of their talk than for the food.

When she lifted her eyes, he held out the platter of hot bread to her. "It's mouth-watering. Have you ever tried it here?"

"Oh, yes." She could have told him she had tasted it several times when she dined here with Josh. "It's anything but light."

"Delicious."

She smiled. "Very."

As they ate, their conversation turned to movies and concerts in New Orleans. Coming last, like the single order of the chocolate crème dessert Brian persuaded her to share with him, was the memory of their first meeting when he rang her doorbell at Chandelle's.

"Sure, it's a cliché," he said, his voice turning to an intimate low, "but talk about a sight for sore eyes. You standing there—"

"Brian!"

Tessa's hand went numb on the handle of her cup. She glanced up to see Simone stopped at their table, her nose tilted at a profile-perfect angle. She had changed into a designer pink suit that gave her a flirtatious, lean look. She laid a hand on Brian's shoulder, a filigreed bracelet dangling on her wrist.

Brian put his cup aside and slowly eased back from her touch. He stood. "I thought you were still at the office."

"And missing out on lunch? I just finished." She gave a little laugh, her gaze flitting toward Tessa. "What a surprise when I just happened to turn around and saw you here."

"Hi, Simone." Tessa saw twin lines crease the flawless skin between her brows. Did she worry that Tessa had broken her promise not to tell Brian about their talk?

Brian pulled out a chair for her.

"And what brings you two together here?" she asked as she sat down.

"Business." Seated again, Brian added, "And celebrating our contract."

"You mean it's signed?" Simone's quick glance darted from one to the other.

Tessa reached for her coffee cup and looked at Brian.

"Better late than never," he said.

Tessa thought the look Simone turned on her now asked, *After all I told you, still you signed that contract?* But she heard her say, "Thank you again, Tessa, for letting me know what a mistake I made when I bought that foyer table. Because of you, I did get my money back."

"I was glad to help," Tessa said quietly.

Simone rested a hand on Brian's sleeve. "Now you can leave her alone to do her job. We've got entirely too much going on at the office."

Brian gestured toward a table in a far corner. "I didn't know our office bunch was here too."

"Yes. Most of us finished lunch. Some are waiting for dessert."

"Let me walk you back there and say hello." Brian got up.

"They'd love it." She rose and linked her arm with his.

He turned to Tessa. "Excuse me, please. I'll be right back."

"See you later," Simone told her, a careless look over her shoulder.

Tessa watched them walk away. A good-looking couple, she didn't deny. Neither could she deny intuition told her she hadn't heard the last of Simone's efforts to get her to give up on redecorating Le Moyne House.

When Brian returned, she'd drained her coffee cup.

"Sorry about the interruption." He settled on the edge of his chair. "Thanks for having lunch with me. I'm sorry it took so long for us to sign those papers. About our talk, now we understand each other?"

Tessa nodded. "Thank you for your trust in me."

"Goes both ways. I'd like to make a habit of meeting you like this." He grinned.

Footsteps sounded.

They turned. Simone again.

"Ready, Brian?" she said. "We don't want to be late for that meeting."

He looked at Tessa. "Are you ready to leave?"

"Yes." She got to her feet, purse in hand. "I should hurry back to the house for a delivery. Nice to see you again, Simone. And Brian, thanks for lunch—for everything."

"We'll walk you out," he said.

"No need. See you later." Her smile included both him and Simone before she turned and hurried away.

As she drove home, Tessa couldn't stop the occasional blurry eyes. She sighed and squinted ahead on the road now flooded with bright sun. Brian had lost his faith when a missionary supposedly fired the shot that killed his wife. He also blamed himself for her death that happened on a trip he planned.

If only she could talk to her parents. But that would have to wait. They'd worry about her relationship with him and his mother's possible reaction when she found out he had hired Lester Chandelle's niece. Besides, they were too involved in their work now. Better, too, not to intrude further at this time on Brian's private life, like that "Maureen—and our—" phrase he hadn't finished.

And Simone? Plainly the woman fed his estrangement from God. She also knew now why Ada couldn't host church meetings in Le Moyne

House.

She began to suspect she and Brian had something in common—disappointment in one's self. She'd assumed blame for being too absorbed in her wedding plans to realize Uncle Lester had a gambling problem and needed help. While her loss of Chandelle's was minor compared to his pain, at times she found it hard to accept that Bible verse about all things working for good to those who love the Lord.

Now her contract was beyond question, and she'd found out Simone's motives for wanting her gone. She had so much as said her mind was set on money and power. The woman saw Brian as her ticket to fulfill her dreams.

She took a deep, calming breath. All should be well if she managed to avoid her and Darrie. When she finished the job, she might even look into a TV spot. Simone had suggested it as a ploy to keep her from signing that contract. Now she would never want to hire her, but another station might be interested in her resume.

Too late she remembered the antique sale on her schedule for today before she'd had that talk with Simone. Just as well, she decided. She couldn't take the chance she'd miss the delivery from Magnolia's and a possible visit with Adrienne.

She turned down the lane approaching Le Moyne House and almost came to a complete stop. A familiar car was parked under the oaks.

Darrie was here.

Chapter VIII

Tessa's foot eased on the gas pedal as she inched toward the driveway. She saw Cede push his red wheelbarrow around a bed of iris blooms. She pulled up under the oak beside Darrie's white sports car.

Cede looked her way, hand going up in greeting. He stopped the wheelbarrow on the walk and ambled toward her. Before she'd got her keys and bag in hand, he was there to open the car door for her.

"Great news," he said. "The new computer came. It's all set up, ready for you. And Chandelle's delivery is on the way. Now you're here, this place will look like its old self again real soon."

"Thanks for the vote of confidence, Cede." Stepping down, she arranged the strap of her handbag over her shoulder. "Darrie's here, right?"

He nodded. "Been upstairs all over the place. Now she's out there." He motioned to the guesthouse. "No telling what she's up to."

Hand on the door, Tessa hesitated. Apprehension needled a trail that began in the pit of her stomach and spread to her chest. If Darrie heard about that contract she and Brian had just signed, the news had likely put a frown instead of a smile on her face. She didn't want to encounter that again.

"Cede, I'll be working in my room for a while. Will you please let me know the minute the delivery truck—?"

An engine roared. Tessa stared as the long, familiar vehicle with dark blue lettering, MAGNOLIA HOUSE OF ANTIQUES, eased toward the driveway. She felt a passing twinge of regret to see the name change but remembered that it carried rare furniture which she and other employees at Chandelle's had added to the inventory.

"I'll get Ada," Cede said.

Tessa took out the credit card from her bag. She dropped it inside her pocket and left keys and bag on the seat of the car. She closed the door and turned to look at the van coming to a stop. Up front with the driver, Adrienne leaned out the window, her sun-blonde hair ruffled in the wind. She waved with that familiar giggly excitement.

The instant the passenger door flew open, Tessa was there. "Oh, Adrienne, it's really you!"

Adrienne slipped out, and their arms went around each other.

"Well, praise the Lord—" Ada began as she and Cede approached.

"Oh, come, Mr. and Mrs. Cede Guidry," Tessa said, "and meet Adrienne Fornet, my very best friend." No sooner had they exchanged handshakes and exuberant greetings than Tessa introduced Poulain, the lean, gray-haired Foreman of Delivery affectionately called *"Capitan"* by his Cajun-speaking co-workers. "And say hello to Neil, Archille, Soco and Pres," Tessa continued, motioning to the helpers, wide smiles all around.

"Bien, fellows, let's get the goods out." Poulain's rousing command brought chuckles as a couple of the men moved in practiced unison, their strong, muscular arms rippling as they opened the double back doors of the truck and let down the slide, ready for the transfer.

"Like old times, eh, Tessa?" said Poulain.

"Like old times, yes. Like a homecoming!"

"Oh, I can't believe it's finally happening." Ada rubbed her hands together as if she couldn't wait to get them on the new acquisitions. "If only Felice could see this. Talk about like old times coming back."

Tessa stood aside with Adrienne. Each antique, carefully wrapped in thick blankets, was placed on dollies. Directed by Ada, they were skillfully maneuvered up the steps, through the halls, and into the sitting room.

As she and Tessa entered behind them, Adrienne flipped off her sunglasses and twirled around. "No wonder you fell for this house, Tess. It's awesome." Her gaze strayed approvingly to the spacious areas and then stopped on the marble mantel. "Beautiful lady. Family matriarch in her youth?"

Tessa stepped forward to direct a mover to the exact corner Ada had indicated. Then she motioned Adrienne aside and whispered, "Brian's wife. Deceased."

Adrienne gave Tessa a long look. "Oh."

Tessa caught her friend's hesitation and the inflection in that single word. Adrienne thought she already had secret feelings for Brian, the widower.

The furniture finally placed to Ada's satisfaction, she offered everyone coffee and freshly fried doughnuts. At the kitchen counter, Tessa signed the bill of sale Poulain presented to her and paid with the credit card. Instead of joining the group for refreshments, she invited Adrienne to tour the house.

First, a private chat in her bedroom.

As Adrienne gushed over the décor there, Tessa changed into a loose shirt and a pair of jeans. She and Adrienne settled on the couch, the open window behind them letting in the refreshing scent of jasmine blooms that flourished at random just outside her window.

"A lot about this place reminds me of Chandelle's," Adrienne said, but her glance lingered on Maureen's framed photo on the table beside them.

Tessa sighed and brushed stray hair from her forehead. "I hope I can help bring it back to life. Keep your eyes and ears open for that Alphonse chair, will you?"

"Oh, always. You'll hear the minute I get a lead."

Tessa blinked at her friend's probing look on hers.

"I don't think I have to ask, but I will." Adrienne's tone lowered to a hush, a habit she and Tessa had when sharing secrets. "How do you really feel about Brian? *Are you . . .?*"

"Don't even go there," Tessa said.

Adrienne laid a hand on her arm. "Something's happened. You're happy and you're not. I see both emotions in your face. Your folks aren't around. If this friend, *moi,*" she touched a finger to her chest, "will do, well, I'm here. You oughta know that."

Words lumped in Tessa's throat until she couldn't hold back a moment longer. She pointed to Maureen's photo. "Brian's wife was killed a year ago in Northern Ireland, of all places. When she and Brian visited there, she got caught in the line of fire between warring groups of people. Some said Christian missionaries were involved. One was charged with her death, but he was never proved guilty. Brian blames himself too. He planned the trip as an anniversary gift to his wife."

"Oh, Tess! How sad!" Adrienne gave a distressed shake of her head. "Do your folks know about that?"

"If they do, they haven't mentioned it. I just learned about it today from Simone. She acts like she's Brian's girlfriend, maybe even his fiancé. Even Ada doesn't seem to know for sure what's going on between the two."

"Of all places for you to get a job—here in Brian's house." Adrienne touched Tessa's hand. "Does he know your parents are over there?"

"Yes, but Maureen's death happened before they arrived. As you know, they've only been in that part of the country about six months. They're missionaries, and they're also helping with a peace movement. Simone wants me gone from here. She says seeing me in his family home upsets Brian because it reminds him of his wife's death. He assured me today she's wrong about that. Things get complicated. Simone offered me a job at their TV station in Baton Rouge."

"Oh, wow! Exciting!"

"But for that, I'd have to tell Brian the lost antiques for this house can't be replaced. And that's not true."

"Poor Brian. And poor you." Adrienne leaned forward. "Maybe you should move out. At least, maybe stay in the guesthouse?"

"That's Brian's home when he's in town." At the mention of the guesthouse, a sudden pricking sensation lurched in Tessa's stomach. If Darrie wasn't still there, she might barge back into Le Moyne House any minute in a fit of temper about something. She took a long breath, eyes lowered. "Brian wants me to live here and work from his mom's office to get the work done faster. Besides, I have no car now and would have to buy one to commute. I need that money for creditors."

"There's got to be another reason Brian wants you here," Adrienne said.

"Don't get any romantic ideas about us. He and Simone *are* probably engaged. She so much as said that."

"And," Adrienne went on, amber eyes giving Tessa a knowing look, "I can imagine how she feels having gorgeous Tess living under his family's roof and redecorating the place."

Tessa gave a hollow laugh. "You should see her. I'm no threat to that glamorous TV personality."

"Females are females, and instinct tells me she's jealous as—well, as any cat could be. Also, people might talk about you living here. Have you thought of that?"

"Oh, I refused at first. When I found out Ada and Cede have an apartment on this floor, I agreed to accept Brian's offer. They're like second parents to me. Brian stays in the guesthouse when he's home. Let's not look for more trouble, Adrienne. I've done too much of that lately."

"Oh, Tess, if there's anything I can do—"

"Just you—well, keep me in your prayers. That I'll soon be able to finish my job here."

"And not fall hopelessly in love again?"

"With a man who might be engaged to another woman? Besides, with a man who says he wants nothing to do with Christianity?" Tessa rested a hand on her friend's arm. "Let's talk about you. What's the very latest with you and Phil?"

"Well, it looks like his army tour abroad won't be up for another six months, would you believe? That's the very latest, as of last night."

Tessa looked at Adrienne's ring and smiled. "But hey, isn't it great to have all this time to plan your wedding? It'll be the grandest ever in Jasmine Hills. That is, with expert help from your matron of honor. Still *moi*, right?"

"As if there's any doubt it's *you*, best girlfriend anyone could ever have. And it'll happen to you too, finding that special guy. Sooner than you think."

"Like Mom says, 'All in God's time.'" Tessa stood, hand outstretched. "Want a quickie tour of the other rooms?"

Adrienne got to her feet at once. "Can't wait."

But as they stepped out the door, Ada called up to say the van was ready to leave. Arm in arm, the two descended the stairs, lamenting too quick an end to their visit. They reached the entry hall and saw the leaded doors open as Cede escorted the movers out, their laughter and chatter like that of old friends.

Tessa and Adrienne followed them outside.

"Thanks, Poulain, and all of you." Tessa's hands went out to the crew as they climbed back into the van. "If we need anything else that might be at Chandelle's—I mean, at Magnolia's," she amended with a quick smile, "I'll be sure to give you a call."

She and Adrienne wrapped their arms around each other.

"Silly us. You'd think we don't talk just about every day!" Adrienne giggled. "Oh, wait!" She scrambled back into the front seat. "Your laptop." She picked it up from the side of her car seat and held it out to Tessa. "You were going to forget it again, weren't you?"

"Thanks so much, Adrienne!" Tessa reached for it and gave her a blown kiss. "'Bye, all of you! Come back soon!"

"Will do, you gotta know that!" Adrienne blew back kisses and closed the passenger door.

Tessa raised a hand to shade her eyes from the bright sunlight and watched as the van backed out of the drive to trail down the oak-lined lane and round the bend toward the highway. Slowly, laptop in hand, she started back toward her car, missing her friend already.

"Great fellas, your old gang," Cede remarked over his shoulder as he headed for his wheelbarrow. "Wonder if Darrie is still in the guesthouse."

Tessa gasped. No time to lose or she might face a repeat of the troubling conversation she'd had with Simone. She hurried to get her purse and keys from her car and, now loaded with the laptop too, she headed for the front steps. She would work in her room as she'd intended and stay out of Darrie's sight.

She crossed the porch. As she pulled the door open, she heard voices:

"I'll check again, but it's gone. I'm sure of it!" Darrie said.

"So?" Ada replied. "That doesn't prove she took it."

"The drawers in that room have always been locked. Sure, the maids clean in there as usual, but they don't have desk keys. Besides, they're honest, like family. Brian gave her full access to the office. Probably to every desk drawer."

"She's innocent, I'm sure of it."

"Why are you taking up for her? Because her parents are missionaries? Where's that money if she didn't take it?"

"Maybe your mother put it in a different place."

"I'll look again. But if I don't find it . . ."

Tessa almost dropped the armload she carried. *Darrie accused her of being a thief.* She dashed forward and saw her accuser leap up the stairs in double time. Ada came around from behind a cabinet. Bottle of furniture polish and cloth in hand, obviously she'd been on her way to capture the tiniest speck of dust on the new antiques.

Her mouth flew open when she saw Tessa. "Oh, dear."

"Ada, I heard Darrie."

"Some mistake." Ada gave a dismayed cluck of her tongue.

"A mistake to blame me, yes!" Tessa said. "I'm going to deal with this right now."

"Honey, she's beside herself." Ada's voice lowered. "Kyle's in trouble again. I feel sorry for her, but she shouldn't be taking out her problems on you."

Tessa hesitated near the stairs and turned back to her. "He darted in front of my car at a stop sign in the city today. He seemed to be running from someone—maybe the law."

"I wouldn't be surprised if he's in some kind of trouble. They're desperate for money." Ada's forehead creased in a frown. "That's why Darrie looked for the cash in Felice's office."

"And she thinks I took it?" Not waiting for the answer she already knew, Tessa bounded up the stairs and didn't slow down until she reached the sunroom. She dropped her bag and the laptop on the couch and then rushed toward the office. Breathless, she hesitated beside the half-open door. Her gaze flitted to the desk with the new computer Cede had mentioned.

Stooped by the bottom drawer, Darrie looked up. She jammed the drawer halfway shut and straightened. "What did you do with our mom's money?"

"I don't know what you're talking about, Darrie." Tessa edged forward, fighting the urge to scream back at her. She scanned the floor littered with files and loose sheets of paper. "I never saw any money. If I had, I wouldn't have touched a penny of it. I'm not a thief."

"Don't play innocent with me."

"But I *am* innocent." Tessa met the coldness in the dark eyes. "You have no proof."

"No proof?" Darrie said. "You're a stranger in this house. You had access. Motive. Like uncle, like niece. Down on your luck, is it? My brother took pity on you and gave you a job. And this is how you thank him? By stealing to pay back your creditors?"

Watch it, Tessa. Don't freak out. A soft answer turns away wrath, the words rushed inside her. "I don't need anyone's pity or help."

"Mom always kept a few thousand in this bottom drawer for emergencies." She slammed the bottom drawer. "Tell me where it is, or I'm calling the police."

Tessa frowned, envisioned men in uniform handcuffing her, the Chandelle name splattered *a la Uncle Lester* in the newspaper, on television. "Please, Darrie, do us both a favor. Don't jump to conclusions right off."

"Do you a favor?" Darrie cocked her head. "Now that's a good one!"

"Call Brian, or I will. Maybe he knows what happened to the money."

Darrie didn't answer. She stooped and pulled out another drawer. She rummaged inside and tossed out handfuls of files.

"You don't want to get the law involved without checking with him or your mom, do you?" Tessa tried again. She caught the instant flush that splashed Darrie's face. Had the word "law" struck too close to home, to Kyle's problems?

The phone on the desk rang. Before she picked up the receiver, Darrie said, "Tessa Chandelle, you stay right there."

Tessa ignored her and started to walk out to get the cell from her purse on the couch. She should call Brian at once.

"It's about time you returned my call," Darrie said into the receiver.

Tessa stopped, her attention full on Darrie.

"You gave your decorator *carte blanche* in this house when you hired her, didn't you?" A moment's silence. "I've been calling you for hours. Why didn't you answer?" She swung around, giving Tessa her back. "Do you know what happened to the money that was in mom's desk drawer?"

Tessa held her breath, hands knotted at her sides.

"Yes, she's here." Darrie glanced back at her, receiver still pasted to her ear. Seconds, and she hung up. "He's on his way. Shouldn't be but a few minutes."

Did Brian, too, think she was guilty? Tessa caught that "gotcha" smile on Darrie's face. She thought his sister seemed more interested in seeing her humiliated in his eyes than in recovering the missing money.

"I never dreamed my brother would give a perfect stranger *carte blanche* in here knowing money was in that drawer. He trusted you."

"I swear I'm innocent," Tessa said softly. "Please believe me."

"I wish I could." Darrie took a long breath. "My brother gave you a job here because he blamed himself for your accident. You know that, don't you?"

Tessa opened her mouth and then closed it. Anything she said would make matters worse. A look around at the mess on the floor and she realized some of the papers might be hers. She stooped and began sorting through one pile, then another.

"The truth hurts, doesn't it?" Darrie smirked.

"Because of my uncle, you're suspicious of me," Tessa said over her shoulder. "But I didn't see any money. Even if I had, I wouldn't have touched it."

"Oh, cut the act. Just today, didn't you agree to keep quiet about your talk with Simone? And what happened? You ran right over to Brian and blabbed everything."

"You're wrong again." Tessa shook her head. "Ask him how he found out. He'll tell you."

Footsteps sounded.

Brian stood in the doorway.

"It's about time you got here," Darrie's tone scolded.

Still stooped on the floor, Tessa looked up and met his gaze.

"I called you several times," he said. "Why didn't you answer your cell?"

"I'd left it in my car." Tessa got up. "The delivery people came up as soon as I got back here. I was in a hurry to meet them."

Brian shuffled a hand through his hair. He looked at the drawers Darrie had pulled out and emptied on the floor. He gave her a long look. "I hope you didn't call our mother?"

"I tried, but I couldn't get her. It's plain what happened. Your new decorator got her hands on that cash."

Brian's gaze shifted to a tiny locked cabinet marked "Private" near the door where he stood. "Obviously you didn't check that one."

"She never puts money in there." Darrie frowned. "She always keeps it in her desk drawer."

Brian took out his key ring and gave her a long look. "Are you sure you're ready for the truth?"

"Why do you think I called you?"

"Well, I have no choice. Mom would understand."

"She'd understand what?"

Brian didn't answer. He selected a small key and turned it into the lock. He pulled out the drawer and flicked long fingers past a neat file of cards.

"You're just wasting time, and you know it!" Darrie said.

Tessa stood rigid and watched Brian. She wondered what went through his head at that moment. Did he doubt Lester Chandelle's niece? Begin to think, *Ah, yes, those Christians?* Or, did he think he should try to protect her because he had hired her and felt responsible for her actions? He pulled out a thin plastic bag.

"Have you lost your mind?" Darrie clutched his arm. "The money couldn't possibly be in there."

"You're right. It isn't." Brian unzipped the bag and withdrew a piece of folded paper. He opened it. "Here's your answer, Darrie." He tapped the paper. "Kyle borrowed the money from our mother before she left.

Drug dealers threatened him. He didn't want you to know —"

Darrie snatched the paper from his hand. "You're making that up to protect Tessa!"

"Wrong." Brian's tone was low, patient. "Mom thought at least I should know."

Darrie stared at the document. "That's a—that's a fake!"

"His I.O.U, her signature and his. She had to file the note here to keep it a secret—from you."

"No! He—or Mom, they wouldn't do that to me!" Darrie glared at the paper.

"Get it together, Sis. Accept the facts." Brian's look scolded. "You know the signatures. You owe Tessa an apology."

"In your dreams!" she swore under her breath.

"Let's put that back where it was." Brian held out his hand.

She flung the paper to the floor.

He picked it up and shook a finger at her. "You'll be back to straighten out the mess you made here. Pull yourself together and head for the station. Have you forgotten you're on camera tonight?"

"This isn't over!" Darrie grabbed her purse from the desk top. She rushed out the door.

Brian eyed the clutter on the floor. Watching his step to avoid the documents, he crossed over to Tessa. "I can't tell you how sorry I am she put you through this. Why didn't you call me right off? If not from your cell, from the house phone downstairs?"

"I don't know," she murmured. "Too stunned, I guess."

"Something like this won't happen again." His arms reached for her. "That's a promise."

The next moment her head was on his shoulder. Tessa couldn't think of anything except the tight safety of his closeness. His cheek lowered to hers. Before she knew it, their lips met, gently at first and then in the raw passion of urgent need. Tessa let go in the moment's dream, lost in an unexpected thrill that made her forget time and place.

"Oh, Tessa, Tessa," he murmured, slowly releasing her.

Their eyes met, held, hers a blur.

He pulled a handkerchief from his pocket. Gently he dabbed at a tear that rolled down her cheek. "Sure you're okay?"

"Yes," she whispered.

"Oh, Tessa." Suddenly his lips were on hers again in a slow, gentle touch. His eyes consuming hers, he pulled back. "Again, I'm sorry," he whispered, "so very sorry for what Darrie put you through."

"Please," she murmured, "let's try to forget—"

"You're incredible." A long moment, and his lips brushed hers again. "You need to rest," he said. "I'll call and come over later. We need to talk."

Fingers trailing hers, he finally let go.

She watched him turn and walk out. Her heartbeat raced. She had let it happen. She was in love as never before with a man who might belong to someone else?

Dear God, what now? The words repeated themselves again and again inside her. She stood in the middle of the room telling herself she must forget about Brian's arms around her, his lips on hers. A determined shake of her head, she tried to concentrate on the floor littered with papers, the half-open drawers and file cabinets.

But thoughts of what had just happened would not go away. Reason told her that to stay here would bring the kind of heartache she had never known before. Besides, accused of robbery, she might have been arrested. No doubt now, Darrie would tell her mother that Lester Chandelle's niece was living in her house and had full access to her office. What then? Cancel her contract with him, could she do that?

At the moment, what should she do? Try to rest as Brian suggested? A deep breath, and she knew there was no way she could lie down and relax. Wait in the office until he came back? He had said they'd talk later. She should have asked what time was later. He expected her to forgive and forget, honor her contract? No matter her feelings for the man, was that what the *Lord* expected of her?

Weary of see-saw emotions, she took a deep breath and started again to pick up the scattered papers and folders. She placed them on the desk, sat down, and began to sort them out in appropriate groups. Better to do that now than to face Darrie later if she obeyed Brian and came back to put the room in order.

When she shifted her feet under the desk, she felt a layer of paper she had missed. She stooped and picked it up. Stiff white cardboard stuck out from a large brown envelope. She pulled out a glossy 8x10 color photograph.

She sat back in the chair, her gaze fastened on Brian and Maureen, the handsome couple posed beside a serene lake, their arms linked, facial expressions in a laughing, holiday mood. Tessa wondered when and where the picture was taken. Judging from Brian's stance, that look on his face she had started to know well, the snapshot could have happened yesterday. She turned it over. A shaky hand had written in black ink smudged in spots:

Brian and Maureen in Northern Ireland the day they found out she was pregnant.

Tessa stared at the last three words. The phrase Brian couldn't finish when they talked at lunch floated back to her. Now she knew he had started to say, "Maureen and *our unborn child.*" She relived the look on his face across the table as she questioned him. He was right. She couldn't know the depth of sorrow he hid.

A double murder. He blamed God—and himself.

She fumbled the photograph back into the envelope, her heartbeat a growing throb at her temples. In more than one of his sermons, didn't her father point out that bad things did happen to everyone, including Christians? Hadn't she learned that truth over the years? The face of the man flashing in her mind now had a bloody gash at the temple, his pregnant wife's lifeless body cradled in his arms. She saw his eyes raised to heaven, imagined his cry, *"Why? Oh, God, why?"*

A distressed shake of her head, and she dropped the folder on the desk, got up, and walked over to the window. The rosy glow of a dying sunset couldn't still the turmoil inside her. Simone had said she made Brian's pain worse every time he looked at her. Should she pack her bags and leave? Or, could she afford to squeeze her budget any tighter than she already had, buy or rent a car and commute?

Her hands gripped the windowsill. She relived the kiss moments ago, his arms around her. That heart-throbbing look on his face rushed over her. In a despairing upward look, she pleaded for an answer. She sat back on the edge of her chair, head lowered. A moment, and she felt it, knew it without a doubt. God had sent her here. She must stay. But why?

Chapter IX

"Tessa?" Tray in hand, Ada hesitated at the door to Felice's office. "I thought you might want this, tea and your favorite chicken salad sandwich."

"Oh, Ada." Tessa sighed and started to get up.

"Your supper. Sit down and enjoy it." Ada walked in and placed the tray on the desk. "Cede is waiting for me. Tonight is church visitation. I couldn't go off before I knew you're all right."

Tessa eased back in her chair. "Just sad for Darrie and Kyle. For Brian too. Like you said, the family has problems."

"Brian told me about your talk at lunch—how Maureen died." Ada gave a distressed shake of her head. "And then what happened in Felice's office. He admires you more than ever for the way you handled it all."

Tessa didn't want either sympathy or praise for herself just then and averted her gaze. "Thanks for the tea and the sandwich."

"You relax now." Ada touched her shoulder. "Cede and I ate an early supper. Later, if you want to talk . . ."

Tessa nodded. "God love you, Ada."

"Keep the faith, honey."

Tessa watched her walk off and wondered once again what she'd do without Ada in this house.

She ate most of the sandwich and then set it aside. Glass of iced tea in hand, she rose and, again, stared out the window. Unlike the disquieting emotions inside her, now evening shadows, that subtle change of faithful guards just before dusk, linked gentle arms across the manicured lawns. *God's peace*, she thought, wishing Brian stood there beside her to look upon it. She must be available when her phone rang and he came by to talk. No telling when that might be. Hours spent today away from his office had surely upset his schedule.

And how, she wondered, would she handle his nearness, that memory of his lips on hers, his arms around her. She must try to push aside those moments. Impulsively, she drank the remaining tea and set the glass aside.

Her mind drifted to her parents. Not the time now to disturb them with a call. They always had that sixth sense to read the slightest sign of gloom in her voice, no matter how hard she tried to be upbeat. Tonight she'd settle for a few quiet moments on the patio and take care to choose just the right words to send them a cheery e-mail. Next, she'd get some work done before Brian called. The sooner she finished her contract here, the better. She looked on the desk where she'd left her notebook of Photos and Needs. Not there.

Frowning, she got down on the floor on her hands and knees to look for it. She found it far out under a chair pushed back against the wall. Some of the pages stuck out the sides. She picked it up and sat back in the chair to check it out. The first couple of pages with copies of her order to Antiques Boutique were missing. She put the book aside and looked around the floor, inside the waste paper basket, under chair and desk. Nothing there.

So where was her order? Darrie, in some kind of vengeance had ripped the pages out and trashed them—but where? She paused, thinking fast. Tomorrow she'd call the dealers she had contacted and ask them to e-mail duplicates of the few orders she had placed. She looked at the new computer sitting on the desk. It was the perfect place to transfer all her records from the notebook without fear of losing them. As for the missing pages of her order, nothing she could do tonight.

She picked up the tea glass and the remainder of her sandwich. Footsteps quick, she went downstairs and into the kitchen. She rinsed the glass, placed it inside the dishwasher and, the slightest sign of an appetite gone, she ran the remainder of her sandwich down the sink. Back upstairs, she locked the office and went on to pick up her purse and laptop she'd left on the couch in the sunroom. Cell phone in her pocket and arms loaded, she headed for the back stairs.

Dusk deepened and lights came on by the patio and the pool. She placed her computer on an umbrella table, along with her purse and notebook and then sat on a cushioned chair beside it. Slowly she opened the laptop and turned it on. She checked for missed e-mails. Whether business-related or from friends, none seemed urgent. Now she would write to her parents. Never had she missed them as she did at that moment.

Her fingers speeding over the keys, she kept a determined upbeat tone to tell them how the job with Brian was coming along and that she'd found needed antiques for Le Moyne House at Chandelle's. She ended with, *Stay well. Love you both and miss you, oh, so much, but know you're in God's hands, doing His work...Tess*

That done, she checked her notebook of "Needs" for the large party room on third floor. As Brian had said, the only missing piece there was the vintage American Steinway grand piano for Felice. A credible lead with a dealer in Memphis required further contact, but plans for that would have to wait. Again she wondered what, if not an angry flare of anger in Darrie's hands, could possibly have happened to the two missing pages of her notebook?

She rubbed her forehead. A break. That was what she needed. Ears alert for her cell to ring with a call from Brian, she got up and paced. Long moments, and the only sounds she heard were early twilight tweets from none-too-subtle birds.

Until came that anticipated call, "I'm coming in."

"Great. I'm on the patio."

Seconds, and the sure sound of footsteps.

She turned.

"Tessa." Brian had changed into jeans and a white knit shirt. He grinned and pointed to the laptop. "Burning the pre-midnight oil?"

"Oh, hi." Her first impulse was to rush forward and wrap her arms around him, her turn to offer comfort now she knew about the other tragedy in his life. But she dared not act on her emotions or mention the photograph she'd seen by accident. Any reference to that would have to come from him if and when he decided to talk about it.

She settled for a casual, "Nice out here."

"How about dinner?"

"Thanks, but I couldn't eat another bite. Ada brought me a delicious sandwich."

He chuckled. "I had a business dinner meeting that seemed like it would never end. That's why I'm so late getting here. Rain check for dinner out, the two of us? Soon?"

If I'm still here, the thought whirled in her brain. She managed a smile. "Promise."

He slipped his hands inside his pockets. "I saw the furniture from Chandelle's. You're doing a fantastic job. I knew you would."

"Thanks." Tessa backed against the umbrella table and tried to smile herself into a sort of limbo, a worry-free zone that would delete the encounters with Simone and Darrie, but more especially his kiss she couldn't forget.

"About this afternoon with Darrie," he began, his voice lowered, "I'm sorry. Very sorry you had to endure that."

Tessa rubbed her forehead. Sights and sounds of the confrontation flashed. "Too bad for her too." She managed to give her tone a carefree lilt. "But maybe it's good the way things happened. We settled some issues." She paused, now surprising herself she could smile. "I found out you still want me."

"Still want you?" Brian shook his head. "Never doubt it."

She made herself laugh, the pretended sound ringing soft and carefree. "Am I glad to hear that. I'm already in love with the house, with Ada and Cede—" She stopped before she could have carelessly let out the words, "with you, too."

He slipped his hands in his pockets. "About Kyle, he's hooked on drugs. He runs around with a rough crowd and has had trouble with the law." He paused and took a long breath. "I'm not sure what to do. I'd hate to see him go to jail. He's family. Darrie is under a lot of stress. I hope you can excuse what happened today."

"Just like that." She snapped her fingers, her quick smile trying to blot the gloom of his words. "And thanks," she added, wanting to change the subject, "for getting the computer."

"Sorry it took so long." He paused and gave her a long look. "Luck was with me the night I showed up on your doorstep."

She tried again for a carefree laugh, telling herself his comment meant he was relieved she could put up with his sister and would continue as his decorator, nothing else. "Didn't I warn you about too many compliments too soon? You'd better wait until you see how the rest of my efforts here turn out."

"That's a finale I can already predict. It'll be perfect." He looked up at the sky, took a couple of steps and stopped behind a chair. Elbows rested on its back, he leaned forward. "Martin and I are flying to Venezuela later tonight. We may be gone a few days. If anything urgent comes up, call me or Margie."

"Oh, yes, your secretary. I'll remember."

"You can have the run of the house." Brian's hand waved in a grand sweep. "No one will intrude on your work. I gave strict orders. This place is off limits to Darrie and Kyle until I get back. Ada and Cede will make sure of it."

Tessa hesitated. "If Darrie wants input?"

"I already warned her to stay away while I'm gone. Trust me. She can't afford to break her word." He crossed the short length of shadowy floor between them and caught her hand, as if to seal another bargain. "I'll call you." He chuckled. "Promise to start answering your cell every time it rings?"

She steadied a smile, once again unable to ignore the heart-touching warm pressure of his fingers holding hers.

"Thanks for giving our project another chance." He released her hand, turned, and walked up to the pool. "We both need a break." He stooped and stuck a hand in the water, rippling it. "That's what I've been doing out here, goofing off. Can't you tell?"

He straightened and pointed to her notebook. "Looks more like you're working twenty-four-seven."

"Don't worry. I like what I'm doing."

"How about a swim?" He worked his shoulders.

Tessa looked at the water drenched in moonlight. With him in that kind of setting? "Thanks, but not tonight. Maybe another time." She picked up her notebook and opened it to the sheet labeled Third Floor. "I thought I had a key to the third floor room, but I don't. I really need one. Unless that part of the house is off-limits to me?"

"No room is off-limits to you. But why the hurry? All work and no play—"

"Would make everybody happy." Tessa remembered she and Adrienne had used that clichéd wordage the morning they said good-bye at Chandelle's. "Especially make your mother happy if the house is completely furnished when she gets back. Didn't you say that might be sooner than you think?"

He chuckled. "Word is it might be *later* than we think. She's still having a great time and plans to visit other places. But she promised to be home by the first of September."

"I might be finished then," Tessa went on, trying to keep his mind off the swim, "and tackling another job in New Orleans."

"Don't feel you have to rush things. If she walked in this minute, she'd be glad just to see what you've already done to the place." Brian stepped over to take a look at the open notebook she held.

His head bent close to hers. She felt his breath on her neck and the touch of his forearm against hers. Like a magnet, the dreamlike hold wouldn't let go. She darted a finger to point out the piano on her chart. Their faces touched. Fire in her cheeks, in his. Somehow she managed to ease away.

He straightened, his gaze full on hers. "I guess I should go. Our plane leaves New Orleans around midnight. Anything happens, anything you need, call at once. Okay, Tessa?"

"Of course." She cleared her throat. "About the key for the ballroom?"

"Mine is in the guest house. Ada has one. She'll give it to you anytime you ask."

"I'll get on it tomorrow." She struggled against his gaze, disarmingly blue in a slash of lamplight. Simone's man, she must not forget.

"About that swim?"

"Yes?"

"A rain check. Soon?"

She smiled. "Sounds great."

"Like I said before, the pool is yours. Whenever you like."

"Thanks."

"The way moonlight touches your face—" He drew closer, now only inches from her. "Tonight you're more beautiful than ever."

Her lips parted, but no words came.

"You're incredible." His tone lowered.

The computer chimed, the surreal moment shattered.

He drew back. "I'd better go. Thanks for today—tonight, Tessa. Until later, take care." He backed off, a hand going up in goodbye as he leaped onto the porch steps and disappeared through an open hallway door.

Tessa sank to the nearest chaise lounge. She couldn't deny it. They were attracted to each other. That warning voice echoed in her head, the one she tried to dismiss. Thankfully, he was gone and would be away for several days. When he returned, she must guard against personal encounters like the one tonight. Maybe it was what happened today that had made them both overly sympathetic to each other and vulnerable to the time alone tonight.

With a sudden start, she got up to check for an e-mail. It came from the dealer in Memphis who periodically informed her of recent shipments of antiques that might interest customers. She'd respond to it later. Nothing to do now but wander around the patio to wait until she thought Brian had left and there could be no chance she'd have to fight temptation again tonight.

Minutes later, purse slung over her shoulder and notebook and computer in hand, she went back into a sleepy house. As she plodded up the staircase, she comforted herself that in the next few days she wouldn't have to deal with Darrie. And Simone? Brian hadn't mentioned the house was off limits to her too. With her business partner away, surely she would be too busy at the office to show up here.

Back in her room, she deposited her laptop and purse on the couch and kicked off her shoes. She took a warm bath, but it didn't quite work the soothing magic she expected. Finally in pajamas and slippers, she continued the nightly routine of filling a paper cup with water to nourish her now healthy jasmine plant in the Zuni jar.

And then again, the computer announced mail. She sat on the couch to check it out. The brief note leaped up at her:

Surprise, honey! Sooner than expected, we might get to make a trip home, though a very short one. Will let you know the minute a date is confirmed.

Her parents went on to remind her they were still working on a plan to help pay Chandelle's creditors. They missed her, and she must never doubt God's love. She felt her eyes grow moist. More than they knew, she wanted to see them. But if, as Simone said, her presence here disturbed Brian, how would he react if he saw two missionaries from Northern Ireland, even if they were involved in a peace movement there? Looking out the window into the misty dark, she doubted that when Brian hired her it crossed his mind that one day he might come face to face with them. Besides, what if they should meet Simone and Darrie?

In bed, she went through a toss-and-turn routine. She couldn't stop thinking the timing for her parents' visit could be wrong. No matter her carefully chosen words, they had understood she needed them in ways she tried to hide. *"What time I am afraid, I will trust in thee,"* a favorite Bible verse she'd learned in Sunday school as a five-year-old, finally lulled her to sleep.

In the following days, those words came to her rescue when she needed them most. At the computer or with phone pressed to her ear, she worked until late into the night.

The insistent ring of the phone early one morning woke her. Estelle wanted to take her to a private estate sale in Ville Platte.

"They have an 1890's French armoire," she said. "If I remember right, Felice had one in the master bedroom."

"Yes. It's on my list."

"Then we should hurry. I know the back roads to my old hometown better than you do. Pick you up in about an hour?"

Tessa didn't have to think twice before accepting the offer. First, she checked her e-mail for a possible change in the delivery scheduled after two o'clock that afternoon. One, from Mr. Forestier, but they should be back in plenty of time to receive it. She lost no time getting dressed and having a quick cup of hot coffee and donuts with Ada in the kitchen.

"You're spending too much time on the job," Estelle said as they headed away from Le Moyne House in her convertible. "Forgive me for saying it, but you look tired."

"Oh, I feel fine. Sure, the work is challenging, maybe more than I expected."

Hands on the wheel, Estelle stared ahead, a tiny frown creasing her brow. "Any time I can help," she said, "all you have to do is ask."

"You're doing it right now. I'm very grateful," Tessa said and wondered if she suspected Simone and Darrie were the main source of her "challenges."

Estelle held her head at a thoughtful angle. "Only last night, Martin was saying he thinks Brian seems happier than he's ever been since Maureen died. What you're doing for him—oh, the *you* being here—has a lot to do with that."

"You really think so?" Tessa wanted to believe her instead of Simone. "I'm trying my best to please him. When I accepted the job, I didn't know about the tragedy in his family."

"Maybe your parents could help him down the road."

"Oh, I don't know about that." Tessa remembered his comment about not wanting church folks in his home. She was afraid it meant he wouldn't want anything to do with her parents. "How would you feel if they came face to face?"

"To be honest, I don't want to think about it."

"Well, Brian hired you knowing what they do. I'll admit Martin and I were surprised when we heard he'd hired the daughter of missionaries. So were some of his other friends. He's convinced you're the best authority on antiques he could find. I think he'll do anything to keep you happy."

"Even be friendly with my parents?" Tessa gave a little laugh she didn't mean.

"Well, I should hope so. He can't blame all missionaries for what one or two supposedly did. My heart aches for Brian. But for his own good and those around him, he's got to get over it."

"Maybe he will," Tessa reflected slowly, "in time."

"Not if he listens to Simone. They spend a great deal of time together in and out of the office. Some think they're engaged. We'll probably know the truth soon."

To Tessa's relief, a highway sign, "Enter Ville Platte," dismissed talk of Simone. Or, so she thought.

After traffic stops and turns, they reached the estate, only to find an early shopper had beat them to the treasured armoire. When Tessa asked the buyer's name, the owner, a balding man with a Cajun accent, laughed. "Man, I shoulda had her handle the sale for me. Simone Duvall, that was her name. Before she left, I heard she'd sold it to someone else for big dollars more than she paid me for it."

Tessa and Estelle looked at each other. They merely nodded, as if no words were needed.

After coffee and a sandwich at a fast food restaurant, they got back on the highway and headed for home. Tessa's phone rang. Ada was on the line to tell her the expected delivery from New Orleans would be on its way to Le Moyne House in a couple of hours.

Estelle smiled. "Great! Let's see Simone try to interrupt that."

When they pulled in at Le Moyne House, the delivery truck was parked in the driveway. The driver, whom Tessa knew as David from previous dealings with Mr. Forestier, leaned against the door of the truck, in his hands a clipboard. Beside him was Ada. They were in deep conversation.

Tessa rushed out of the car.

Ada, shaking her head from side to side, motioned her forward. "Reproductions. He says that's what you ordered. Come, look."

"Absolutely not, David!" Tessa said. "I specified I would accept antiques only. Nothing but antiques."

"But see here," David said, "is a record of your second request: 'Cancel order for antiques to Le Moyne House. Change to reproductions only.' And there is your signature, or at least, it looks like it is—*Tessa Chandelle*."

Tessa studied the new order. "It's an imitation, not my signature. I don't understand how this could happen. When a client asks for antiques, I never compromise. Mr. Forestier knows that."

"He was surprised you would change the order." David tapped the sheet. "Don't worry. He'll be glad to straighten this out."

"I'm so sorry," Tessa said. "I'll call him right away."

"See you soon." David got back into the truck and drove off.

"I heard everything." Estelle came up from behind her. "Unbelievable."

"And yet, believable." Tessa remembered that two sheets in her notebook with that order vanished the day Darrie accused her of being a thief—*like uncle, like niece.* What else did Brian's sister have in mind?

She left Estelle in Ada's company and went upstairs to call Mr. Forestier from Felice's office.

Ada's friendship, along with Estelle's, boosted her spirits in the following days.

Brian had promised Darrie would stay away.

She didn't.

Somehow she knew when a furniture delivery would be made and showed up with a supposed expert in antiques at her side to check every new acquisition. Not wanting to create further animosity, Tessa made no mention of that to Brian. Feverishly she worked the phone and computer and traveled about the state to follow up on ads for estate sales. Too often, cherished pieces fled the market before she got there or old, established houses reported they must contact other places to accommodate her requests.

Other worries multiplied. If she had to choose a substitute piece, would Brian's mother like it? Darrie frequently insisted on another replacement heartily endorsed by her expert. If Tessa simply listened and didn't agree or tried but was unable to follow her suggestion, Darrie put her hands on her hips, gave a disbelieving shake of her head, and walked off. In spite of what Brian expected, Tessa wondered if she secretly reported to their mom what was happening in her house. Just what was going on behind her back and Brian's too?

"Forget about her. Just do your job the best you can," Ada told her.

Sensible advice, Tessa argued with her fears, but not easy to follow.

Still no exact date from her parents as to their anticipated visit. "Things happen," her mother said over a phone call, "and talk is it might have to be postponed for maybe three or four months. But it'll come, all in God's time."

With that news, Tessa began to think her work at Le Moyne House might be over when they arrived in the States for a visit.

Her schedule gaining momentum, sometimes she accepted Gene's invitation to ride with him when he happened to have a photo assignment in the town where she needed to attend an auction.

"Boss-man might not approve, you with me," he'd say with a laugh. "But, hey, that's his problem. You're being spared all that driving. Besides, we're having fun and saving on expenses." He looked at her with a teasing gleam in his eyes. "Agree?"

"Agree." She would smile back, hoping he understood they were friends, nothing more.

During Brian's frequent calls from Venezuela, she shared her successes in finding certain rare pieces. He applauded her but seemed more interested in hearing about the little happenings in her day. In turn, he chatted about places he visited, people he met, where he stayed, and even laughed about how much he missed a New Orleans fixin' of his favorite Cajun shrimp dinner. She came to feel she knew him better than she'd ever known Josh.

Late one night, his voice unusually intimate, he said, "I don't know what I'd do without you." He only meant he needed her help to redecorate his mother's home, that stern voice inside her warned again. Another voice, memory of his lips on hers, said something else she must forget? A deep sigh. If only she could find that Alphonse chair for him…

Almost two weeks had flown by since he'd left. The morning work brought her into Felice's office earlier than usual for an important conference with a New York dealer via the computer. Her latest "prize find," as she dubbed each hardest-to-locate piece, was a French Renaissance bookcase, subject as usual to approval upon delivery.

Other contacts included a late morning call from her accountant. "I hate to tell you," Greg said, "but creditors are becoming more and more impatient."

"When Brian gets back from his trip, I'll ask for another advance," she told him. "Until then, there's nothing I can do."

"I understand," he said. "I'll try my best to calm them down."

"Thank you, Greg. I appreciate you more than I can say."

She glanced at her watch. Twelve o'clock. On her schedule that afternoon was a promising estate sale in New Orleans. She turned off the computer, locked the office, and started downstairs for lunch with Ada which was usually a sandwich or a salad over a friendly chat.

At the kitchen entrance, she stopped, surprised to hear the relaxed sound of the bass voice that laughed with Ada. Coffee cup in hand, Brian leaned against the counter. In none of his calls had he mentioned he'd be back today.

"Am I interrupting?" She tapped lightly on the door frame and smiled.

Brian straightened. "Tessa. Your phone is so busy these days. I couldn't get a call through to you this morning."

"Hi." Tessa's pulse raced at the quick sparkle in his eyes.

"The Prodigal Son returns." Ada laughed as she bustled around the stove. "But no fatted calf. Only broiled shrimp with brown potatoes and avocado salad."

"Sounds great," Tessa said.

Brian set his cup on the counter and grinned. "Glad to see you take time off for lunch, Tessa."

"Your CEO," she nodded toward Ada, "insists on it."

More soft laughter.

Ada turned to Tessa. "While waiting for lunch, why don't you show Brian your latest purchases? Especially the writing table." She looked up at him. "It's a French Henri like the one that once belonged to your Grandmother Le Moyne."

"It came in yesterday." Tessa took the bait, eager to talk about work, which would help her manage the excitement of seeing him there. "Come check it out."

"You didn't tell me about that." Brian followed her into the study.

"A day for surprises for both of us. For you, that 1890s piece." She stepped over to the table and rubbed her hand over its smooth walnut surface. "I hope your mother won't mind the pale water spot and the couple of tiny indented marks."

Brian shook his head. "You don't have to worry about those."

She stood aside, watching his reaction, the kind of far-away look that came over the faces of Chandelle's customers when they found a treasure which reminded them of other times, other people in their lives. "And in here—" She nodded toward the next room.

At the entrance, Brian stopped, one hand propped on the door frame. "The parlor chair set, the four pieces." He shook his head in a kind of disbelief and then walked in slowly. He paused by the lady's chair and stroked the back, his manner pensive. "Just as I remember it."

As he remembered Maureen sitting there? Simone believed he should be encouraged to forget the past. Yet here she was bringing it back to him. *But it's what he wants*, she told herself. She tried to lighten the memories with casual chatter, as if she were on the phone with him, telling him about other furniture coming in from trusted contacts.

Brian's gaze swept over the room. "Mother will get the surprise of her life." A moment, and he turned to her. "Any big plans for today?"

"Oops." She sucked in her breath and checked her watch. "I'm going to an estate sale in New Orleans this afternoon. It's at Mr. Forestier's shop."

"Then ride there with me." Brian touched her arm. "We can leave right after lunch. I've got to be at my office around three o'clock."

Tessa tried to hide a burst of excitement and casually flicked a strand of hair from her forehead. "Well, if I wouldn't be—?"

"Imposing?" Brian grinned. "Seems I've heard that one before. Again, the answer is you've got to be kidding."

"Lunch, you two," Ada's voice rang out.

"Now that's what I call a real homecoming." Brian smiled Tessa back toward the kitchen.

He meant Ada's cooking, of course. Tessa promised herself she'd remember that all the way to New Orleans and back.

Chapter X

Tessa slipped into a light blue pantsuit and a soft multi-flowery blouse, a go-anywhere outfit for working comfort. As she inspected her makeup and hair in the mirror, a high color flooded her face, a sure sign her heart was desperate again to overrule her brain.

When she sat beside Brian in his white Porsche, the sun was high and bright, the sky cloudless. A glimpse of paradise, she blithely told herself, but then the thought nagged, *a fool's paradise*?

She ignored the question. This trip would be a pleasant business adventure, just what Brian wanted for both of them. Just what she wanted more than she would admit even to best friend Adrienne. She would remember that and relax in the passenger's seat while she waited for Brian to start the conversation.

He flipped a Harry Connick, Jr., CD on the player and gave her a side glance. "Now this is the life. Music and a ride down country roads. Reminds me of the day we drove up together to the house for the first time."

Not daring to deal with the "together" word, Tessa shifted in her seat. "Beautiful weather then and now. Like you said it usually was in Venezuela?"

"Absolutely." Brian settled back and started talking about the problems of management versus labor in the oil refinery business. As the miles multiplied, she gained new insights into the man, convinced he was a commanding presence at any business meeting. Brow furrowed, he went on to speculate at length about national and international news. Tessa listened with consummate attention, surprised and flattered that he spoke to her of such matters. He seemed pleased she kept up with world affairs and didn't hesitate to express her opinion.

After a brief pause in conversation, he grinned, as if in sudden thought. "I got a call from Mom last night. She said she met a 'nice' man."

"Oh, that's great."

"Whatever makes her happy. She's a good judge of character." Brian tapped the wheel playfully and chuckled. "After all, she did say 'yes' to my father when he proposed. Of course, I'm sure this fellow traveler she mentioned is just a friendly attraction. Nothing more."

Like it is with us? Tessa wanted to say. Too keenly aware of the way he threw back his head when he laughed and his broad shoulders a touch away, she clung to the words, *friendly attraction, nothing more.*

"I know you said you wanted to surprise her," she said, "but don't you think the news could leak out that you hired a decorator?"

"Possible, I guess." Brian's tone sobered. "But I hope not. I asked the household and our closest friends to keep quiet about it."

He didn't mention he had promises from Darrie and Simone to keep his secret, and she didn't dare ask. It was enough she had to cope with his nearness, leaving her vibrantly alive and defenseless at the same time.

They approached St. Charles Avenue in New Orleans. Brian braked for a light. According to a sign on a bank building, the mid-afternoon temperature had climbed into the 90s. With the words, Tulane University, emblazoned across their shirts and backpacks slung over their shoulders, groups of students moved briskly down sidewalks or waited for public transportation. A scattering of other folks, doubtless both locals and tourists, meandered, some holding wide umbrellas against the sun's rays.

A streetcar clanged to a stop. "That look, that sound." Tessa sat up taller for a better look at the now rare public conveyance and smiled.

"Brings back memories, does it?"

"I'll never forget one of the best days ever with my parents. They took me for a ride on that streetcar. It was my sixth birthday."

"A bit of a sentimentalist?" Brian's tone teased.

She caught the serious, thoughtful gaze he slanted her way. "Takes one to know one?"

They exchanged smiles. Onward again with a turn here, another there, Brian finally pulled up in front of the white, two-story antique shop crested with the sign: FORESTIER ANTIQUES. Pink azaleas lined the walkway that led to the steep flight of steps and a wide veranda. A young couple holding hands waited at the white double entry doors with intricate moldings and designs clearly visible from the street.

Tessa gathered her notebook and purse, unbuckled her seatbelt and stepped out.

"Hey, wait up." Brian came around to take her arm and start toward the pale brick walkway.

At his side, Tessa wondered what searching for antiques would be like with him.

The front door opened. Notebook and pen in hand, a dark-haired young woman stood at the front door. Tessa had never seen her before. She welcomed the pair ahead of them and then waited as Tessa and Brian climbed up the porch steps.

"I'm Brian Le Moyne, and this is Tessa Chandelle."

"Miss Chandelle, Mr. Le Moyne, I'm Andrea Drost." Gray-blue gaze on Tessa, she added, "I hope you know we only have real antiques here, no reproductions."

Tessa stared at the woman, a sudden flush in her cheeks. Did she recognize her as Uncle Lester's niece? "Real antiques are what I want," she said. "Nothing else."

"Then, welcome," Andrea said.

"I'll be at the office." Brian released Tessa's arm. "Call me when you're ready to leave."

Head held high and shoulders back, Tessa followed the woman into a wide mahogany hallway that led to a large room filled wall to wall with advertised treasures.

"Thank you, Miss Drost," she said, still reeling inside from the possible implication she was like her uncle.

But soon she shrugged off the thought and mingled with other shoppers who strolled around, absorbed in the variety of rare treasures. She recognized some of the valuables which, she had no doubt, were a few hundred years old. Others, though prized, she judged had only recently qualified for the antique label.

She spotted the console table in a corner. It might be the very one Ada had said ranked second to the Alphonse on Brian's list of Most Wanted.

A tall young woman in tight jeans and floral blouse ran her fingers over the surface of the piece. Mr. Forestier stood nearby to answer her questions. Tessa held her breath for fear the table would be gone any minute. But at last the would-be customer shook her head. "Wish I could afford it," she said and walked off.

"Ah, Tessa," Mr. Forestier said haltingly, a tremor in his voice. "We're still looking for that Alphonse you want."

"I appreciate that, sir. Now I'd like to check out this console."

"Oh, but you should. You must be convinced it's the real thing."

Tessa applied the usual drill to authenticate an antique piece. Then, with a smile she couldn't hold back, she said, "I'll take it."

"A fortunate find for you. I haven't seen one like this in several years." He walked her to a small room that served as an office.

After the transaction that included a certificate of authenticity, Tessa told him Cede would pick up the piece within the week. The news that she'd found it, the thought soared, should make Brian's day—or even his month. Time forgotten, she indulged another look around.

More than an hour flew by before she called Brian and stood outside by the street to wait for him.

He pulled up within minutes and got out to open the car door for her. "That smile on your face," he said, "I don't have to ask. You found something."

"Yes, and just one look at you, I'd say you're celebrating something too. You go first. What's up?"

He didn't answer but closed her door and circled around to climb back into the driver's seat. He paused, hand on the ignition. "What an afternoon! We just settled the strike at Acadian Oil."

"Congratulations!" Tessa clapped her hands. "Now, more good news. I found that console table for the family room."

His gaze widened on hers. "Not the one that was handed down from my great-great grandmother?"

"Yes. According to Ada, no doubt about it. Cede can pick it up tomorrow."

"Fantastic!" He reached for her hand, his thumb stroking hers. "Mother won't know how to thank you. And neither do I."

Lost in a triumphant moment, Tessa sat back. "And I won't know how to thank both of you for trusting me with the job."

"Your reputation," he said, "is what got you the job. We are the most fortunate ones." Brow raised, he went on, "Now I have a question. Martin and Estelle called right before I picked you up. They're dining at Antoine's tonight and asked if we'd join them. I told them I'd check with you."

"Oh, yes," she said, "dinner with them sounds great." Tessa's thoughts raced, processing the invitation. She would enjoy seeing Martin and Estelle again. Besides, the event would mean more time she'd have to spend with Brian, a truth she could admit only to herself.

"They'll be glad to hear that." Brian gave her a quick look. Then, gaze intent on the traffic again, he nosed the car down Canal Street.

The city screamed with five o'clock traffic at its peak. With practiced skill, he made a left turn off the street, narrowly missing pedestrians who dared ignore lights and whistling policemen. He maneuvered into the narrow little streets of the French Quarter, past small, colorful shops, or elaborate ones labeled "Antiques." Tessa had often browsed through most of them with her parents and later alone just days ago.

"The past and the present," Brian mused.

"And I'm the sentimentalist?" Tessa smiled.

"Like you said," he bantered with a glance her way, "takes one to know one."

Tessa concentrated on the scenery as they went past Spanish courtyards hidden behind gates and balconies with iron-lace balustrades. Farther down a side street, a policeman rode on horseback. Fleetingly, Tessa glimpsed another sign: Le Moyne-Duvall TV station. She wondered if either Simone or Darrie was on camera at that very moment.

"At last, here we are." Brian whisked the car into a parking space in the Hotel Monteleone garage.

Tessa sat forward. "What are we doing here?"

"I want to touch bases with Margie, my secretary." Brian slipped his car keys into his pocket. "This is where I have my executive-suite. While I check messages, you can freshen up before we meet the Arceneaux couple."

Brian reached for his cell on the dash board, punched a number and held the phone to his ear. "Margie, I'm coming up with Tessa."

Eager to see his "other world," Tessa stepped out of the car before he could come around to open her door.

They slipped through the private entrance to the lobby. Headed for the elevator, Tessa glanced at the dazzling chandeliers that hung from the ceiling. She and her mother had admired those on stopovers when they made buying trips to the city.

As Brian stuck the key into the door to his suite, it opened. A petite brunette greeted Tessa with a quick smile.

"Finally we meet, Tessa. I'm Margie. Welcome," she said and motioned her inside. "I hear you're the kind of decorator everybody is looking for."

"Thank you, Margie. But that might not be always true." Tessa smiled and glanced up at Brian as they walked inside the room.

"I second the rumor." He grinned and walked over to a desk.

"I just got back from a trip downtown to get office supplies," Margie told him. "Some messages are there on your desk." To Tessa, she said, "Make yourself at home. If you'd like to freshen up, the bathroom is down the hall, that door to your left. Please excuse me. I've got to get back to work."

At once she went over to a small corner table with a computer. Brian had already pulled out the chair by the large desk near a window. His phone shrilled. He sat, rippling through a pile of notes with one hand while the other held the phone to his ear.

"Too bad." He looked at Tessa. "Martin and Estelle can't make dinner tonight after all. You still game?"

"Certainly, if you are," Tessa said.

"Let's do it," he said. "The evening would be quiet, relaxed. We wouldn't be out late." Back on the phone, he said, "Another time then, Estelle. We'll miss you two."

Brian clicked off and turned back to his messages on the desk.

Eager for a refreshing alone, Tessa headed for the bathroom.

She pushed at the unlocked, slightly open door and stopped. Simone stood before the mirror, washing her hands in the basin on the counter. She wore a short, blush-pink skirt and blouse, her hair a shimmer of curls piled on top of her head.

"Oh, I didn't know—" Tessa began.

"Tessa?" With a twist of the faucet's knob, Simone shut off the water, a frown creasing her brow.

"I'm sorry." Tessa backed off.

"What are you doing in Brian's suite?" Simone reached for a towel on the rack to dry her hands. "Is he here too?"

"We just walked in. I attended an antiques sale. Please excuse me." Tessa turned and started toward the office space.

Simone rushed out past her, hand outstretched toward Brian at the desk. "Darling, so glad to see you!"

"What's going on, Simone?" He didn't look up. "Shouldn't you be at the studio?"

She walked up to him and put a hand on his shoulder. "Sweetheart, I'm the bearer of good news."

"If it's about—?"

"You have no idea!" Simone gushed.

"Excuse me. I'll freshen up downstairs and wait in the lobby." Tessa headed toward the door out of the suite.

"Just a minute, please, Tessa?" Up at once, Brian stopped her with a lift of his hand.

"You're busy, and I can wait elsewhere in the hotel," she said.

"No." Brian gave an urgent shake of his head. "That's not necessary."

She hesitated. No doubt she had walked in where she didn't belong. Clearly that sullen look Simone gave her said she didn't want an audience.

Brian turned to Simone. "What's on your mind?"

She clutched his arm. "Our good friends, those network guys, Rhoden and Saunders, are in town. They want to see both of us."

Brian's face clouded.

"Darling, you've got to make time for them." She clutched his hand. "You know they're top brass with connections all over the world. They want to do business with us. You mustn't ignore them."

"They can't just show up here without—" Brian gently disengaged her fingers from his.

"But they did call at the studio, and I invited them down. You were away. It was up to me to look out for the business. Please, can we talk in private?"

Tessa didn't need another hint. She retraced her steps to the bathroom. No need to hurry, she told herself as she freshened her makeup. She had to hand it to Simone. The woman undoubtedly had a key to the suite and knew just how to get her way with Brian. Dressed as she was, she probably expected an evening out with him and the visitors. Tessa felt trapped. Dinner-for-two? She must forget about that now.

When she dared return to the sitting room, Brian motioned her aside. "Do you mind if Simone and a couple of business friends have dinner with us?"

"No problem for me," she told him. "But I don't want to interfere with you and your business friends."

Simone chimed in. "I just talked to Gene. He'll join us too. He couldn't stay away when he heard you were with us, Tessa."

Brian gave Tessa a raised-brow look. Not knowing what to say to Simone's obvious insinuation, she smiled, flirting with a spurt of girlish excitement. Maybe Brian was jealous? Immediately she dismissed the giddiness as impossibly wishful and even foolish.

In the hotel dining room, Gene arrived with the guests Simone introduced as Carl Rhoden and Paul Saunders. Both were in suit and tie. Rhoden stood lean and suave. Saunders, balding and ruddy-faced, had the look of an elderly man. Their jovial demeanor made it plain they fancied a rare fling along with business in the Big Easy. Sitting between Rhoden and Brian, Simone seemed determined not to disappoint her guests as she joked about certain "hot spots" they should visit.

Tessa found Gene, though cordial, rather subdued. Perhaps, like her, he felt uncomfortable with the visitors. She sat between him and Saunders, opposite the others, and sipped from a glass of lemonade. Brian said little, but he appeared the genial host and offered a frequent husky laugh. Simone talked incessantly, her hands moving, often touching his. While he didn't seem to respond with any particular emotion, he didn't discourage the gestures. Tessa couldn't be sure he enjoyed the evening. Toward her, he seemed restrained, overly polite.

They had barely ordered dinner when he pulled out his cell. He checked a message and frowned. He looked at Tessa first, and then at the others. "Sorry, folks. Please excuse me. Business guys upstairs. It will be quick talk. Hopefully," he added.

Simone seized his hand. "You need me?"

"Not yet." He got up. "I'll be back soon as I can." He paused. "Don't wait for me if you're served before I get back." Tessa caught the subtle nod toward her just before he walked off.

"Tessa Chandelle." Rhoden smiled and shook his head. "Why isn't a gorgeous young woman like you working for us in front of the TV cameras?"

Startled, Tessa glanced from him to Simone. Had she put him up to this? "Thank you for the compliment, Mr. Rhoden. Maybe someday I'd like to try that."

"Just what I suggested." Simone looked at Rhoden. "She'd be great with a show on antiques. She had a dreadful accident, several weeks ago, wasn't it, Tessa?" She turned a brief moment to Tessa as if for confirmation. "She lost her car and a job interview. Brian, the darling that he is, felt sorry for her and offered her work redecorating Le Moyne House. He even gave her a room under his roof."

Saunders snickered. "That Le Moyne is no fool."

Tessa ignored him and smiled politely toward Simone. "You know I met Brian when he came to Chandelle's looking for that Alphonse chair. My years of experience in the antique business impressed him. That's why he hired me to redo his home after that hurricane episode." She paused, a shake of her head toward the listeners. "And surely you know he's lived in the guesthouse on their property or in his apartment here in the city for some time now. I stay in the main house with his other employees, Ada and her husband Cede." She kept a smile and turned to Rhoden, then to Saunders. "Of course, Simone is right about the accident." She savored a gleeful moment, knowing she hadn't let Simone get away with a twisted version of why Brian hired her. "But to all of you who think I could do it, I appreciate your suggestion about a TV spot. Like I said, maybe in the future."

Simone leaned forward as if she'd reply, but the waiter arrived with dinner. The visitors raved about the feast of oysters in champagne, shrimp saki, and poached red snapper with crawfish sauce. Hoping Brian would show up any second, Tessa took her time eating the grilled chicken salad.

Halfway through the meal, he hadn't returned.

Tessa rose, excused herself, and made her way to the ladies' lounge.

The place was crowded, but she found a spot at the lavatory counter where she could go through the motions of brushing her hair and refreshing her makeup. She hung around the lounge, hoping when she got back Brian would be there, the party ready to break up.

But when she returned to the table, she found Gene alone and the table cleared of dishes. He stood and pulled out her chair.

"Where is everybody?" Tessa asked.

"Another business emergency for our boss," Gene said. "Simone and the guys left with him."

"Any idea when they'll be back?"

Gene shrugged. "None at all. He said he called your cell, but you must have turned it off. Then he phoned me. He says you can wait for him in his suite."

"What about you, Gene? Do you intend to hang around here?"

He drained his water glass. "Afraid not. I'm heading back to my trailer. But I'd hate to leave you here alone."

"You won't have to. Since Brian is tied up, no telling for how long, I'd love to ride back with you." She took out the phone from her purse. "Let me make a quick call to let him know."

Brian didn't answer. She left a message, snapped her phone shut, and smiled at Gene. "Ready?"

Together they walked out of the hotel, found his truck, and headed for home.

During the bumpy ride that reminded Tessa of her old-model car, she found little to say and wondered if Brian, too, was disappointed that their plans for the evening fell apart. She encouraged Gene to talk about his work. His excitement soared when he told her he wanted to write an article for a national magazine, complete with photographs of the swamp behind his trailer.

"Ardoin's plantation—the legend—will be in the background." His laughter bubbled. "That will be the pièce de résistance for an editor. You know the formula—mystery, lost love. That sort of thing goes over big with readers. By the way," he shot her a glance, his tone bubbling with mounting excitement, "I hear his house is full of rare antiques. Wanta check it out with me sometime soon?"

Tessa frowned. "Thanks, but no. Brian warned me to stay away from that swamp. Besides, I hear the owner himself could be dangerous. He doesn't like visitors, and Brian said the man has used a shotgun to keep them away."

Gene slanted her a quick look. "Yep. Some even say he's senile. Pining away for his bride that wasn't. She left him at the altar, so goes the gossip. More good fodder for my article."

"I heard that curious boaters who try to visit the place sometimes get scared and turn back," Tessa said. "Others get stranded for days on the bayou. Some even lost their lives before anyone knew they were missing."

"Oh, the stories about Ardoin and the swamp." Gene shook his head. "Lots of them nothing but gossip. True and false. But like I said, what fodder for an article!"

"And how do you know some of the talk is just that, false rumors?"

"Gut feeling is all I can go by. As for those water hyacinths, they could mess up a boat's motor and stop it cold." His shoulders squared, and he chuckled again. "But if you know swamps and bayous like I do, it's smooth sailing."

"So what's the secret?" All attention now, Tessa played along with him.

"Commonsense. Just look at the water. If it's high, you can't see the underbrush. Go to the low spots. Whirl your way around places you know to avoid. That simple—well, almost. A country boy born and raised in the bayous and swamps of Evangeline Parish learns certain things about safety in those waters almost from the cradle. My boat and I are invincible. And I know how to talk to eccentric Cajun folks. I've never met one I couldn't make friends with."

"So you say." Tessa smiled at his bravado.

The truck roared through the small village of St. Pierre, past the church, and then up to Le Moyne House bathed in moonlight. But instead of stopping there, Gene nosed the truck down a side lane.

"Where are we going?" Tessa's voice rose in shock.

"A little adventure, do you mind? It's early yet." He pointed to a trail that wound down an incline. "It leads to the swamp, the bayou in the middle. Want to see my famous boat?"

Tessa sighed, caught in his boyish enthusiasm. "Well, if you insist."

"I'll turn off the lights." Gene eased the truck to a stop at the end of the lane. "The moonlight is bright. You'll be able to get a real good look. Maybe even dare a ride with me."

"Don't count on it." Tessa laughed as they got out and began a quick and playful descent down the trail. "Besides, I see clouds floating around."

"Nothing to worry about." Gene pointed to a motorboat anchored near the bank of the wide, swampy bayou. "See it?" His voice was a low, excited echo on the night air.

Tessa stood still, absorbed in shimmering moonlight that outlined the boat and sprinkled the still water with the illusion of diamonds. The higher humidity dampened her skin and smelled of dead leaves and plant decay. Frogs croaked and other night creatures sang in various keys, while cicadas droned in their usual monotone.

"Talk about mystery, intrigue," she mused.

"And straight ahead," Gene said, "across the water, Ardoin's plantation. Just look at the faint lights shining through the windows."

"The place looks spooky, haunted." Tessa vaguely remembered seeing it from far off with Brian the day they drove in from St. Pierre.

"Haunted?" Gene faked a shudder. "Imagine a close-up photo on a night like this. One day soon, I'll have the time and luck to get one. I've taken the boat out to scout around for other scenes to shoot. In fact, I've got quite a portfolio already."

"But getting inside the house," Tessa asked, "how will you ever do it?"

Gene gave a determined shake of his head. "Knock on the door and wait until someone answers. I can be patient. Imagine charming the elder recluse and getting an interview. After all these years, I'll just bet he's eager to tell his story. No editor will be able to resist it. And, I remind you, Tessa, you'd go bananas over those antiques. Word is he's got 'em stored away. You should be the one dying to go there."

"Dying, did you say?" Tessa echoed with a giggle. "That's what scares me."

He looked from his boat and back to her. "How about a ride, just a short one? The water's down. Our lucky night."

"You're pushing it, Gene."

Gene stepped out to the boat, climbed in, and turned on the ignition. "Come on," he called over the motor's roar. "Don't be a spoilsport. The minute you tell me to stop, I'll bring 'er back in. Promise." He reached a hand to pat the space behind him.

Debating, Tessa chewed her lip and considered Gene's pleading little-boy look. Why not make him happy? Besides, what did she have to go home to? She'd hoped for an enjoyable evening, and it had been anything but that so far. Why not take a break and cut loose? Since he'd been raised on a bayou, it stood to reason he knew the swamp well enough to keep them safe.

She stepped forward and gripped his hand. Her heart pounded as she let him help her inside the swaying vessel. "I've lost my mind," she said with a nervous little laugh. She settled down behind him, hands quick to grip the sides of the boat.

Off they dashed in a whirl of laughter, swerving around trees, forming smooth arches and then straightening in the rippled moonlight.

A cool breeze flirted with Tessa's eyelashes and hair. "What a trip!" Her voice rang out. "I love it, Gene!"

Frolicking moments, and then sudden blackness swooped over the moon. Tessa looked up to see darkening clouds swirling around. "Gene," she cried, "let's turn back—now!"

"Oh, but it's wonderful out here. The clouds will pass. Just relax. Enjoy!"

"No, Gene." Fear licked up her spine. Distant thunder and thicker clouds rolled in, dark sweeping over the water. "Please, Gene. Let's turn back. You promised—!"

"Okay. Your slightest wish, my command." Slowly Gene turned the boat around and nosed it back to shore.

Tessa's heartbeat slowed, and she brushed stray hair from her forehead. "Okay, for a while, Gene, that was fun."

"Didn't I tell you?" He caught her hand to help her out.

Tessa scrambled onshore, her breath coming in short gasps. She watched Gene anchor the boat as sudden moonlight broke through the clouds, for an instant almost like early morning sun.

"Want to go out again?" Gene chuckled.

"Better not," she said.

Laughing, they relived the excursion as they headed back to Le Moyne House. Although she doubted Brian had returned home by now, Tessa sent her gaze in a quick sweep over the driveway and the parking area under the oaks as they stopped before the mansion. No sign of his car. She couldn't deny a tugging wave of disappointment.

"The evening turned out great after all, didn't it?" Gene said as he escorted her up the steps to the front door.

Tessa caught the serious look on his face. "Oh, yes. Thanks so much, Gene. Both rides were fun. Good luck with your other swamp tours and that proposed interview."

"You're beautiful, Tessa," he said, his voice low and intimate.

She opened her purse and fished out the house key. "And you know just what a girl wants to hear." She smiled and stuck her key into the door lock. "Good night, Gene. Thanks again for everything. You're a very nice guy, a great friend."

"Yeah, that's me—Mr. Nice Guy." With a grin and a wave of the hand, he sauntered off.

Tessa stood still and watched Gene climb into his truck. A moment, and it roared away in now paling moonlight. *Gene,* she thought, *a truly nice guy for a really lucky girl someday.*

Her cell rang. She stepped back from the door and fumbled the phone out of her bag.

"Tessa?"

"Oh, hi, Brian."

"Just wanted to make sure Gene got you home okay," he said, his voice hurried.

"Yes, thanks." She smiled at his concern.

"Sorry about dinner."

"I understand. Things happen."

"I'm flying out to New York tonight. Saudi Arabia later. Don't know for how long. I'll call you. Take good care."

She stared at the phone that fell silent in her hand. A day of ups and downs, she would tell Adrienne. She gazed at the moonlit grounds and listened to the lulling sounds of nightlife shutting down in one place only to start up in another. Memories of the serenity here, she reflected, like those she treasured from Chandelle's, might be why Brian didn't want to let go of this house.

She dropped the phone back into her purse and leaned against a porch column. Why, she asked herself, did she think about the softly absorbing look in his eyes on hers when he sat across from her over breakfast at Mignon's, and the way his strong fingers curled around a coffee cup. Now she wanted to feel those hands holding hers the way they had in Felice's office when Darrie accused her of theft. More than that, she wanted to have dinner with him—just the two of them. She wanted to hear him say he and Simone were no more than friendly business partners. Besides, she wanted a kiss that meant more to him than a sudden impulse in sympathy, like that moment when Darrie accused her of theft.

A deep sigh, and she let herself into the quiet, sleepy house. After an emotionally draining day, she looked forward to the privacy of her bedroom. She needed time alone to process tonight.

She had barely stepped into the hallway before Ada emerged from the kitchen, eyes flashing excitement.

"Tessa, honey," she said, "your parents are here."

Chapter XI

"Here?" Tessa echoed.

"Oh, no." Ada gave an emphatic shake of her head.

"So where are they?"

"In a cottage near New Orleans. They came on mission business, they told me. They're so excited. Your folks seem to have everything under control. They called your cell, but you didn't answer. They left a message with directions on where they are staying."

"Thanks, Ada." On the instant, Tessa regretted the bayou tour with Gene. She stuck a hand in her purse for the cell and bounded up the stairs.

Breathless, she entered her bedroom, kicked off her shoes, and headed for the couch. Her fingers rushed over the familiar numbers. Phone pasted to her ear, she heard her mother's fervent, "Dear, we can't wait to see you."

"Oh, Mom! I'm so sorry I missed your call. Why didn't you let me know sooner you'd be coming in?"

"We would have, but we only had a couple of hours to pack and board the plane. We're last-minute subs to the Foreign Missions Board Peace Conference."

"If it weren't so late," Tessa said, "I'd drive over to see you right now!"

"Tess, it's Dad."

"Dad, hi. I can't wait to see you and Mom."

"Yes, you can. Don't you dare get on the road this time of night. Wait until tomorrow. And, Tess, before we leave, we'd like to meet your client, Brian."

"I'm afraid that won't be possible. He's in New York and may be out of the country for a week or two."

"Too bad. We have only three days here." Tessa heard the fall in her father's tone.

"We want to spend as much time with you as possible," her mother said. "And maybe we can get a quick look at this mansion you're redecorating? A deacon friend here is letting us use one of his cars."

"Oh, yes, you must see the place. And I need your advice, both of you. But just being together, Mom and Dad, that'll be great. We have so much to talk about."

Back and forth the conversation went as they made plans for the next day.

Tessa didn't feel she should use a Le Moyne vehicle for personal reasons. She dialed Adrienne to tell her about her parents' visit and her transportation problem.

"Would you believe the Lord works in mysteriously wonderful, practical ways?" Adrienne said. "Tomorrow I have to meet with an antique dealer in New Orleans. I can pick you up in the morning and drop you off to meet your folks."

Too excited, Tessa hardly slept. Tomorrow she would talk face to face with her parents. They might have time for a visit here. Seeing the antiques she'd purchased from Chandelle's to replace losses would please them. She would ask if they remembered anything about the Alphonse chair. Maybe fortunate both ways, she'd get to show off the antiques and enjoy their visit without the risk of an uncomfortable situation with Brian.

Before dawn the next morning, she was up to pack an overnight bag. The sun barely a wink over the horizon, off she went with Adrienne who flirted with the speed limit as they headed down the interstate. She didn't need the written directions on the sheet in her lap. She'd memorized every twist and turn as well as the exact mileage to their destination.

The moment they swung onto the designated street, she spotted the number on the white frame house reserved for their stay. The yard was outlined with greenery on the sides, and a weeping willow centered the yard.

Tall and slim in khakis, her father strolled about and absently swiped a leaf from a bush. He looked up as they turned into the driveway.

"He can't wait to see you," Adrienne said.

Tessa loosened the restraining seatbelt. The instant the car stopped, she opened the door and slid out into a pair of embracing arms.

His cheek, smoothly-shaved, pressed against hers, a slight catch in his whispered, "Tess, sweetheart."

And then there was her mother out the front door and rushing toward her. Her wavy, gray-black hair had a freshly combed look, her petite form accented by a floral skirt and white blouse.

"Mom!" Tessa said, their arms going around each other.

"Room for one more?" Adrienne joined the now tight family circle. "All this hugging is nice, and I'd like to hang around," she said with a laugh. "But I'm a working gal, you know. Duty calls, and I gotta run." She broke loose and dashed back to her car. She poked her head inside and held out Tessa's overnight bag. "See y'all later."

Tessa rushed to get the luggage and waved Adrienne off with blown kisses. Her father relieved her of the suitcase as the three entered the cottage through the back door and the smell of strong coffee brewing.

Her mother pointed to the hallway. "The bathroom is first door to your right."

Tessa hurried inside for a quick freshening up.

As she came out, the doorbell rang.

"Want me to get it?" Before her mother could answer, Tessa turned and headed for the living room.

She opened the door. There stood Simone and Gene.

"Oh, hello—?" Surprised, Tessa looked from one to the other.

Notebook in hand, Simone stood back. Her smile engaged as if their last conversation had been a friendly exchange and Tessa might have expected them here. She wore a light grey pant suit and a string of pearls at her throat, her hair in a casual fall around her shoulders.

"We have an appointment for an interview with your parents," she said.

"An interview?" Tessa stared at her.

"I just learned about it myself this morning." Gene, in everyday slip-over brown shirt and blue jeans, shifted his camera from one shoulder to the other. Tessa couldn't tell if his somber expression was in apology for not calling her as soon as he found out about the interview. Or, for some reason he didn't look forward to filming it?

"Good morning, Miss Simone Duvall and—?" Monette said as she and Boyd walked up. "We're the Chandelles."

"Gene Dupre, our photographer," Simone said.

"Welcome. Glad to meet you both. Do come in." Monette stepped aside as they entered, handshakes all around. "We didn't get to tell our daughter about your call last night for this appointment. You're a little early, but that's no problem. We're all set up here in the living room for you." She motioned Simone to a stuffed chair. "You can sit there, if that suits you, and we'll sit on the couch facing you. How about coffee first or a glass of fruit juice?"

Simone smiled. "Thank you, but we're on a tight schedule, as surely you are. We should start right off if that's fine with you."

"We're ready when you are. Anything we might do to accommodate you, don't hesitate to ask."

Tessa stepped aside and caught her mother's "Not to worry" look toward her, a reminder that to be interviewed before a camera was nothing new to her parents.

But you don't know Simone Duvall, Tessa wanted to say. No telling where this interview would lead. A *"Please, God"* going up in silence, she eased away from them toward a stool in a corner of the room.

Simone settled in the indicated chair, notebook on her lap. She put on her professional smile for the Chandelles who sat on the couch opposite her. Gene stood off to the side, his camera poised to focus on them.

"Comfortable? Ready?" Simone looked at the two Chandelles side by side on the couch before her.

They nodded. A moment, and a pinfall kind of quiet.

"Mr. and Mrs. Boyd Chandelle, missionaries, now in Northern Ireland working closely with a Volunteers for Peace movement," she began, "we welcome you here in New Orleans and appreciate your time to speak with us." She went on to mention their background in the antiques business and said their daughter Tessa had followed in their footsteps as a home decorator. She quoted glowing words from other newscasters who had interviewed them during their missionary work in Africa and Kenya.

Tessa began to relax. She'd misjudged Simone?

"Now," Simone went on, her tone professionally controlled, "I'll get right to the point of your work in Northern Ireland. Exactly what are you trying to do for the people there? What would you say is their biggest problem? Might it be animosity among people of different religious beliefs?"

Tessa's hands tightened on the sides of her chair. She saw her father lean forward, eyes wide on his interrogator as if startled by the unexpected first question. Her mother shifted in her space. Tessa knew too well from her hands moving together in a clutch on her lap that she had gone on sudden alert for what was yet to come.

"Great question, Miss Duvall. Intolerance of religious beliefs and in all phases of daily life happens there and to some degree in all parts of the world. Even right here in our own United States. Even within families, I'm sad to say." Her father paused and cleared his throat.

"But let's talk specifically about Northern Ireland, since that part of the world is your assignment now," Simone pressed. "How bad is the problem there today, Mrs. Chandelle?"

"Others who have been there longer than we have, and legal authorities as well," Monette glanced at Boyd, as if for confirmation, "say conditions have improved in the past three or four years. But we do know fighting still happens there at times between people of opposing faiths."

Boyd nodded. "Our work in coordination with that of the Volunteers for Peace movement is dedicated to helping people tolerate each other's views. As my wife just said, animosity there, as you put it, seems to be improving."

"Can you tell us exactly how you and your fellow workers try to improve relationships, Mr. Chandelle?"

Boyd sat forward. Eyes intent on hers, he talked about serving food to the hungry in their homes or in food courts, helping with both money and personal skills to establish and teach in schools, orphanages, and hospitals. "Every day," he said, "we try to live and show our love for God. As we help others accept our Heavenly Father, our own faith grows. We hear and can testify that yes, people are beginning to tolerate one another's beliefs as never before."

"But news reports contradict your statement, Mr. Chandelle.

Relationships have not improved noticeably even with your charitable and well-intended efforts."

"Then you have information that contradicts what we and others in the mission field experience almost every day. As I just mentioned," Boyd went on, "intolerance does exist there and is always possible when folks don't respect one another's religious beliefs, no matter in what part of the world. Through the years, a history of the place tells us, people have lost their lives in bitter debates over their religious beliefs. Yes, even today, at times officers are sometimes injured or killed while trying to stop hostile group meetings. Some disagreements are subtle, others still more open."

"More open? And become more physically hurtful to one another? For instance, as in the murder of Maureen Le Moyne, the wife of Brian Le Moyne from our own St. Pierre?"

Tessa gripped the sides of her chair. She pressed her lips together to keep from blurting, "Stop it!" Where was Simone going with this interview? Why did she want to revive talk of the tragedy in Brian's life? Next, would she work in a question about Uncle Lester?

Her mother hesitated and again glanced at Boyd.

"We were not there then," he said. "Sad to say, we only recently heard about that particular tragedy. We know nothing about it except what we read in the papers or learned from fellow workers, none of whom had first-hand knowledge."

"But a missionary was charged in her death, wasn't he, Mr. Chandelle?"

"Yes. However, as you probably know if you've read news reports— and doubtless, you have—he was not proved guilty."

"Yet he carried a weapon—a gun?"

"So we read and hear. As I said, I cannot speak with authority. Neither can my wife. Again, we were not there when that supposedly happened at the hand of a missionary."

"Supposedly?"

"As a news reporter, Miss Duvall, surely you know that whoever fired that fatal shot has not been identified."

Simone paused, pursed her lips, and then asked quietly, "Do missionaries usually carry guns?"

"Not to my knowledge," Boyd said.

"Nor to mine," Monette added. "My husband and I don't even own a gun."

"Brian's wife was pregnant." Simone spoke slowly, the words like contemplated hammer strikes. "That means two murders were committed by the accused missionary. Correct?"

Boyd drew a tolerant breath. "Once again, Miss Duvall, those are the reports we read and heard. We cannot shed any light on who committed the tragedy. Nor, it seems, can any legal authority."

"And Brian Le Moyne should just forgive and forget?" Again, Simone's slow, measured words.

"He's always in our prayers." Monette sat forward. "Our hearts ache for him."

"A tragedy—" Simone's tone took on a note of disbelief, her words once again slow and measured, "allegedly caused by people who are supposedly dedicated to promoting love and peace and goodwill all over the world." The shake of her head from side to side and the incredulity in her lowered tone seemed to emphasize her conviction that what had happened to people like the Le Moynes was not unusual. "Those who preach the words, 'Thou shalt not kill,' obviously don't always practice what they preach. Wouldn't you say they might alienate rather than convert people to their gospel?"

"Miss Duvall," Boyd leaned forward, his gaze steady on hers, "doubtless that does happen at times. We are not perfect. Sometimes we fail in our mission. We need forgiveness as does every other human being on earth. Our mission is not to 'put down' anyone's belief. It is to do our best to try to share the love of God by showing we love and respect everyone regardless of race, culture, or religion and to encourage them to do likewise." He paused with an emphatic nod of his head. "I repeat, God commands us to promote love in His name, not hate. That's what we try to do."

"With guns, sir?" Simone asked quietly.

"No, Miss Duvall. By preaching and practicing God's commandment to love thy neighbor as thyself. To show others the same kind of tolerance and respect we want for ourselves."

"As was shown to Brian Le Moyne and others left to mourn the loss of loved ones? In his case, a wife pregnant with their first child? And the guilty go free?"

"Miss Duvall—" Boyd began.

"You don't have to answer that." She looked down at the notebook in her lap. "One more question, please. Do you sometimes wonder if you might not be more helpful to people back home, including family members?"

Boyd took a long breath, a shadowy look in his eyes. "If you're referring to my brother Lester, the answer is yes. I did not know about his addiction until it was too late. He didn't have my support. For that, I ask for his and God's forgiveness. Please understand, Miss Duvall, that at this time I would rather not have any further discussion of such a personal matter."

Tessa gripped the sides of her chair. So this was Simone's purpose for the interview, to revive talk of Uncle Lester?

"Thank you, Mr. and Mrs. Chandelle." Simone nodded and smiled. "We are grateful that you two try to spread love and peace wherever you go." She got up, hand extended to him and then to Monette.

Tessa heard it in Simone's words, the condescending tone and manner. She felt she had made her point and saw no need for further questions. Her parents? Surely, her mind sped on, they were aware of their interrogator's motive in every question to which she subjected them.

And yet, "Thank you, Miss Duvall," she heard them say in unison.

Gene lowered his camera. He glanced back at Tessa and gave what she took as an apologetic shake of his head.

He stepped up to her parents. "I know your work is very difficult at times, Mr. and Mrs. Chandelle. You are in my prayers."

"Thank you, young man," Boyd said.

Tessa got up and stepped forward. Words burned on her tongue, but she hesitated. Her parents would not want her to try to get back at Simone for the way she conducted the interview and made matters worse for her family. Better to smile and join the group.

Gene caught her hand. "Enjoy the visit with your folks. I'll call you later."

Simone put on a smile. "See you, Tessa."

Gene let Simone precede him out the door. They headed for their car in the driveway.

"Oh, Mom, Dad." Tessa's arms went around them. "I'm so sorry. For you two, and for Brian. I had no idea—"

"Whatever the woman's motive in bringing up personal matters and whatever happens now," her father said, "we have to leave it all in God's hands."

"Yes, that's what we must do," her mother said. "Now let's have breakfast."

And forget about the interview for now? Tessa would try to do just that and not add to her parents' worries about how Brian would react when he heard it, as surely he would when he returned home. As for Simone's motive? Plain as mid-morning light angling through parted window blinds in the room. Anything to get Brian to send her packing and away from Le Moyne House. She'd made good her threat.

They headed back into the kitchen. Monette pointed to a maple corner table set with green, leaf-shaped placemats, paper plates, cups, knives and forks, as well as a squat jar of strawberry preserves and a pot of coffee. She picked up the padded kitchen glove from the counter and opened the oven to take out a warming skillet with scrambled eggs and another with smoked sausage. She handed those to Tessa to place on the table. Next she found a platter of golden toasted bread, another of pancakes. Different flavors of syrup already centered the table, along with plastic cups of butter and sugar.

"A breakfast extraordinaire," Boyd said with a chuckle.

"Ada and Cede would really go for this," Tessa said.

"No thanks to me." Her mother smiled. "Deacon Brown's wife down the street, the angel, did the cooking." She gestured to the refrigerator. "She even stocked it up for us."

They took their places at the table and held hands. Her father offered thanks to God for a safe trip and the chance to visit with their daughter.

As her parents suggested, Tessa tried to forget about the interview with Simone and concentrate on breakfast with them. The past few months, too absorbed with her own problems, she hadn't given much thought to their work except for positive news reports she heard now and then.

While they served their plates, she caught a familiar interplay of glances between them. Something was on their minds, and it concerned her. She must wait them out.

Her father cut into the sausage on his plate.

Tessa noticed lines of fatigue on his forehead. "You look tired, Dad."

He smiled. "Time zones. We'll adjust, and then we'll have to fly back."

She couldn't be sure she'd ever been told the entire truth about the trials they faced every day, no matter in what part of the world their mission led them.

"Oh, Mom, Dad," she said, putting down her fork and looking from one to the other. "I'm sure your work is heartbreaking at times. Ada and Cede pray for you. I think I told you that a couple of years ago they heard you speak at one of their church meetings."

"Your Ada and Cede sound like fine Christian people." Her mother reached to choose a bottle of syrup to drip on the pancake in her plate. "We'd love to see them too."

"You have a lot in common," Tessa said. "Even love of antiques."

Her father's sturdy fingers stroked the handle of his coffee mug. He was ready to talk about Brian and her work in his home, she just knew it. She wanted to tell them everything, but not yet. For now, their conversation should be about happy times at Chandelle's. While she spread honeyed butter on a slice of toast, she tried to decide which incident to bring up from the "old days." Now might be the time to mention her dream for a new Chandelle's.

"I have a couple of questions," her dad broke in on her thoughts. "Did Brian know that you're our daughter when he hired you? That we're missionaries in Northern Ireland?"

Tessa's hands tensed on the sides of her plate, all thought of food gone. "Yes. He heard talk at the party the night he came to Chandelle's looking for that Alphonse chair."

"Strange he would hire you," her father went on. "From what we heard, he's bitter toward God and Christians."

Tessa looked down at her plate. "Yes. He even admits that."

"Have you seen signs of that in the way he acts? How he treats you and other people?"

"Never, Dad."

"Well, thank the Lord for that," her father said.

"I wanted to tell you about the sadness in the Le Moyne family," Tessa began slowly, "and I know now I should have. Somehow, I just couldn't over the phone or in an e-mail. I was afraid you'd worry about me, and you shouldn't. Things are working out. I like my job. I do feel sorry for Brian."

Her father nodded. "We understand you tried to spare us, but we read your heartache between the lines and heard it in your voice over the phone. At first, we had no idea what the trouble could be. We finally decided it was only because of trying to cope with creditors and the loss of Chandelle's."

"What do you mean by 'at first,' Dad?"

"One night we decided to check old newspaper clippings. We needed to find out what happened between religious factions there before we arrived. Oh, we had heard stories, but we wanted more information. We wondered if our peace efforts were making changes for the better. If so, how much better."

Tessa tensed, her gaze locked on his face.

"That's when we discovered the news about the Le Moynes. We called some friends here to try to find out more about Brian."

"And then we talked to peace-loving citizens in Ireland who recalled the tragedy," her mother added.

Tessa picked up her coffee cup and then set it down with a soft thud. "So you've known everything about Maureen for some time now."

Her parents exchanged glances.

"Probably not everything, but here's what we learned," her mother said. "She and Brian were visiting relatives and tracing her roots. They didn't realize they had crossed over into a neighborhood where a hundred or so people were gathered outside a public building in a bitter religious dispute. The article said a few missionaries visiting there tried to make peace between them. But things got emotional. Voices grew loud with threats. Shots were fired. The missionaries were said to have taken up arms also. Two were blamed for Maureen's death."

"Both denied it," her father pointed out, as he had earlier in the interview. "No one could prove without a shadow of doubt either of them had pulled the trigger that took her life. But anyway, one of them bore the brunt of the blame and was called back home." He shifted a piece of toast from one side of his plate to another and then looked at her, the food before him seemingly forgotten. "You know Brian's wife was pregnant at the time?"

"I learned that by accident too," she said.

"We dug deeper," her mother added. "We had to because you work for the man and live in his home. Reports say Brian still believes the accused missionary fired the fatal shot. His wife died in his arms. He even had a superficial injury."

"A scar on his left temple," Tessa said. "It was one of the first things I noticed when I met him."

"We were shocked by what we read and heard." Her mother sighed and absently smoothed the paper napkin beside her plate.

"I'm sorry I didn't tell you everything I knew from the beginning." Tessa gave an apologetic shake of her head. "Instead of sparing you, I worried you terribly. I see that now."

"We could have told you what we found out about the man. We kept quiet for the same reason you did with us," her father said. "We didn't want to upset you."

"How Brian must suffer." Her mother's tone became sorrowfully reflective. "And always will."

"Sometimes I don't think even he knows what's really going on inside him." Tessa shifted in her chair. "He says Christianity is a fairy tale."

"We've held many a circle of prayers for him," her father said.

Tessa looked from one to the other. "Mom and Dad, he's the kindest, most considerate man you could ever meet. Like I told you, he might have saved my life when I had that accident. The better I know him, the more I see how compassionate he is. Always willing to help others, like those poor people in New Orleans who went through tornados and hurricanes." She stopped, afraid she'd come on too strong in his defense and alerted them to certain feelings for him. She shrugged. "At least, that's how he seems to me." Mug in hand, she got up for a coffee refill from the pot on the stove. "Either of you ready for a second cup?"

A dual "No, thanks," then silence except for the squish of her footsteps on the linoleum floor as she stepped back to the table. They seemed to wait for her to comment further, but she couldn't decide what to say. She leaned back in her chair and took a sip of coffee.

Her mother touched her hand. "If there's anything we can say or do to help you cope, no matter what comes up, we're here for you. Surely you know that."

"I'm having a few problems. He has a sister. She wants their mother to sell the family home, not have it restored with those antiques as it was before the fire. She and Brian have had words. She wants me out of there. To make matters worse, her husband is into drugs and causing her a lot of trouble." She blinked off and took a deep breath. "Simone is Brian's business partner. She wants me gone too and begged me to tell him those lost antiques can't be replaced. But I can't lie to him."

"Of course not," her mother said.

"Some think she and Brian are engaged. Ada says that's not true. Her harassment stresses me at times. But I'm dealing with it."

Her father's gaze lingered on her mother. "We're trying to heal wounds in another country while folks are hurting right here at home. Isn't it ironic?" He sighed and turned to Tessa. "Like I said in that interview, take your Uncle Lester, for instance. I didn't even know my own brother needed help." He paused. "As for those creditors, Tess, they're our responsibility too. We'll find a way to settle with them."

"I know, Dad. The debts are eating up our savings and part of my paycheck, but our accountant still manages monthly payments to everyone. When I finish the job for Brian, I have something else in mind."

She laid a hand on his. "You shouldn't worry. Not yet, anyway."

"Don't overdo the work," he cautioned. "We're family. Never forget that. As always, you can share any of your problems with us." He paused and gave her a studied look. "One more thing, Tess. Be careful you don't get involved," he stopped, took a deep breath, "uh, emotionally with someone if your values are different."

Tessa stared down at her coffee cup. She knew it. Dear Dad, he remembered her heartache over Josh and didn't want her to go through that kind of pain again. Her cell rang. Relieved, she reached for it but paused to make sure her parents wouldn't mind if she took the call.

"Go ahead." Her mother nodded. "It might be important."

"Honey," Ada said when Tessa answered, "is this a good time to ask your parents if they'd like to come out and see the house?"

"But Ada, the way Brian feels—I mean, didn't he say—are you sure?" Tessa lowered her tone, almost a whisper, and paused. After all, she had no doubt her parents could probably hear every word she said.

"I knew what you were going to say, but your parents are an exception. They are welcome here any time," Ada assured. "They love antiques. Besides, the place is so quiet now with everybody away. Cede and I would be honored if they could drop by."

"Oh, Ada, that's what I was hoping for. But they don't have much time, you know. Let me check—" She covered the phone with her hand to relay the message, glancing from her mother to her father.

"We'd love to visit with her and her husband," her mother said. "And yes, your dad and I must see Le Moyne House."

"We have only three days here," her father said. "Maybe we could come over just before we catch the plane. It's an evening flight."

The invitation became a priority with headshakes and smiles.

Other calls trilled, for Boyd, for Monette, and then off they went to meetings. Many people had heard about their visit, and their interview on television with Simone became a main topic of conversation among pastors and church members as well as the general public. Tessa shared her concern with Ada that Brian would relive his deepest heartache the moment he learned about the interview or heard a replay.

"Let's not worry about it," she said. "Leave it in God's hands."

Tessa tried to follow Ada's advice, a replay of what her parents had said after the interview.

She accompanied her parents on speaking engagements. Not only did she want to spend extra time with them, but she also wanted to find out more about their work. And, once in a quiet moment, she reminded them that her goal remained the same—one day to open another Chandelle's House of Antiques. She would follow in their footsteps and sponsor church socials there as they had done through her growing up years.

"Just don't let that plan consume you or think you have to fulfill a childhood dream to please us," her father said.

"Honey, like you've heard us say so many times," her mother added, "the Lord can use you wherever you are and whatever you do. Every day brings an opportunity to help someone."

But if He had given her a mission at Le Moyne House, Tessa thought with regret, she had failed.

Too soon for her and her parents, they repacked their bags. She must return to her work, and they would fly back to Northern Ireland. But first, in the borrowed vehicle, their scheduled visit to St. Pierre. Tessa prayed Brian had not yet heard about the interview with her parents and would not return before they were gone.

But fear nagged. Had Simone already told him about it in a phone call?

Mid-afternoon that Friday, she and her parents arrived at Le Moyne House.

"I can understand why you took the job here," her father said as they walked up to the front porch.

"Like you said, Tess, it looks like Chandelle's," her mother added, "but grander, at least from the outside."

Ada opened the door at first ring as if she'd been watching for them. In her dressy, iris-blue dress and white lacy collar, Tessa thought she looked like she deserved that CEO label Brian had bestowed on her. Beside her stood Cede in dark trousers and a white shirt open at the neck.

"Ada and Cede Guidry, my parents—" Tessa began.

165

"Welcome, Mr. and Mrs. Chandelle!" Ada said. "How nice to see you again. Please do come in." Smiling, she reached first for Monette's hand and then for Boyd's.

"Our pleasure and honor, Mr. and Mrs. Guidry," Boyd said.

More handshakes all around, and Ada, followed by Cede and Tessa, ushered them down the hallway.

Again, the doorbell rang. Ada hesitated and glanced at Tessa.

"I'll get it." Tessa walked back and opened the door. She tried to hide her surprise when she saw Pastor and Mrs. Maynard from Ada's church.

"I hope we're not intruding," the pastor said. "We heard your parents would be here this afternoon. May we come in and say hello?"

"Of course, Pastor and Mrs. Maynard. They'll be glad to meet you." Tessa stepped aside. "Please come in."

When she turned to close the door behind them, a well-dressed young couple, Deacon and Mrs. Hudson, whom she'd met at a church social, climbed the porch steps.

"Good afternoon. Any chance we might come in and shake hands with your parents?" the deacon asked.

Before Tessa could answer, Ada appeared, her arms extended. "Welcome!"

And then, up the walk and toward the porch, other folks appeared. Seven, eight—Tessa lost count of the faces she'd seen at church, others new to her. They introduced themselves first to Ada and then to herself as representatives from sister churches. All were eager to meet the Chandelle missionaries Simone had interviewed on television and wanted to learn more about their work in Northern Ireland.

Tessa and her mother exchanged glances.

As Tessa helped Ada find chairs for them, she sent her a helpless, raised-brow look. A quick nod said she understood Tessa's concern, but how could they refuse to let the new visitors inside to meet her parents? Besides, Brian was out of town.

"Make yourselves comfortable, everyone." Ada's smile circled the group. "Coffee will be ready in a few minutes."

Murmurs of "Thank you" flowed. Tessa's parents were quick to shake hands in welcome. "We're humbled by your kind presence," her father said.

Tessa struggled against a war of nerves. What if Darrie and Simone had heard that her parents would visit here this afternoon? Would they show up too? Though Ada displayed the face of a gracious hostess, Tessa sensed the woman's concern about the unexpected turn of her invitation to the Chandelles. She noticed the coffee server on the table and a platter of those famous pecan-and-chocolate cookies, treats Ada had prepared to celebrate a quiet time with the two missionaries. Now more cups and saucers were needed for the extra visitors.

Tessa rose to help Ada with added refreshments and shot a desperate glance toward her mother.

In response, her mother smiled at the pastor's wife next to her. "I think I should get another chair, just in case." She rose and ambled over to Tessa. "Dear," her tone lowered, "what's wrong?"

"Brian gave orders," Tessa murmured. "Ada says it's okay for you and Dad to be here, but he forbids clergy meetings in this home."

"Then we'll leave and others will follow," her mother whispered. "We *are* pressed for time—"

"Let me show you the house first," Tessa said. "We'll invite the ladies to join us."

"But make it a quick tour."

"Quick tour?" Ada caught the words and nodded, as if thrown a lifeline. "Of the house? Good idea I'll take care of things here." She stepped up to the group. "Ladies, Tessa wants to show her mother the rooms she refurnished. The Chandelles have to leave soon to catch their plane. Would you like a look too?"

Smiles eager, they rose.

Tessa led them through adjoining rooms. At her side, her mother noted certain acquisitions from Chandelle's, often exclaiming, "Oh, yes, I remember this one." Others mentioned having admired the furnishings before the fire and declared Felice could only be overjoyed when she saw her home restored to its former grandeur.

"Now if only we could find the Alphonse," Monette said.

Back downstairs, Ada and Cede rose to direct everyone to chairs waiting for them and then joined Tessa on a couch behind the group.

"Yes, life in Ireland is improving every day," Tessa's father was saying. "Community centers offer folks a chance to form new friendships."

"We have our problems here, too," Deacon Hudson observed.

"You're right, Hugh." Pastor Maynard nodded. "No matter where, we've got to fight intolerance, poverty, discrimination. All we can do is live what we preach." On went the conversation about trying to lead others to an acceptance of God's love.

Monette glanced at her watch, then at Boyd. "I'm sorry to interrupt, but time is slipping away. We do have a plane to catch."

He nodded and straightened as if to get up. The conversation sped on with Pastor Maynard taking out a large, stuffed envelope from his coat pocket.

"We got up a collection to help fund the work you're doing," he said. "We're blessed to deliver it in person—"

Footsteps sounded in the hallway. The group turned.

Wearing jeans and a plaid shirt, Brian strode in, briefcase in hand. The puzzled look on his face etched lines that turned to steel. His eyes narrowed, roved the visitors, and stopped on Ada, then Tessa. *So this is what goes on behind my back?* Tessa could almost hear him say.

He turned from Tessa, who stood at once. To Ada, her hands knotted in her lap. Next, to the group.

Tessa's pulse pounded at her temples. "Brian, I'd like you to meet my parents."

Smiles undaunted, they stood, hands extended toward him.

"Mr. Le Moyne—" her father began.

A flush crept over Brian's clean-shaven face, fire burning in his cobalt eyes. "Mr. and Mrs. Chandelle," he nodded curtly, his gaze shifting toward the staircase as he strode past them. Each thump up the stairs echoed through the otherwise pin-fall quiet of the room.

Ada's mouth hung open. She got up, made a couple of starts after him, obviously reconsidered, and stopped. Close behind her, Cede frowned, hands helpless at his sides. A murmur among the visitors said it must be late, they should be going, so nice to meet the Chandelles, and their prayers would go with them. Everyone, including Tessa's parents, started toward the front door, the envelope with the love offering left on the table beside the empty cookie tray, a forgotten casualty of the afternoon.

Ada's eyes welled up.

Tessa patted her shoulder. "I'll see the company out."

The deacon and his wife, followed by other late-comers, crossed the porch in silence, eyes lowered.

"It's plain the man needs our prayers," Boyd said. "He bears a burden on his heart, and he can't shove it off. In his place, who knows how any of us would feel?"

Monette shook her head. "How sad for him. We represent the very people he blames for the death of his wife and child. He's still in pain. Who wouldn't be?"

"Yes, you can put yourself in his place," the deacon added as he and his wife hesitated with the group on the concrete driveway.

"Invaded his home," Boyd said. "Let's face it. That's what we did. His heart isn't ready for us yet."

Tessa listened, eyes darting from face to face. Coming from the gallery, Ada rushed past her and handed Boyd the envelope that had been left on the table. "I'm so sorry," she said, her gaze wandering to the remaining guests who stood around, apologetic themselves. "Please, you must excuse Brian."

And he must excuse Ada and me, Tessa's mind raced on. She took a deep breath for courage. "Mom and Dad, give me a few minutes. Wait out here or in the car, please. I have to let him know how sorry I am for what happened here."

She charged back into the house and up the stairs, sure Brian had closed himself up in his mother's office. She'd knock, hoping he would let her in to apologize because she and Ada had let people into his home they knew he didn't want there. But when her glance caught the sunroom's open door, she saw him sitting at a desk, his briefcase open before him.

Afraid she would lose her nerve any second, she called, "Brian!"

He turned and looked at her.

"Ada and I didn't plan the affair here this afternoon," she blurted, meeting the hard look in his eyes as she entered the room. "We were as surprised as you were. I can explain how it happened."

"What's to explain?" He lowered his gaze and shuffled papers. "I know what I saw."

"This is your home. We had no right to let in people you don't welcome here."

"I'm sorry about your parents." Still he didn't look up.

"And they're so very sorry, too, about the meeting they didn't expect." She paused, gasping for breath. "They did leave an offering to help spread peace in the world."

"Peace, as in that interview?" Now his gaze challenged.

"That was Simone's idea. Not theirs or mine, please believe me. I'm sorry you had to relive that tragic event in your life. They are too."

He didn't answer. Gaze lowered again, he slid papers back into his briefcase.

"The people here this afternoon came with a love offering," she went on. "They want to help so what happened to your family *and to you* never happens to anyone else. Should Ada and I have told them they weren't welcome here?"

He snapped the briefcase shut. "Excuse me. I have work to do."

"I don't doubt it, but I'd appreciate an answer to my question."

He surged to his feet. In two steps he crossed over to her and grabbed her arms. "What do you want me to say? Oh, it's great they were here? I lost my wife and yes, our unborn child, because of people like them. Christians, they all call themselves? Believers in what? In murder? You tell me!"

"They're human beings, sinners like all of us. I can't know their hearts."

"Well, I do! Why are they different from *you*?"

Tessa saw the swell of the veins on his temples. Her own face caught fire, her breath in short gasps. "Because I—?" Words tripped on her tongue, stopped. She'd almost said, *"Because I'm in love with you?" At a moment like this? How could she tell him that now? And what difference would it make to him?*

"Well?" he demanded, his jaw tightening.

"Those people who came here today love you." Words gushed in a torrent she couldn't stop. "They miss you and need you. They want you back with them, Brian. So do Cede and Ada. We're praying for you, for peace and love and understanding all over the world, for professed and unprofessed Christians—"

"Forget prayer." Distress flashed in the flaming blue of his eyes. "Nothing can bring back my wife and child."

"What happened to them is too horrible for words." Tessa's tone lowered, her gaze never leaving his. "But can you try to let go the bitterness and forgive them? If you don't, you're giving in to those who killed your loved ones. You're—you're becoming one of them. You hate people because of their beliefs. Can't you see that? Not only did they take your wife and unborn child, you let them take away your faith too."

He opened his mouth, his face flushed with a kind of anger warring with need. "I'm just supposed to forgive and forget? Move on, fall in love with someone else—with you?"

"Fall—in love—? *With me*?" she stammered.

"Yes, with you!"

"And I—with you—" Her voice lingered in a sudden soft whisper. Eyes on his, she couldn't, didn't want to pull away.

Before she knew it, his mouth approached hers, demanding. Just before their lips met, he stopped. He held her there, fire in his eyes. A moment, and he released her.

"Like I said, I've got work to do." He turned, grabbed his briefcase and rushed out.

Hand to her throat, Tessa watched him disappear down a staircase. She started to hurry out after him and then stopped. What could she say? Or do? No question about it now. Again she'd fallen in love with the wrong man. *And he with her—the wrong girl? He was Simone's fiancé?* She shook her head and took a deep breath. She was losing it, drifting off into fantasy land. A land he knew as well as she did they could never share. That's why he'd changed his mind about the kiss? Had rushed out? Hand to her mouth, she let out a whispery, *Dear God...*

The sound of a door closing somewhere in the house snapped her back to reality. She must forget an impulse of the moment between them. She'd come up here to apologize to Brian, not to exchange an impossible *I love you.* To assure him she regretted the incident in his home, hoped he might accept the visitors' apologies for being there without his invitation. Yes, that was what she wanted. But it wasn't going to turn out that way. She must get back to them.

She hurried down the stairs and out the front door. Her parents stood near the car with Ada, Cede, Pastor and Mrs. Maynard. The deacon and his wife were gone, as were the other visitors.

"Tess, honey?" Her mother reached at once for her hand, the lines on her forehead deepening. "Are you all right?"

All right? Am I all right? Oh, sure. I'm in love with the man—and he's in love with me? Just what you warned me against, just what I knew I shouldn't let happen. She shook her head. "I couldn't reach Brian. I don't think anyone can right now."

Pastor Maynard fingered his chin and stared at the ground, his manner reflective. "The man can't understand how the Lord let it happen. Le Moyne money poured into the mission fields for years to work for peace there." He hesitated and looked up at Boyd and Monette. "The very spot in Ireland where she was killed." Another pause. "How Simone could bring back all that pain in her interview with you two is beyond comprehension."

Boyd sighed. "Believe me, we don't understand it either. We are deeply troubled for him."

A knot formed in Tessa's stomach. *Dear Heavenly Father, how could You let that happen? How can You say all things work together for good when innocent people are killed in Your name? When their loved ones are made to suffer again and again?*

Ada's hand reached first to Monette and then to Boyd in good-bye.

"You're always in our prayers," she said.

More goodbyes between the Chandelles and the Maynards, and Ada walked her pastor and his wife to their car.

"Tess, we have to leave it all in God's hands—" her mother began.

Tessa heard the concern in her tone and saw it in eyes that searched hers with the tenderness she knew too well. She slipped one arm around her mother and the other around her father. "Don't worry. I'll be fine here."

Her father shook his head. "Never doubt that. The Lord will see to it."

Numb with tears held back, they embraced. Tessa stood aside as they climbed back into their car. She watched them drive off, hands lifted in good-bye. How *could* she stay here and "be fine" after what she'd just discovered *about herself. And, could it be, what Brian had discovered about himself?*

Chapter XII

That night Tessa dreamed she fled Le Moyne House.

Zuni jar tight in one hand and clunky suitcase in the other, she bolted up and down the narrow streets of New Orleans. Her pulse throbbed at her throat. Ahead, blinding sun turned into dark, foggy mists. She stumbled. So tired, so sleepy. A room to rent? Veiled elderly women shook their heads behind iron-latticed gates and pointed fingers to No Vacancy signs dangling from closed doors. She cowered, eyes wide on the parade of shapeless forms that disappeared into mysterious little courtyards shadowed in alternating mounds of dark and light.

"Why, God? Why?" a despairing voice boomed. So near, so far.

Round and round she raced in an endless maze. Her leg muscles screamed in fiery pain. Breathless, she dropped her suitcase on the sidewalk and sat on it to rest. From somewhere, the drumming of footsteps grew louder and closer. Holding hands, Brian and Simone whizzed forward in a blinding flash of light. She shaded her eyes with both hands and screamed, *"Brian! . . . I'm here! . . .It's me, Tessa! . . .Brian . . . Brian . . ."*

Head high and eyes forward, he ignored her. Simone's laughter rang out in a fading echo followed by a shriek over her shoulder. "Look back there, Tessa. A church! Go pray, silly girl. But it's me Brian loves. *Me* Brian loves." She dropped Brian's hand. Veering back, she poked a jasmine sprig under Tessa's nose and then tossed the bloom into the street. A car streaked by and crushed it under its wheels. Tessa's gaze darted to the Indian jar in her lap. The plant had vanished.

She woke up screaming, "No!" and jolted to a sitting position. Her gaze flew at once to the Zuni pottery safe by the windows.

She heard a knock at her door and stiffened. "Who—?"

"Tessa, it's me, Ada. Can I come in?" The door inched open. "Honey, I heard you cry out. Are you all right?"

"A bad dream. I'm sorry. Come in." She swung her legs to the side of the bed and sat hunched, gulping deep breaths to quiet the pounding in her chest.

Ada stepped inside and gave her a searching look. "Sure that's all?"

"I'm fine. Really."

"You worried about Brian? About what happened yesterday?"

Tessa rubbed her forehead. "How he must hate me now."

"Hate you? Oh, no." Ada approached the foot of the bed. "It's himself he hates."

"Hates himself?" Tessa's eyes widened.

"He was rude to your parents and everyone else." Ada sighed. "The poor man just lost control."

Tessa looked toward the windows, bright sun mocking the gloom inside her. Both of them had lost control yesterday. About the meeting in his home. Alone, they both said words they regretted. *About love? A kiss that didn't, couldn't happen?* "I can't face him today."

"You don't have to." Ada shook her head. "He's gone. He left early this morning. Not a word to anyone. I just happened to hear the copter and looked out as he lifted off."

"That proves it." Tessa brushed a strand of hair from her eyes. "He can't bear to see me either."

Ada's hands flew to her hips. "Now, you listen to me. It's not you upsetting him. He's been his own worst enemy ever since Maureen died. In fact, the whole family's been torn up." She paused and moistened her lips. "Only Felice kept the faith. But it got to where she couldn't cope anymore with where the family is headed. She needed a break from them. That's mainly why she went abroad. I thought so the day she left, and I think so now."

"I have to accept the facts, Ada. I pray for Brian—for me, that I'll help him somehow. But everything turns out wrong, except finding pieces of furniture that can't bring him happiness. Not really, not the kind he's looking for. You said so yourself the day we met."

"He's been in deep pain. We know that."

"Of course he has. Even inviting my parents here was a mistake. Oh,

Ada, to think of Le Moyne money supporting a mission dedicated to saving lives. And Maureen and their unborn child losing theirs, *maybe at the hands of*—I can't even say the word."

Ada settled on the side of the bed. "Look here, honey. Like I explained to Brian late last night after he'd cooled off a tad, I'm partly to blame for getting those church folks here. Sure, I knew you wanted your parents to visit and see the house. But I called you and suggested it. Besides, I let on to a couple of friends at church that we expected them here yesterday afternoon. Am I sorry that's probably how word got out? That some took it for an invitation to drop in with a love offering? Reflecting now, the answer is NO."

"You're not to blame for anything that happened." Tessa took a deep, slow breath. "Of all times for Brian to come back early from his trip—" she hesitated. "Then showing up here at the very time members of the church dropped in. I wonder—"

"If Simone called to tell him they were in town? I don't doubt it for one second. She didn't worry that Brian would be hurt all over again hearing how Maureen died. And she acts as if she's in love with him?" She looked off toward the window, brows squeezed in a frown. "She and Darrie got their heads together. They planned that interview, and then somehow they found out your parents would be visiting here today. God forgive me for judging them. As for those church folks, I'm not surprised they wanted to meet your parents and present them with a love gift to help with their work."

"I shouldn't have taken the job here," Tessa said. "I've caused nothing but trouble in the family."

"You get off that guilt trip. We must put all those doubts and fears behind us. Sure, we all hurt for Brian. But it's high time he let go that bitterness and stops listening to those like Simone who keep feeding it to him. It'll destroy the man if he doesn't. How far I got trying to get that message across, I don't know." Ada touched Tessa's hand. "You let God deal with Brian in His own good time. Keep your end of the bargain like you've been doing and stop worrying." Ada paused. "We Christians," she added with a nod, "we must trust that all things—"

"Please stop, Ada. Right now, I have trouble with that verse."

"Of course you do. All Christians face doubts now and then. God understands that."

Tessa gave her a faint smile. "You and my parents, Ada, have so much in common."

Ada stood, her chin going up. "Why don't you get dressed and come down for breakfast? Besides, messages are waiting for you by the kitchen phone."

"Thanks for being here for me, Ada."

"I didn't say anything you haven't thought of yourself. You just needed to hear it from someone else. Glad I came by when I did." Ada hesitated. "Brian did come by to talk to me after everyone had left. He asked me to be sure to continue to be here for you. To make suggestions when you needed them about any furniture replacement. I assured him I would do my best as he had asked me from the start to help you whenever you might ask."

"Oh, Ada." Tessa got up, hesitated, and went into her friend's open arms.

After that treasured time with Ada, she watched her walk out and wondered how long rebounding from that nightmare would have taken without their talk. More than she'd known, she needed to be reminded she couldn't live with regrets and what-ifs.

Her mood somewhat calmed, she got up, determined to make the best of the day. She glanced toward the door and saw a piece of paper off to the side on the floor. She had no idea how it had landed there. Lucky that Ada hadn't slipped on it. She walked over and picked it up, the words leaping up at her:

Tessa,

I'll be gone for a while. Unexpected business out of town. Good luck with our project. Don't work too hard. Ada promised me that she will be ready to keep on helping you with any question you might have regarding the furnishings or anything else you might need.

Until later,

thanks.

Brian

She stared at the words. Read them again. No word that might even hint he remembered the kiss that almost happened. She wondered if thinking about it now bothered him as much as it did her. No matter how hard she tried, she couldn't forget that, for a moment, he had left her too dazed to think or speak from her head. But then, he'd probably said words he regretted too, like the way he said he loved her? And words she'd said, too, and now should regret?

She slipped his message inside her Notebook of Needs. Why write instead of call? Because he didn't want to talk to her? As for herself, if she'd waited, she might have lost the nerve to challenge him about losing not only his wife and unborn child but also his faith in Ireland. Only he could decide how to work through what she'd said. And she had a decision as well—how to deal with feelings for him she had been obviously unable to control. She knew what it had to be. She must finish her work here as quickly as possible and then move on.

She brushed off a scatter of tears and made her bed. Then she picked up her parents' latest gift from the nightstand, a purse-size, leather Book of Psalms. Slowly she paged through it at random. Her eyes fell on Psalm 143:8: "Cause me to hear thy loving kindness in the morning; for in thee do I trust; cause me to know the way wherein I should walk; for I lift up my soul unto thee." Clasping the small volume to her chest, she pleaded softly, "Lord, forgive the times I doubt Your word. Please show me how to share it with everyone I see today and every day. Especially with Brian—when we meet again."

She closed the Bible and put it back in place. Now she must get to work.

Moments later, dressed and ready to walk out of her room, the house phone rang. She stepped to the bedside table and glanced at the caller ID, *Simone Duvall*. Brow furrowed in a disquieting chill, she stared at the name of the woman in her nightmare and picked up the receiver.

"Simone?"

"We've got great news."

"Great news?"

"Darrie and I are parked in the driveway. Can you come out and meet us?"

Tessa hesitated, her fingers twisting the phone cord. Good news from Simone and Darrie? "Yes. I'll be right there."

With visions of last night a renewed turmoil floating in her head, she hurried down the stairs. As she went through the hallway, Ada called from the kitchen, "Simone and Darrie pulled up in the driveway. I wonder what they're up to this time."

"I'll know soon. They want me to meet them there."

Tessa pushed the door open and walked out into bright sunlight. The familiar car was parked under the oak swirling mossy trails nearest the driveway. Simone leaned against the driver's side of her car, hands plunged into her pockets. She wore dark glasses, a sunflower- colored pant suit with a string of gold beads at her throat. Beside her was a smiling Darrie in jeans and a blue-knit top.

"Hi, Simone, Darrie." Tessa stopped before them. "What's going on?"

"We came to say we're sorry." Simone pulled off her glasses, as if to let Tessa look into her eyes and see that she was sincere.

"About what?" Tessa's glance shifted between her and Darrie.

"We heard my brother insulted your folks yesterday and everyone else here." Darrie frowned. "How awful that must have been for all of you."

"But that didn't surprise me," Simone said.

"Oh?" Tessa couldn't stop a challenging smile. "You expected that?"

"Knowing him as we do, yes," Simone said. "In your place, I'd run away from here. Get as far off as I can."

In my nightmare, I did just that, Tessa wanted to say.

"Seeing your parents—missionaries—well, surely you can understand that would upset him," Darrie said. "Now maybe you'll listen to us."

"Listen to you?" Tessa's brow arched in a questioning look from her to Simone. "About what?"

"Accept a job at our TV station in Baton Rouge." Now Darrie flashed a cajoling smile.

"You could work as a newscaster," Simone said.

"Or have your own weekly show on antiques," Darrie added. "Wouldn't you just love that? And how proud your parents would be."

Lips parted, Tessa looked from one to the other.

"Perfect for you, like I knew first time we met." Simone's tone lilted, as if the sky was the limit if Tessa accepted their offer. "Negotiable salary. Soon you'd have a great audience. For the station, a big asset with added viewers tuning our channel every time you're on. What's more, the Chandelle name respected again. Which is what you want most of all, right?"

"I appreciate the offer." Tessa stepped back and glanced from one to the other. "But like you both know, I have a contract to honor here."

Simone broke into a half-laugh, her brows going up in disbelief. "You can talk about honor? When Brian insults you and your parents in front of everybody?"

"I signed a contract—"

"My brother wants to relieve you of that." Darrie's smile fled, hands knotting at her sides. "He's too kind to tell you that."

"He left me a note." Tessa took another step back. "He says I should go ahead with my work."

"Of course, he'd say that," Darrie said. "I know my brother. He's too much of a gentleman to tell you to pack up and leave!"

The blush on Simone's cheeks turned a quick red. "I can't believe you still want to torture him. Don't you have any pride? Any professed Christian love?"

Tessa blinked, struggling for a civil tone. "That's why I won't break our contract. Like I told him from the start, if he changes his mind, all he has to do is say the word."

"Say the word? His actions speak louder than words! Can't you understand that?" Simone threw up her hands. "You're determined to keep torturing the man in the name of—righteous Christianity! Like those people who took the life of his pregnant wife and unborn child." She made an abrupt turn and gripped the car door open. She looked back at Tessa. "You'll regret your decision, I swear it!"

"Don't you regret yours," Tessa couldn't stop the words, "to interview my parents on television? Make Brian relive the worst tragedy of his life?"

Simone climbed into the driver's seat and slammed the door shut. She turned on the ignition. Darrie gave a dismissing wave of her hand and rushed for her place on the passenger's side. The car sped away.

Tessa stood still and looked after them. Could they be right? Maybe she didn't know Brian as well as she thought she did?

Slowly, she went back into the house. Ada was nowhere in sight. For that, she was glad. She couldn't talk at that moment about her conversation with Simone and Darrie. No matter what the two threatened, she knew what she must do, whatever the cost.

Chapter XIII

Back in her bedroom, she dialed Gene. "I need photos. Would you have time to meet me downstairs at the house for coffee and a chat?"

"You're in luck," he said. "Be there in a few."

Armed with a packet of photographs and the Notebook of Needs, she went downstairs. Shelling peas, now Ada sat on a rosewood Lincoln rocker in a corner of the kitchen. "Breakfast, Tessa?"

"Only orange juice for me," she said, "and I'm getting it, thank you. I called Gene. I need duplicates of some photos. He'll be over any minute now. I hope you don't mind."

"Mind?" Ada smiled. "That young man is always welcome here."

Tessa was relieved that Ada made no mention of Simone and Darrie's visit. Her friend always seemed to know when to ask questions and when to keep silent. She got a glass from a cabinet and stepped up to the refrigerator for the pitcher of juice. Her glass filled, she perched on a stool at the counter, taking an occasional sip. She'd left not only her cell number but also that of Le Moyne House with some choice antique dealers. She found several responses in a clip by Ada's cookie jar. Glancing over them, her eyes lit up now and then with an occasional, "Great!"

"Looks like we found the Queen Anne walnut bureau and the *papier mâche* table for the library," she said.

"Like *you* found them," Ada corrected as the doorbell chimed. She set her pan down and pattered toward the foyer.

"Come on in, Gene," Tessa heard her say. "Coffee's waiting."

"Hi." Tessa looked up as he entered, camera hanging around his neck.

"At your service, Tessa," he said, his unshaved face awash with a broad grin.

Tessa slipped off the stool. "Thanks so much for coming, Gene." She opened the cabinet above the stove and took out a cup. She filled it with Ada's steaming black coffee. Smiling, she set it on the cream and sugar tray already on the table and sat down. She patted the chair next to hers. "Enjoy your coffee while we check out some treasures."

"I haven't seen those pictures in a long time myself," Ada said.

"Then join us."

Seated between them, Tessa listened closely as Ada and Gene pointed to photographs and exchanged a running commentary about the handsome look of the first floor rooms. With a dreamy excitement, Ada spoke of the "old days," enthusiasm building when Tessa flipped to the close-up of the scenic wallpaper adorning the right foyer entrance. It showcased a magnificent palace nestled against a background of soft blue sky and pink-tinged clouds. The foreground boasted luscious greenery and flowers, while elegantly dressed ladies and gentlemen in various poses surrounded party tables and chairs.

"Marie Antoinette's garden," Gene said. "With your connections abroad, Tessa, you should be able to duplicate that."

"Done." Tessa smiled and turned to other needed items, matching them with the responses she'd just received from dealers. As her two helpers offered suggestions about various photos, she jotted short notations for follow-ups. Finally, she pointed to a shot of the Alphonse chair. "No word on this one yet."

"Brian's favorite chair," Ada murmured. "Maureen's last gift to him."

Tessa's hand tightened on the pen. She recalled the eager look on Brian's face when he first showed her the photo that night at Chandelle's and then the shadow that clouded his brow when she said it was sold.

Ada got up, eyes squinted in reflection. She reached behind her to tighten the sash of her white apron. "Maureen got it from the old plantation owned by the Veillons south of town. Only one other like it, they said."

Tessa jotted a note to research a possible survivor of that family.

"They said they got it from someone who found it in a king's castle in Spain. Did they make that up? We don't know." Ada smiled. "I'll never forget the king's name. Alphonse, same as my grandfather's."

"That piece tops my list of priorities." Tessa met Gene's stare and then attempted a careless laugh. "You know the drill—aim to please the boss."

Gene shrugged. "Can't argue with that."

Tessa broke eye contact. She had no doubt Gene suspected she had another reason for wanting to find that chair for Brian.

"Now, look at these." Ada pointed to photographs of paintings by master artists. "You'll find some others stored in the barn. They're scorched, but Felice couldn't make herself throw them away."

"Good she didn't," Tessa said. "I'll take a look. Maybe they can be restored." She quickly scanned those on hand. She selected a group of photographs and turned to Gene. "Five copies of each, please?"

He nodded. "You got it."

"I can send photos via the internet, but hard copies are better to hand to dealers. And don't forget to give me your bill." Tessa smiled. "Now I'm going to the barn to check on those paintings."

Gene followed her outside. "Anything else you need—anything I can do—just ask, Tessa."

His low, intimate tone startled her. She avoided his gaze, not wanting him to guess she was beginning to suspect his feelings for her went beyond friendship. "You make my work so much easier," she said, assuming a businesslike manner. "You're always there with a helping hand any time you're needed. You're a definition of the word *friend*." Not waiting for his response, she waved a goodbye hand and walked off toward the barn.

Later that morning, Tessa headed for New Orleans, notebook and photographs on the seat beside her. The car's trunk held four paintings she thought could be redeemed. She had prepared a list of antique dealers, certain one of them would know a reputable artist skilled in restoring oil paintings.

In New Orleans, she parked her car and made her way on the sidewalks through tourist groups, some wearing shirts or blouses stamped with out-of-state logos. She shaded her eyes in the direction of Mirbeau's Furniture and remembered that company's ad in the paper a few days back for a "a sales person of proven talent in the antiques business."

She debated whether to take time out right now and apply for the job. While her last contact for employment there had been disappointing, she couldn't forget she'd be out of work when she left Le Moyne House. She must try to get her hands on extra dollars to strengthen her bank account and help satisfy the remaining creditors.

But could she even think of subjecting herself to a working environment with people who might not be trustworthy, such as whoever had twisted Brian's message with Mirbeau's after her accident? She sighed. No business place could guarantee all their employees were of sterling character. And then there were other kinds of problems that could come up in any job, such as that recent encounter with Simone and Darrie.

An application with a television station must be off her radar screen for now. Since she had refused Simone and Darrie's supposedly "generous offer," no telling what they had in mind when Simone said she'd "regret her decision." She drew a deep, unsettling breath.

A glance at her watch, and she decided she did have time for a stop at Mirbeau's. Besides, Mr. Nilas might know a reputable artist to redo the paintings.

Upon entering the store, she noticed an area of collectible antiques mixed with pieces from the better lines of modern furniture. Before asking about the job ad she'd seen, she took notes on a few items that might be suitable alternates for minor pieces she had not yet replaced.

"So good of you to drop by, Miss Chandelle."

She found herself face to face with Nilas, a short, paunchy man with thinning hair combed crosswise on the top of his head.

"Mr. Nilas." She nodded and returned his smile.

"Just the other day I came across your résumé in our files." His dark eyes softened in a friendly manner. "I'd like to talk to you. If you have time now, would you step into my office?"

"Yes, thank you." Tessa could hardly believe their meeting of the minds.

"A pleasure," he said as they entered his office, "to talk again with someone from that fine antique house, Chandelle's."

Tessa smiled, grateful for praise she wanted to hear. She was ready to forget their last disappointing conversation and settled in the chair he offered.

Seated behind his desk and, in a relaxed, off-the-cuff manner, he asked about her employment with Brian. "It's too bad that accident nixed our interview. But from what I hear, you're doing an excellent job for the Le Moynes. We already filled the spot for a sales person. But I think you're the right person to be in charge of our new decorating service. Now, I have to be honest. The job probably won't last more than six months, nine at the most. Interested so far?"

Tessa hadn't expected even a part time job. "Yes. Please tell me more."

"A client of mine is converting some old homes into efficiency apartments. We're combining resources mainly to help a number of homeless hurricane victims. If we start this temporary decorating service, he wants us to do the work. You'd get a professional rate on a place there if you like." He went on to explain further details about the work.

When he quoted a salary, Tessa shook her head. "I'd be on the lookout for work after I finish your project. An apartment for a temporary home is all I would accept from you. I would like to donate my time as you and the builder donate your resources. It's the least I can do for those in need."

"That's very generous of you. I didn't expect you to do that. The extra money will go for a good cause."

"I'll be glad to help. My work with Brian should be over in a month or so. Is that time frame a problem for you?"

"Not at all. It should fit our schedule just fine." He opened his desk drawer and pulled out a folder. "This copy outlines the kind of work we plan to do." He handed it to her. "Look it over. I'd appreciate your response within a week."

"Thank you, Mr. Nilas." Tessa worked the folder into her purse. "I have no doubt my answer will still be yes. You'll hear from me soon. And now," she went on, "I do have some paintings for Le Moyne House that were damaged in a fire. Do you know a reputable artist?"

"To restore them? Absolutely. He's the best of the best." He scribbled a name and an address on a slip of paper and handed it to her. "But he isn't in today. Try him in the morning."

Eagerness held, and two days later, the paintings were in the hands of the recommended artist. Besides, she had signed an agreement with

Nilas and his partner for the charitable project. Work would begin as soon as she completed her contract with Brian.

Now if only she could hear from *him*.

At Le Moyne House, she set a work pattern Ada called "back-breaking." Added renovations called for the services of wallpaper and picture hangers, as well as carpet installers.

"Talk about meeting yourself coming and going," Ada remarked.

"And you're right there with me as CEO," Tessa told her as they joined in a laugh, remembering Brian's comment when he introduced them.

Daily she rose early for a light breakfast and then secluded herself in Felice's office for a couple of hours to scan antique journals and the classified sections of the *New Orleans Times-Picayune*, always careful as usual to try local antique shops first and then others in some part of the state. She researched any chance for a needed special piece, no matter the odds, on her computer and phoned before she drove off to check it out. She listened to those whose judgment she trusted most, especially Ada, when they said: "This is probably the closest you can get to what you want"; or, "Let me check with my contacts in Paris or London, Fresno or Minneapolis."

From Brian? Silence. Ditto from Simone. Darrie still came by to check on every piece of furniture, pad and pen in hand to take notes. As usual, if she and Tessa met in a room or on a staircase, she might ignore her and rush off in a different direction.

She did hear from Margie. Invitations to the welcome home party for Felice would be mailed out from her office, she said, and Ada had already told her the piano Tessa ordered for the ballroom had arrived.

"Brian says you're not to worry if the house isn't completely furnished," Margie assured her. "Ada will handle maid service, and I'm in charge of everything else."

"Just when is the party?" Tessa asked, phone pressed to her ear. It was easy for them to say, "Don't worry," but she had things to do yet, a reputation to uphold. *Or prove*, the thought needled.

"We're shooting for six weeks from Saturday, from seven o'clock to ten," Margie said. "All Brian asks of you is to be there to meet his mother and socialize with the guests."

All he asks of me? Why didn't he tell her that himself? Now and then she considered dialing his cell, but each time she drew back her fingers from pressing the numbers. Did his silence mean he was still upset about her parents' interview with Simone, their visit with church folks in his home? She could only try to shrug off the worry and continue her rigid schedule to try to please his mother, as well as him, with restored furnishings in their home. At church services when the pastor asked for unspoken prayer requests, her hand always went up. Her own daily petitions ended not only with a plea for Brian's happiness again in the Lord, but also for the entire Le Moyne family to return to the faith Ada said once sustained them.

With a better idea of a party date and schedule, she had even less time for social outings like the occasional coffee break with Estelle or Gene at Café du Monde in New Orleans. The morning "Sold" signs sprang up on Duvall property, she worried aloud as she helped Ada in the kitchen.

"Does that mean this place will be next? If Brian and Simone marry—?"

Ada's hand went limp on the silverware she rinsed at the sink. She looked out the window. "Who's to say? All these years, I was sure I knew Brian." A quiet sadness tinged her voice. "Maybe I didn't. It's hard to think Simone could take Maureen's place in his life."

Late in the evenings when Tessa couldn't sleep, convinced she had failed Brian or he would call her, she tried to concentrate on the Royal Doulton china set she needed and the long list of collectibles yet unfound. Often she lingered on the front porch and stared out on the moonlit driveway, hoping she'd see him pull up in his car or hear the drone of his copter bringing him home. She blamed herself because he stayed away, certain he would never forgive her for inviting her parents there when church leaders appeared for the kind of meeting he had strictly forbidden. For him, that moment, added to the interview with Simone, had dealt another blow to a wound that wouldn't heal.

And for herself, too, words they'd exchanged that led to an impulsive and impossible declaration of love, a near kiss they both wanted…

Back from a shopping trip one afternoon, she found Estelle in the parlor standing by the mantel to examine a pair of red candlestick holders with cut glass pendants.

"Oh, Tessa, I never thought you or anyone else could do it." She gestured to the latest acquisitions. They included a Louis XV walnut provincial sofa in a subdued beige floral design, a pair of Adams-style cane armchairs with handsome royal blue velour cushions, and an oriental rug with a pale gold background.

"You approve?" Tessa asked off-handedly, the thrill of compliments dulled.

"The place almost looks like it did before the fire," Estelle marveled. "Felice will positively adore you."

"We mustn't forget Ada has been a big help. Always at my side when I needed advice."

"Of course." Estelle nodded. "As for Brian, he's proud of you, and grateful."

Tessa's smile wavered at the mention of Brian's name. She rebounded quickly and pointed to the entry hall with the standing walnut clock Mr. Forestier had found for her.

The *piece de resistance*, by David Pain.

"The end here is in sight," she said. "Margie tells me Brian has set a date for the party. Do you know *exactly* when his mother will be back?"

"The exact day is iffy, as Martin understands," Estelle said. "But he thinks it'll definitely be a few days before her welcome-home party. Brian must be terribly busy not to call you himself."

Tessa shrugged. "He told Margie I shouldn't worry about anything."

Days flew off the calendar. Late one morning in New Orleans after a consultation with Mr. Nilas about her part in the coming project, she had a few minutes to spare before an unexpected luncheon date Estelle had planned for them. She wandered out to the wharf by the river and watched barges and freighters plow through the dark Mississippi waters. The sky a steel blue, the sun hot on her face and bare arms, a vague kind of restlessness came over her. She ambled about, staring but seeing little.

Tourists crowded around one of several gates for a ride on the *Orchid Bloom*, a pleasure boat. She fought a sudden impulse to cancel her date with Estelle and lose herself with the crowds for a carefree outing.

But fantasy must wait.

She headed down Toulouse Street, then Royal, and moments later she was in the Monteleone's Le Café where her friend waited for her.

"There they are." Estelle smiled. "Come along, Tessa."

"*They?*" Tessa echoed. Her heartbeat stopped and then raced as she realized they neared a table occupied by Martin and *Brian*. Right off, she wanted to take a backward flight, but her feet moved ahead as if she had no control over them. "I thought it was going to be just the two of us. You didn't tell me—" she murmured.

"I'll explain later," Estelle whispered.

Brian saw them first and got to his feet. Tessa met his gaze, something there she read as between a welcoming smile and a question. But if a question, what? Uncertainty froze a faint smile on her lips.

Martin, too, stood at once. As he helped Estelle settle beside him, he said, "Two beautiful ladies, Brian. Aren't we the lucky ones?"

"I'll second that." Brian pulled out a chair next to him for Tessa.

She managed a soft, "Hi," and quickly shifted her focus to the safety of Martin's friendly grin. As soon as everyone was seated, the waiter brought the menus. Tessa's fingers gripped hers for support, and she looked down in blind concentration. She heard Estelle order a chef's seafood salad, while the men wanted squab with stuffing and a rich *crème* sauce. After a moment, Tessa said that, like Estelle, she, too, would try the seafood salad.

Martin and Estelle immediately began a light conversation about the goings-on in St. Pierre. Brian's remarks were subdued, though now and then his shoulder or his hand moved disturbingly close to Tessa's. She wanted to pull away from the electric draw of him, but she remained still, as if glued to the chair.

"Tessa, I hear you're doing a fantastic job at Le Moyne House," Martin said as the waiter appeared with their orders.

"Thanks." She glanced at Brian. "It seemed slow at times, but the job is almost done."

He turned to her, his tan coat sleeve brushing her arm. "I stopped by this morning, but you had just left. The place looks great—like home again. I'm afraid you've been working too hard."

"Oh, not at all." Tessa made light of his comment. "I enjoyed every minute. I want the house as near normal as possible for your mom when she gets back."

"Which will be when, Brian?" Estelle reached for a slice of French bread.

"That's not settled," he answered briefly, "but she'll be here a few days before her party."

"I suppose you know," Martin said with a laugh in Brian's direction, "your soiree will set me back a tidy sum. Estelle is shopping for a new gown. *Another* new gown."

Brian seemed not to have heard him. Now his glance lingered on Tessa and trailed to her lips. Like her, he couldn't forget that near-kiss the day of her parents' visit at Le Moyne House. She managed to shift her gaze down to her plate.

On the foursome ate, Martin and Estelle now trying for relaxed talk, while Brian and Tessa made only minor comments.

Finally, plates pushed aside and coffee cups in hand, Brian turned to Tessa. "You and I need to talk."

"About the house?"

"That's not what I meant."

"You two, please excuse us for a few minutes." Estelle got up. "Martin and I must say hello to friends over there before they get away."

"We sure do." Martin stood and walked off with her.

Brian's gaze held Tessa's now, and he reached for her hand. "About the meeting with your parents, please tell them I'm sorry. I hope they can forgive me. To them and everyone else there, I was rude."

"You were hurting." Tessa blinked at the now familiar, shadowy look on his face. "Seeing my parents must have brought back so much pain for you. All of us, we felt terrible about it. The visit in your home shouldn't have happened without your permission."

He shook his head. "No, you might have been right, what you said." He rubbed a forefinger back and forth over her hand. "The way I acted— it was on principle or out of a sad memory." His shoulders lifted in a deep breath. "Or feelings I couldn't talk about, admit—" He paused, eyes steady on hers.

His tone lingered. *Feelings he couldn't admit? Still couldn't admit, and for her?* Tessa glanced down at her their hands now linked. She didn't know what to say. Too often she had relived that afternoon. In his place, what would she have done, or said? Hurtful memories had surely taken over, piling inside his heart and mind.

"I've been doing a lot of thinking." He hesitated. "Maybe you're right. Maybe I'm becoming too much like those I've hated. I've tried to forgive, but—"

"I can only imagine how hard it must be for you." Tessa felt a sudden torrent of words inside her battling to be said. "For the longest time, I couldn't let go the bitterness I felt toward my Uncle Lester. It took time and much praying before I accepted that if I was going to be forgiven, I had to forgive others. In your case, it must be so much harder."

Now he held both her hands, the pained look she had come to know so well in his eyes was fixed on hers. "You've been there for me from the moment we met. It was almost like I'd known you forever. You're more important to me than—" His fingers tightened on hers.

Tessa's breath went on hold. What else was he about to say?

"I wish I could undo what I put you through that afternoon."

"And I wish I could undo what *I*, what *we* put you through." Tessa felt her heartbeat soar in a rush between joy—and sadness. He was here to apologize, nothing else?

"When you hurt someone," he went on, his tone reflective, "you hurt yourself too. None of you deserved to be treated with disrespect."

"And neither did you. It was all—oh, so unexpected, the way things happened." Now her tone, uncontrolled, was a near whisper.

The waiter started to clear the table. Out of the corner of her eye, Tessa saw Martin and Estelle stop to exchange helloes with other diners nearby.

His gaze never leaving hers, Brian slowly released her hand. "I'm glad we had this time together. You don't know how much I've wanted to see you and apologize for the way I acted. I thought we should talk in person instead of over the phone. To tell you the truth, several times I started to call you or send you an email. I was afraid you didn't want to talk to me or hear from me." He paused. "I wouldn't have blamed you if you had walked away from our contract. But, knowing your dedication to our contract, I was not surprised you—well—you kept your word."

"I've felt the same way about you," Tessa said, her tone whispery.

"Finally seeing you like this—well, I can't tell you what it means to me."

"I've wanted this too, Brian." Once again, she couldn't break away from the luminous blue of his eyes. She'd wanted to hear his words of apology for that ill-fated afternoon with unexpected visitors in his home, had prayed she would, and had longed to say to him that she, too, regretted her part in his pain, in *their* pain. But now she felt only a confusing joy and sadness. For what was yet between them? Or, was she lost in some daydream kind of world again?

"I'm back at my apartment in New Orleans," he said. "You're not to worry about the party. Just plan to enjoy it. As I said earlier, the place looks super already. Mom will be grateful to you."

"As you had suggested, Ada had a big part in trying to get the house back like it was."

He nodded, his hand tightened on hers. "But you were the real pro." A shake of his head, and he said, "Let's keep in touch now that we had this talk. Call me any time—day or night, okay?"

"And you do the same. I need, want to hear from you."

"Take care. Very good care." A gentle stroke, and he let go her hand.

She nodded. "You too."

Another long look between them, and he stood. He gave her shoulder a lingering touch before he walked off to join Estelle and Martin.

A moment, and both men glanced back to nod goodbye while Estelle headed back to the table.

"Ready to go?" she asked Tessa, hesitant hand on Tessa's shoulder.

"When you are." Tessa pushed back in her chair. A loneliness she couldn't describe wrapped around her.

"Brian asked me to arrange this luncheon date," Estelle said. "He had the bill charged to his account. He was afraid you'd refuse to see him if you knew he'd be here. The man was desperate to apologize for the way things turned out when your parents visited in his home."

Tessa stood. "What happened wasn't just his fault. We needed to talk it out."

"Then you're not upset with me?"

"We both owe you thanks. You did us a favor."

"Now will you return the favor?" Estelle smiled. "Go shopping with me? I'd like your opinion on a couple of gowns I saw at La Belle Madame's on my last trip here."

Tessa managed a smile. "Wherever you lead, I'll follow."

Minutes later in the dress shop, she waited while Estelle modeled the two pieces she'd chosen and then was consumed with indecision. Tessa voted on the loosely fitted, blue-toned silk creation that almost hid even the slightest sign of her friend's midriff bulge.

"Your turn." Estelle shook her finger. "I saw you eyeing that gorgeous jade creation over there. Unlike anything in my size, it's on the half-price rack. Lucky you!"

Tessa gave an exaggerated little sigh. She'd have no peace until she did as her well-meaning friend asked. She headed for the dressing room, carrying the fitted chiffon with off-the-shoulder ruffles. Seconds later when she saw her reflection in the mirror, her lips parted in spontaneous approval.

"It accents your tan and your slender hips. And oh, it brings out your eyes. You've got to get it." Estelle stepped back for a long look. "It's perfect for the party. And what a bargain!" Tessa dawdled before the mirror. She imagined dangling earrings in a matching color and reached to unzip the back. "I love it. Thanks."

As they stepped out of La Belle Madame with their purchases, Estelle said, "Maybe you haven't heard—?" She paused as if unsure whether to continue.

"Heard what?" Tessa asked.

"Simone says she and Brian have a big announcement to make sometime soon."

Tessa's heartbeat skipped and then raced. "Their engagement, you suppose? Surely not at Felice's welcome-home party. Doesn't seem like the right time to do it."

"Talk about a guessing game. Martin confirms something big *is* happening with Brian and Simone. They've held a lot of top-level meetings with business executives from New York. Rumors are the two may have decided to go nationwide with some kind of business deal. Maybe Brian finally caved in to Simone's pressure." Estelle's brow wrinkled. "I just don't know what it's all about. Brian has changed, though."

Tessa was torn between wanting her to go on and wishing she wouldn't.

"He and Simone work close mainly at the station and with other business companies. Their families have been co-owners for years. Besides, she's part of Brian's past with Maureen, as you well know by now." Estelle hesitated. "I don't think anyone really understands the woman. Today when somebody asked her if she's engaged, she smiled and said, 'You'll find out soon enough.' Even with Martin, Brian's grown awfully quiet lately about his private life."

"Whatever happens," Tessa said, "I hope they'll be happy."

"Like I said, something's going on there. But what, who knows."

Tessa had been and was now more than ever in a state of confusion about that near kiss the day of her parents' visit to Le Moyne House. It had been a moment of desperation, of need for both of them. And what about the passion she'd seen in his eyes just moments ago when they talked. If he loved someone else, how could he consume her with such a look?

Tessa tried to tell herself to face reality. No matter what he felt for her or she felt for him, weren't their lives headed in different directions?

While she drove back from the city, the magical memory of her reflection in the green chiffon dress dimmed. How she looked at the party wouldn't matter. One thought consoled. Marriage to Josh would have been a mistake. What she'd felt for him had been nothing more than fantasy. Now though she knew true love, she must be prepared to let it go.

As she approached Le Moyne House, her hands relaxed on the wheel. She sat forward, her gaze embracing the fiery glow of setting sun behind oaks and pines, a dream-like finale that lit up the lane. At the upcoming party for his mother, she and Brian would say good-bye. She sighed, struggling to ignore the flicker of doubt that all things worked for good if one loved the Lord.

She turned down the lane that led to Le Moyne House.

Her foot hit the brakes. Once again, Darrie's car was in the driveway.

She let out a short breath. If the woman wanted to confront her about something, the sooner, the better.

Chapter XIV

Darrie met her at the front door. Her purse dangled from her shoulder, and she clenched loose sheets of paper. "Did you get the draperies for the sitting room?"

"Oh, hi, Darrie. No, not yet." Tessa headed toward the stairs.

"Not yet?" Darrie echoed.

Tessa glanced back at her. "That's right."

"Do you realize how much still needs to be done and how little time you have before Mom comes home?" Darrie shuffled the papers in her hand, working to fold them and slip them into her purse.

Tessa wondered what the papers contained. Then again, none of her business. She halted on the bottom step of the staircase. "I marked my calendar. I'm trying my best to hurry up the job. As you can imagine, I meet myself coming and going."

"When do you plan to be out of here for good?" Darrie's face flushed. She snapped her purse closed. "I mean, be through with everything?"

Tessa ignored the needling and squinted. "I wish I could give you a definite date, but I really can't. We knew from the start this wouldn't be an easy job."

"The Alphonse for the library?" Darrie's stare sharpened. "Do you have a lead on it?"

"Not yet." Tessa shook her head. "But I haven't given up." She smiled and waited. She'd learned from the moment she met Darrie and heard her conversation with Brian that whatever else weighed on her mind wouldn't be long in coming.

"No matter what my brother says, I'm sure you know it's not necessary for you to be here when Mom gets back. We have your phone number. She can get in touch with you if she has a question about any of the pieces you substituted." She turned as if to leave and then looked back at Tessa. "Oh, and please don't disturb my things. Some are stored in the bedroom across from yours and some are in the barn." She tapped her purse. "I have a record in here of everything Kyle and I brought over."

"Don't worry." Tessa met the sharp look that said she still considered her as dishonest as her Uncle Lester. "I won't go near your belongings. As

197

for your mom's party, I want to meet her and know how she feels about the house. Besides, your brother expects me to be one of the hostesses." To Darrie's flustered look, she added, "Anything else you think I should know?"

"That's it for now." Darrie flounced off.

Tessa turned and hurried up the stairs. She wondered why Darrie would store personal belongings in the house. Did she plan to move in as well? Maybe she and Kyle could no longer afford to live in New Orleans?

Force of habit, she headed for Felice's office. She sat at the desk and flipped through odd notes in a compulsive rush, hardly registering what she read. Events of the past few months were too much for her. At the moment, she couldn't understand how her coming here had worked for her good, except to provide another lesson in the price of rash decisions mistaken for answered prayer.

Perhaps it also helped her to realize again Josh would have been the wrong man for her. During a recent phone call, Adrienne had commented, "I haven't heard you mention his name except maybe once or twice since you've been at the Le Moynes'. It's really as if he's out of sight, out of mind."

Adrienne was right, but could she forget Brian? She stroked the edge of the desk and remembered the night she accepted his job offer. He not only opened this room to her but also his heart. And then there was their impulsive declaration of love with a near kiss the afternoon her parents visited here. She drew back, once again determined to blot the impulsive moment from her head. Just that, maybe, an impulse with no longevity?

She reached for the phone and dialed Gene's work number. "Want to meet me at the site of the new Jolie Fleurs apartments around seven?" she asked. "I'd like your opinion on some items there. After that, I'll treat you to dinner." She paused, her tone lowered in a hint of laughter, "Your favorite oyster po-boy at your favorite fast-food dive."

"You got it. But I'll pick you up, okay? Can't wait," he said, laughter in his tone.

Somewhat soothed by the prospect of seeing the place Mr. Nilas had said she could call home whenever she wished, she took a few minutes to jot an inventory of personal items she'd stored in Jasmine Hills that would give her new quarters a touch of home.

Much later, and just before his workday ended, a grumbling painter with a tired slouch and a heavy Cajun accent let her and Gene into one of the apartment buildings. Tessa's spirits lifted when she toured the units to be furnished. One south corner apartment, her choice, offered a pleasant view of well-tended yards with shade trees and a rainbow of blossoms.

Over the promised oyster sandwich later at the drive-in, Gene said, "Tessa, I think you'll be happier away from Le Moyne House."

Startled by his comment, Tessa's brows went up in question, her eyes meeting his. Did he expect more than friendship from her? She gave him a quick smile. "Oh, I love my work here, Gene. Besides, I've made many new friends. You're one of them, the best anyone could ask for."

"Well," he began, slowly returning her smile, "I'm glad I'm included in that list."

Mirbeau's remained open late that night. As planned, they dropped by the furniture department. In his usual caring demeanor, Gene helped her select the basics for her new living quarters. When she indicated the apartment and furnishings she'd chosen, Mr. Nilas reached inside his desk drawer and pulled out a key. He handed it to her and said, "Good choices. We'll deliver within the week. After that, you can move in as soon as the apartment is ready."

Back at Le Moyne House, Tessa tried to relax in a warm bath. Seeing what would be her new living quarters had not worked the long-term magic on her mood she'd expected. She dawdled as she applied a moisturizer to her face, her thoughts turning to the night by the swimming pool when Brian's cheek had touched hers by accident. But it was the near kiss the afternoon of her parents' visit in his home which shattered any possible doubt she had fallen in love with him.

She gave herself yet another stern look in the mirror.

Rushed days left her little time for romantic dreams. She worked long hours supervising workers and receiving calls from Brian now, which usually came late at night. They talked about what was going on in their lives and drifted on to childhood memories, sometimes in sober tones and sometimes in laughter. Tessa felt she already knew him better than she'd ever known Josh.

All too soon, only nine days remained before the party. Mid-morning found her and Ada at work in the kitchen while maids polished the upstairs rooms. On the table lay a tray of water goblets.

"I hope Brian's mother will be pleased I found these glasses," Tessa said.

"She will." Ada wiped her hands on her apron and stepped up to the stove for a second cup of coffee. "Since she's been back—?"

"*She's back?*" Tessa swung around to face Ada. "Where is she? Brian said she wouldn't be here until the day before the party."

Ada clapped a hand to her lips. "Oh, my. I goofed but good. Brian didn't want you to know. He was afraid you'd worry she might show up before you're ready. She won't." Ada shook her head. "Please don't let on that I spilled the beans."

"Oh, I wouldn't do that." Tessa blinked hard at the goblet in her hand. Brian knew her well. Already she felt the start of that dreaded tailspin. "You might as well tell me everything you know, Ada. Where is she?"

"She arrived in New Orleans a few days ago. Now please listen to me. Don't worry." Ada patted her shoulder. "She's staying at the Monteleone. Brian told her *I* was getting the place cleaned up and didn't want her around just yet."

Tessa tried for a deep, calming breath. "How is she? Have you seen her?"

"Oh, no." The corners of Ada's eyes crinkled in a little smile, but then she looked off with a wistfulness Tessa didn't understand. "We just talk on the phone. She says she loved the trip, that it was as if 'God planned it,' her very words. She looks forward to other vacations abroad. I'd say she's happy again, almost like her old self."

"I should move out of that bedroom. Brian once said it was her favorite room." Tessa dipped another glass into soapy water and glanced over her shoulder at Ada. "She might want it freshened up for herself after the party."

Ada sipped her coffee. "Oh, she likes her old bedroom best, the one nearest her office."

"It'll be a miracle," Tessa mused, "if she doesn't find out before the party what went on in her house while she was away."

"Oh, that might happen, but everyone is being extra careful not to spill the beans. Even Darrie seems a little excited about the surprise. She'd never admit it. And, I hate to say it, but you never know what she's got up her sleeve."

"She's storing some of her things here. Is she moving back too?"

"Oh, no. She found a smaller rental in New Orleans. She'll be living alone for a while. Kyle's going into rehab." She hesitated. "When I heard how tight money is with them, I thought she might try to pressure Felice again to sell this house. But the way Brian helps her and Kyle—well, I don't think she'd want to cross her brother. Unless, it's behind his back and there's no chance he'd find out."

"I'm glad things are working out for them." *Rehab, where Uncle Lester should have gone,* Tessa thought as she wiped the last goblet in the set.

Ada drained her coffee cup and set it on the counter. "You worked a miracle here, honey. Felice wanted her home back. She'll get it, thanks to you, and Brian, of course. I can't get over it. The mansion looks almost exactly like it did before the fire, only fresher, brighter. And Felice didn't have to lift a finger to get it done. She won't be able to thank you enough."

"I pray you're right. Now if I could just find that Spanish chair for Brian. Which reminds me . . ." Tessa dried her hands on a paper towel and reached for the telephone. "I should call Mr. Forestier again. He's one I haven't checked with lately. He just might have a lead by now."

But when he answered, he told her he didn't.

On the day of the party, Tessa rose early in the morning. Dressed in jeans and a sleeveless shirt, she stood by the open window in her room and embraced the gentle light of dawn and a cloudless sky. *"Dear Lord,"* she whispered, *"thank you for letting me be a part of this household. Please bless Brian and every member of the Le Moyne family today and always as you gather them back into Your loving arms."*

No time to linger. For tonight's finale here, she wanted perfection. From the bedside table, she picked up her "To Do" list and went down to the kitchen for a cup of coffee with Ada and four maids hired to help with last-minute details.

Promptly at ten o'clock, the expected time, they directed a steady stream of caterers into the ballroom and helped arrange tables and settings for Felice's welcome-home festivities. The musicians would be coming around five o'clock in the afternoon. "A Chandelle's kind of party atmosphere" was Tessa's dream for the event. This one, a privately sad farewell for her, would celebrate Felice's welcome home.

After a late lunch, Ada declared she was tired and needed a nap. Tessa and the maids started a final check of each room. Around four o'clock, Tessa was alone in the second-story hallway. She paused to rearrange a bouquet of yellow roses in an urn. The house phone rang on a nearby table. She thought it might be Brian who wanted a tour of the house before Felice arrived and hurried to pick up the receiver.

"Miss, uh, Tessa Chandelle?" The man's voice on the line sounded thin and weary, one Tessa didn't recognize.

"Yes. Tessa Chandelle speaking," she said.

"I, Miss, I'm . . . Joseph Ardoin." He paused, his breathing labored.

The Mr. Ardoin, of Ardoin's Plantation? Tessa straightened, pressing the phone tight to her ear. "Yes, Mr. Ardoin? Are you all right, sir?"

He ignored the question. "I live just across the, uh, bayou." Again, a pause and a gasp for breath. "Ardoin's Plantation. You know . . . you know where it's at?"

The heartbroken recluse? All attention, Tessa said guardedly, "Yes. What can I do for you, sir?"

"It's what . . . what . . . I . . . can do for you, Miss."

"Do for *me*?" Tessa frowned.

"Yeah. Uh . . . your ad . . . in the *New Orleans Picayune*. You need a . . . chair." His breath seemed short again. "Spanish chair, huh?"

"Well, yes. A King Alphonse. Do you know about it?" Tessa asked.

"Sitting on it . . . The very one . . ." He coughed and then cleared his throat. "The Veillons . . . they had a pair." The scratchy voice trembled. "I . . . I bought one. That lady, Brian's wife . . . well, she got the other."

The Veillons, just as Ada had said? Nothing wrong with the man's mind? Tessa swung around in a suppressed whoop of joy, the phone cord pulling at her shoulders. *Thank you, dear Lord.* "You're sure, Mr. Ardoin?" she cried. "You're positive the chair is a real Alphonse?"

"Yeah, it's the one . . . you want." He paused, letting out an apparent gasp for air. "Uh, another lady . . . she wants it . . . real bad too. But the Le Moynes, such good old neighbors—"

"Please, sir!" Again, the man sounded—*sane. She could believe what he said.* Terrified she'd miss her only chance to get the chair for Brian, she begged, "I've just got to have it."

"Only if . . ." the raspy voice faltered, "only if you come . . . come right away, Miss."

Mind in a spin, Tessa rubbed her forehead. How could she even get to the plantation and bring the chair back? Ada had said the helicopter had taken off before sunup. *But to risk losing the chair?*

"Will you hold it for me?" she pleaded.

A croupy cough. "Sorry, Miss . . . have to be fair. . ."

"Wait, please. If I come over and pay you for it, could I leave it with you until I can get it home?"

The ear-splitting cough again. "My nephew, he's here . . . in his helicopter. He'll . . . deliver . . ."

"Oh, thank you." An excited tangle of nerves surging inside her, Tessa said, "I'll be there quick as I can. Promise you won't sell it to anyone else?"

"One hour. Or the other. . . the other lady . . ." The phone clicked off.

What now, Tessa? She swished her hair to one side of her neck, thinking hard. How to get there was the question. Inspiration struck. Gene. *His boat! Perfect.* She dialed his number.

When he answered, her words rushed, "I need help. Would you believe Mr. Ardoin just called from his plantation? He has the Alphonse! I have to get there within the hour. If we don't, he'll sell it to someone else who wants it as bad as we do. You've got to take me over there in your boat. *Right now!*"

"Not so fast," Gene stopped her. "The man might not be in his right mind. Maybe you can't believe him."

"Oh, but I can! He makes perfect sense. His place is full of antiques. Didn't you say I should be dying to get there?"

"Well, yes. But right now I'm on special assignment, about sixty miles or so from you. Anyway, Darrie doesn't want anyone else for the shoot—"

"Beg her to get a sub for you. She'll do it!"

"I'm telling you, Tessa, I couldn't get there in time to help you, no matter what. Minutes are ticking away as we speak."

"Give it a try, please. Darrie knows what that chair means to Brian. You get your interview, I get the Alphonse. We both win!"

"Listen, Tessa, there's absolutely no chance I can get away. Please understand that."

"But, Gene, Mr. Ardoin said—"

"Sorry. I gotta go. See you tonight."

"Wait!" Tessa pleaded. "If I find someone to take me there, could we use your boat?"

"Yeah, but at the last minute? You don't have the time either. Give it up or ask Ada to help you decide what to do."

"See you tonight," Tessa's voice dropped. "You can take me to my apartment like we planned?"

"Sure. Soon as the party is over." He clicked off.

Since Ada was asleep, Tessa didn't think she should bother her. Besides, her gaze had strayed out the window and landed on Cede. He ran a hand mower around an incline of azaleas. Just the man to take her to Ardoin's in that boat? In a gush of excitement, she told the maids she must leave at once to get the Alphonse. She added no further details about her plan except that she hoped to be back within an hour or so. As soon as Ada woke up, they should give her that message. She made sure a blank check was in the wallet inside her straw bag and then flew down the stairs. Outside, she rushed to jump into her car parked in its usual place under an oak tree.

She whizzed down the lane, left arm waving out the window in Cede's direction. She halted near him in a squeal of brakes. His face screwed up in surprise, he approached the car.

"What's going on? Some emergency?" He pulled out a handkerchief and mopped the sweat from his forehead.

"It's the Alphonse chair. I just found out I can get it right now, but I have to hurry. It's at Ardoin's plantation. If I get there within the hour, it's mine. Imagine, so close, right under our noses *all this time*."

"And how do you know that?" Cede asked.

"Mr. Ardoin himself called." She added quickly, "He sounded just fine. He knows all the details about the chair."

"Hard to believe the man phoned you." Cede gave a doubtful shake of his head. "So how do you plan to get there?"

"I called Gene, but he can't leave work. He says it's okay to use his boat. You know where he keeps it anchored, don't you?"

"Yes, sure, but—"

"It's our one and only chance for that chair. Think how happy we can make Brian."

"Now, Tessa, I don't know." Cede rubbed his hands together. "How you gonna get it back here?"

"His nephew is there in his helicopter." Tessa gave him a "no-problem" smile. "He'll fly me back home with it. Isn't that *luck*? We can always get the boat later."

Cede removed his straw hat, ran grass-stained fingers through his hair, and glanced toward the bayou. "Does Ada know about this?"

"No. She's taking a nap. I don't want to wake her up. I told the maids I'll be back soon."

"Well, now—" Cede hesitated, his brow furrowed.

Tessa's hands chopped the air between them. "You don't know how long I've prayed to find this chair."

"And if I don't take you there?"

"I'll have to find another way."

"Like how?" Cede's thick, caterpillar eyebrows shot up. "Don't tell me you'd take that boat out alone?"

"No," Tessa baited with a smile. "That's why you'll take me, right?"

Cede's shoulders lifted in a deep breath, then relaxed. "Well, I guess I don't have any choice, do I? Ada would want me to help you. Yeah, she'd be glad to see Brian get that chair. Okay. Let's go."

With Cede beside her in the car, Tessa zigzagged down one trail and then another to the place she remembered Gene anchored his boat. She slid the car under a towering oak and parked. As they flung open their doors and got out, she caught the start of a smile on Cede's face. *He's excited as I am*, she thought.

Cotton ball clouds laced with black swatches dotted the sky, and the August sun beamed hotter than any scorcher Tessa remembered. Discomfort aside, her excitement soared when she spotted Gene's boat partly hidden by low-slung oak branches near the water's edge. A long-necked blue heron launched itself from its perch near the stern and flew off with a reproachful backward look, leaving behind the sounds of a muted screech. Then, sudden, uneasy quiet.

"See it?" Tessa cried. "It's just waiting for us." The air clung to her face, oppressive and still. Only then did she realize that, in her hurry, she'd forgotten to grab a straw hat. She didn't care. Nothing mattered except getting her hands on that chair first.

She watched Cede approach the boat and tackle the outboard motor like a schoolboy eager to play hooky. Soon it roared and, once seated in the narrow space behind the wheel, he extended a hand to help her climb in behind him. Her heart hammered with a wild kind of joy defying any hint of dread. Cede swung the vessel around as easily as Gene had done the night of their moonlit ride. Now they headed in a westerly direction, toward the plantation, away from spotty greenery and clots of lilies on the pulsing water.

"Will Brian ever bless you for doing this!" Tessa cried above the sound of the motor.

"Ada won't believe her eyes." Cede chuckled as if the farther they got away from home, the more he got into the spirit of their adventure.

"Brian won't either." Tessa stared straight ahead, hot wind tearing at her face and hair. "What a surprise if he's home just in time to see that copter land with his Alphonse."

Cypress trees and sightings of leafy growths on the water disappeared. The boat gained speed.

And then it slowed. Tessa glanced back at Cede.

Ear cocked, he frowned and bent forward. The motor sputtered. The boat slowed to a crawl, and his hands froze on the wheel. Tessa leaned over the side of the boat. Hyacinths fluttered in soiled blue beauty just below the surface of murky water.

"Oh, Cede. Do you think—?"

The motor choked and then died.

Cede rubbed his neck. "We're stuck. I don't just think it. I know it."

Tessa looked around at the mocking stillness about them and shaded her face with her hands. Perspiration rolled down her cheeks, sunlight doing a steady burn on her bare arms and legs.

"I shoulda known, shoulda been more careful." Cede pulled off his straw hat to fan his face.

"It's not your fault." Tessa's shoulders slumped. "What now?"

"For sure, we need help." Cede inhaled a long breath. "Get Ada on the phone. Let me talk to her."

Tessa fumbled to open her straw bag and rummaged inside. "Oh, no." She let out a frustrated cluck of her tongue and looked back at Cede. "I forgot my cell. I can't believe this! *My mind! Where was my mind? I lost it...!*"

Cede gave her a blank stare and shrugged. "Now don't worry. Someone will come along. Bound to, sooner or later."

But *when*? Tessa did worry and slapped at mosquitoes. They'd never make the plantation on time. Her one chance to get the chair lost within the next half hour. *The party tonight. Felice's homecoming. Brian had warned her not to venture out like this, as had Gene only minutes ago.* "Gene will guess where we are," she told Cede, struggling to sound upbeat.

"Yeah." Cede leaned over and rippled his fingers among hyacinth blooms. "But no telling when he'll be back from the station."

Right, Tessa thought. She watched a carefree pelican ease in flight above them and land on a far-off balding cypress tree branch. *Flight. If only the copter had been available.* She sighed and glanced down at a string of bubbles in the muddy water. *Snakes?* She shuddered and pulled back to wrap her arms around her chest.

"We'll be okay." Cede rubbed his hands and studied the sky. "No rain in sight. Now that's a relief. And, like you said, Gene's gonna figure out what happened. God will take care of us."

Minutes passed. Tessa checked her watch again. Almost an hour gone.

A sudden booming "Aha!" shot through the sultry quiet. Tessa jerked sideways to see a pirogue glide toward them. A tall, muscular stranger in blue overalls and wide-brimmed straw hat stood in the middle of the craft, push-pole in hand.

"Well, praise the Lord," Cede exclaimed.

Half rising, Tessa waved frantically. "Help! Please, help!"

"Cousin Jacques," Cede yelled.

"Your cousin?" Tessa stared back at him.

"For true." Cede nodded.

Tessa clasped her hands together. "Thank you, God." She watched as the man slowed the small pirogue alongside the boat in the swirling water, his sharp black gaze fixed on the bottom of the boat.

"Aha," he repeated, as if sizing up the situation, and then turned to Cede.

The two men carried on in Cajun French. Tessa's glance darted from one to the other as she struggled to interpret every shake of their heads and hands. Of one thing she was certain, the big-eyed looks on their faces as they pointed to the hyacinths edging both sides of the boat meant trouble.

Finally Cede turned to her. "He'll take you to Ardoin's and then come back for me. His pirogue isn't big enough for the three of us. Besides, it's pretty old. It's sprung a few leaks. But he worked on it and says it seems okay now."

"So let's go." Rising to her feet, Tessa smiled at a solemn Jacques.

"I'll meet you soon as I can," Cede said. "Right off, you call Ada from Ardoin's phone to let her know you're all right."

"Don't worry," Tessa said.

Cede shook a finger at her. "Be sure to wait for me. Don't get in that helicopter alone with some stranger. I'll meet you there and ride back with you. I'll take care of Gene's boat later."

"Thanks, Cede. I hear you." Tessa reached for the hand Jacques held out to help her into his pirogue.

He nodded to the narrow seat behind him. She sat, rigid at first, purse on her lap and hands clutching the sides of the vessel. With a playful salute toward Cede, Jacques push-poled away, slowly at first, and then gained speed as they drifted farther into smooth bayou waters.

Tessa's spirits rose again, but this time to guarded heights. Would she be there in time to beat that other lady who wanted the chair? But if not and she was still there, she could tempt her by offering to buy it from her by doubling the price she'd paid. Whatever it took, if a deal was at all possible, she'd go for it.

Long minutes later, it seemed, and Jacques coasted alongside the bank that fronted the plantation.

"*Bien.*" He held out his hand to Tessa.

Bag slung over her shoulder, she gripped his strong fingers and jumped easily to shore.

"*Merci,*" she said and waved.

"*Au revoir, Mam'selle.*" He tipped his hat to her and gestured back over the waters. "Cede."

She nodded and smiled. "*Merci*, again."

As the man push-poled away, she surveyed the house, not startled by its run-down appearance. Even the barn, which was off to the side of the house, was battered at the sides, the roof caving in. From what she'd heard about Mr. Ardoin, no surprise he was too frail to maintain the house, barn, or grounds. But no help from family or friends? A helicopter here, he'd said? None in sight. That down feeling rushed over her again. The other woman had already beat her here and bought the chair? Now his nephew was taking her home with the prize?

She doubled her steps up the walkway, a curve of broken bricks that led to the front door. She climbed the three concrete steps, and then, just as she reached for the corroded knocker, the door opened.

A stooped, gray-haired woman in a faded blue housedress stood there. Her eyebrows rose in a startled look.

Tessa smiled. "Good-afternoon, Ma'am. I'm Tessa Chandelle. I'm here about the Spanish chair. I hope I'm not too late."

"Excuse me?" the woman said quietly, a touch of Cajun-French accent coloring her tone.

"This is the Ardoin home, isn't it?" Tessa asked.

"Well, yes, it is. And I'm Mable, Mr. Ardoin's sister." She pursed her lips and gave Tessa a long, appraising stare. "There's no Spanish chair here."

"But there is. Or was," Tessa said. "Please, just let me talk to Mr. Ardoin. He's expecting me. He called me about the Alphonse."

Mable shook her head from side to side. "It is not possible my brother called you. Besides, sometimes our phone works, sometimes it doesn't. Today it is not working."

Tessa frowned. Maybe this woman didn't know about her brother's private business or might even suffer from some kind of dementia. "But Mr. Ardoin did call me. He said he has an Alphonse chair for sale. Are you sure he didn't sell it to someone else?"

Mable exhaled a tolerant breath. "Believe me, *ma chére,* I am telling the truth. You are mixed up." She opened the door wider and stood aside. "It is so hot out here. Come in and see for yourself. We have just plain furniture. A phone, yes. Look there on the table by the couch. Dead."

"Thank you." Tessa entered, her shoes squishing on the bare wood flooring. "I'm in an awful hurry. I don't mean to offend you, but the elderly man who called me said he was Mr. Ardoin of Ardoin's plantation."

Mable shook her head. "That cannot be."

Tessa's eyes darted around, searching corners. But as far as she could tell, the place was sparsely furnished. No obvious signs of an Alphonse or antiques, and no other person in the room. Had he sold it and this Mable didn't know?

"Could I talk to his nephew, the one who has the helicopter?"

Mable frowned. "A helicopter? A nephew. Just him and me is all. No other family member."

"But he told me—" Tessa began.

"No, no. Oh, you are so mixed up."

Tessa stared at her. "But your brother said— "

"I am telling you the truth. No nephew, no other person here but him and me. Nobody has been here today, not yesterday, not the day before." Mable released an impatient sigh. "And I know every stick of furniture my brother ever owned. If you're looking for a fine antique, you're looking in the wrong place."

Tessa frowned. "I did get a call from someone who said he was Mr. Ardoin."

Mable gave an impatient shake of her head. "You keep saying that. Well, let me show you why that cannot be true. Come." She flicked a finger and walked toward a doorway in the back of the room.

"I'm sorry to bother you, but this chair is so important—" Tessa followed her down one hallway and then another, on to a flight of stairs. They went by wide open doors, and Tessa threw hurried glances inside the sparsely furnished rooms. No sign of an Alphonse or other antique furniture. An eerie feeling spiraled inside. She recalled every piece of gossip she'd heard about Mr. Ardoin. *What if*—?

They entered a large, airy room furnished with a bed and a table beside it with a coffee pot. Mable nodded toward the south wall and stepped up to the elderly man who sat in a wheelchair. His face was turned toward the window that overlooked the bayou. "Here he is, my brother."

"Oh, so he's the one who called me." Tessa felt a renewed flutter of excitement. Her gaze took in the frail gentleman in khaki trousers, a white shirt and a black bow tie. His hands rested in his lap. At his side, a small white towel bulged, as if something lay beneath it.

Mable put a hand on his shoulder. "Big brother, Tessa Chandelle is here to see you. She said you called her. Tell her she's wrong." She motioned Tessa to step forward. Then she stood aside, her brow furrowed.

"Hello, Mr. Ardoin." Tessa smiled and walked up to him. "I came for that Alphonse chair."

His gaunt face, framed by scraggly grey hair, turned to her, a little-boy look in watery, sea-foam eyes.

Tessa stepped closer. "Mr. Ardoin?"

His lips parted in a trembling grin. A sudden move and he jerked out both hands for a steel-like grip on hers. "Oh, my Julianne, my love! You're back. I knew you'd come!"

"No, no, sir. I'm not Julianne—" Tessa tried to pull away, but his hands held tight. "I came for the Alphonse chair." She turned to Mable. "Tell him I'm not who he thinks I am."

Mable rushed up to him, her smile cajoling. "Let go, big brother. She's not your Julianne." Her fingers struggled with his, but she couldn't loosen his hold on Tessa's hands. "This girl is a stranger. Let her go, I say. Julianne will be here later."

"She *is* my Julianne!" The man's hard fingernails dug deeper into Tessa's flesh. He elbowed Mable aside. His chest swelled in a long breath, and he looked down. In a decided heave, he struggled to his feet. The wheelchair screeched off behind him. The towel slid off his lap. Tessa saw it then, the gun.

It exploded as it went crashing to the window panes.

Shattered window glass.

Fragments spewed down the man's back and clinked to the floor.

Tessa screamed.

The man's grip tightened, vise-like on hers.

"Let the girl go, I tell you!" Mable yelled, her hands shaking his shoulders free of glass fragments.

"No!" Tears flooded his eyes. A trembling smile, and he reached a hand to caress Tessa's cheeks. "My love, my sweet Julianne."

"Please, don't—" In a sudden jerk, Tessa managed to pull away from him. She backed off toward the doorway.

Eyes fixed on her, he staggered. A heart-rending cry, and he fell to the floor.

On his hands and knees, he looked up at Tessa. Tears flooded his face. "Oh, Julianne. Why did you leave me, Julianne?"

"I'm not her. Believe me, Mr. Ardoin!" She looked at Mable. "Is he— will he be all right?"

"Yes! Go, now!" Mable waved her off. "Hurry." She knelt on the floor and cradled him in her arms. "It's okay, it's okay. Hush, now. Julianne will come. Real soon."

"I'm so sorry." Tessa couldn't stop the tremor in her voice. "Mr. Ardoin, Miss Mable—please, forgive me. The broken glass—the window—can I help?"

"No! You go. Quick." Mable gave a distressed shake of her head. "Don't come back! He's so confused. That gun," she murmured, "how he got a hold of it again…"

Tessa stumbled away in a blind rush down one hallway and then another, toward the front room and out the door. On the walkway, she stood still, hand on her chest to quiet her heartbeat. She or one of the Ardoins might have been killed or hurt. She muffled a *"Dear Lord, please have mercy on them! And please forgive me for…for…"*

Her breath in tattered gasps, she couldn't finish her plea. She started down the walkway, her gaze scanning the bayou. No sign of a boat with Cede and his cousin. No sound of a copter overhead. Everywhere stillness and fading sun.

A trembly sigh, and she looked at her watch. Six-thirty. Guests would soon be arriving at Le Moyne House. And the musicians? Ada counted on her to be there to guide them upstairs when they arrived. She should have let the maids know she was going to the Ardoins' in hopes of getting that chair. They would have told Ada. Now only Cede knew she'd come here. He and Jacques had problems with the canoe or he would be coming for her. As for Gene, he might be late arriving for the party due to some other assignment. Maybe no one at Le Moyne House knew where she was.

She pulled a tissue from her purse and wiped droplets of perspiration from her face and neck. A shady spot under an oak beckoned in the corner of the yard. Slinging her straw bag over her shoulder, she went to the tree and leaned against the trunk. She prayed someone else, if not Jacques, had rescued Cede. He or Gene should come for her soon.

For now, nothing to do but wait.

She squinted into the silent distance. Not only had she endangered the Ardoins tonight as well as herself, Lester Chandelle's niece had also ruined the homecoming party for Felice. Besides, hadn't Brian warned her to stay away from this plantation? That special moment in her career she had struggled to earn? Lost, too, because of her impulsive, foolish act.

"Oh, Tess," she could hear her father say, "you'll never learn when to use your head instead of your heart."

Chapter XV

Setting sun.

Twilight.

Tessa slapped at mosquitoes buzzing in her ears and slid down to a sitting position against the yard tree, her back stiff against the trunk. Her dry throat ached, and her hair lay hot and pasted on her neck. She drew up her legs and cradled them against her chest, her gaze locked on the somber bayou waters flecked with glistening moonlight. *How long, oh, Lord?*

Dark deepened and showed pinpoint stars. She pictured party guests walking up to the entry doors at Le Moyne House. Inside, there would be talk about her and Cede. Gene—she hoped, not Brian, whom she didn't want to face now—soon to their rescue?

Owls hooted and, from somewhere, dogs barked. On the ground behind her, the flutter of leaves. Snakes, the thought leaped, and no telling what or who else might lurk in the shadows. She scrambled to her feet. Her gaze veered back to the house. Light in the windows, but silence there. No way could she dare knock on the door and ask to go inside.

Moments, and a low but sure drone shattered the quiet. She jerked and looked up. *A helicopter. Please, God, let it be someone coming for me.* Half-crying, half-laughing, she waved frantically as the copter dipped and then made a gradual slow lift upward and away, finally out of sight.

Head down and now too weary for tears, again she sat, her gaze shifting from the bayou waters for a possible boat and then to the sky for an approaching plane.

Unsettling quiet. She glanced at her watch.

Almost eight-thirty.

A moment and, ear inclined, she thought she heard it again, that soft but sure roar of a plane. She jumped to her feet. Hands waving as before, she ran back and forth on patches of grass or dry ground. The helicopter lowered and continued to descend. No doubt about it this time. Someone was coming for her.

The plane landed near the crumbling skeleton of the barn, swirling dust in a swathe of light from a lower window in the house.

On the passenger's side—no mistaking the profile—*Brian*.

Her gaze fixed on the helicopter door. It opened, and he jumped out. He wore a white dress shirt and dark trousers, a tie loose at his neck. His hair wind-rumpled, he bounded toward her.

Eyes misty, she rushed to meet him.

"*Tessa!* Are you all right?"

"Yes." She went into his open arms.

"If anything had happened to you—!"

"I'm sorry," she whispered. "So sorry."

"Gene told me what you were up to." He held her back, a touch of reproach in his tone. "Why didn't you listen to me?"

"Where's Cede?" She changed the subject before he could pursue it.

"A crew just brought him and Jacques home. The pirogue started to leak." His voice trailed on the stifling night air. "The guys are okay. Let's go." He wrapped his hand around hers and led her in a half-run toward the waiting aircraft. "At least you told Gene about that call." He paused and helped her climb inside the plane. "Too bad you didn't let me know." His strained voice grew louder over the engine's roar.

"I wanted to surprise you," she said.

"You did, all right."

"Welcome aboard," the pilot said.

Tessa caught the man's amused smile as he watched her and Brian settle behind him.

Their elbows touching, Tessa swallowed the throb of guilt in her throat, only too aware of the strained look on Brian's face. She had disappointed him, worried him. No way would she tell him about Mr. Ardoin's gun that accidentally went off and might have hurt or even killed one of them. The aircraft lifted. Slowly it roared away. Her hands tightened on her bag for comfort.

"The call turned out to be a hoax," she admitted finally, her tone defensive. "Someone tricked me."

Brian stared out the window. "I could have told you that."

"You *knew*?" Tessa frowned at his profile.

He massaged his jaw. "Yes."

"How?"

"The man is senile. He couldn't have called you. I warned you about him. Why didn't you listen to me and just take off like that? I've been worried half out of my mind."

"Okay. I said I'm sorry."

She leaned away from him. Her head ached. Knots in her stomach grew tighter the closer they got to Le Moyne House. Who might be waiting to see them land? Surely Ada and Felice must be upstairs with guests. Would Darrie and Simone be outside, pretending to be worried about her?

She held her breath as the helicopter descended on the strip near the barn. When the craft came to a standstill, she braved a look around. Artificial lights mixed with moonbeams flooded the area. She saw a flock of cars parked up and down the lane and driveway. A few people hung around the walkway, obviously waiting for the copter to land as she and Brian had done her first day here. Would they rush forward, want to talk?

But she didn't want to meet anyone. Not now.

"Folks have been worried about you," Brian said. "That Ardoin is known to keep a gun at his side. You could have been hurt."

"Well, I wasn't. So, please, I just want to forget..." *Tell him the gun did go off? Never!* No telling how he would react.

The helicopter's growing whir made it hard for them to hear each other. He motioned to his ears. "I need to talk to you. . . "

"Please, later..." her voice rose. "Those people out there...tell them I'm fine."

The plane landed in a rise of fluttering debris.

Their fingers barely touching, Tessa went through the motions of letting Brian help her out.

She waved toward onlookers, not able or even trying to make out any of the faces. She headed off in a run toward the back entrance to the house. New tension fired up every little nerve in her body. Any talk tonight should have been about the honoree, not about Lester Chandelle's niece.

Behind her, she heard Brian call, "Mom is waiting to meet you—!" His voice trailed off.

Meet his mom? She couldn't do that now. Upset as she was, no telling what words might come out of her mouth and ruin tonight even worse than she already had. She gave him a dismissing wave of her hand. Breath in sharp gasps, she headed toward a back door. Finally there, she pushed it open and rushed inside, up the stairs to her room. She entered and closed the door, shutting out the vague sounds of music from the floor above.

She stood still, heart pounding, thoughts a jumble she tried to clear. No way could she dress and show up last minute for the party. She should stay in her room until it was over and she had gained back some control of her nerves. That would be best for everyone. Later, she'd meet Felice. Then, as she and Gene had planned, he'd take her to her apartment.

As for Brian, what must he really think of her now? They hadn't meant to spill out their feelings for each other the night her folks visited here. That was a mistake, the result of an impulsive moment he doubtless wanted her to forget—and she must. *So Gene was right, the sooner she walked out of this house, the better for her? For Brian too?* He knew as well as she did their lives were going in different directions.

She tossed her purse on the bedside table and rushed to open the armoire. She yanked her two overnight bags from the top shelf and flung them on the bed to pile in her belongings. A flurry of hot tears scalded her cheeks as she emptied chest drawers and jerked garments off hangers. But when she saw the dress, that jade chiffon, she hesitated. "*Mom is waiting to meet you,*" Brian had said.

Could she do it, miss the entire party? Brian's mother expected to see her there. But how could she handle talk or pity, even inquiring looks about her foolish escapade at the Ardoin's? In the back of her mind, one of her mother's favorite sayings unreeled in a flash: *Some things in life are so hard to do, they're easy. You have no choice.*

She drew a quick, relenting breath. No time to lose. She smoothed the jade dress and then gathered the accessories she had chosen to wear with it.

All things work together for good. . . ? Her faith far from even a mustard-seed size, she dragged her packed bags over by the marble pedestal table that held her Zuni jar. Luckily, she told herself, she'd already made sure Felice's office and desk were in order, photographs neatly stacked in a drawer, along with the house keys and Mirbeau's number where she could be reached if necessary.

Momentum held while she dialed Gene's phone. He answered against the background noise of chatter and laughter upstairs. When he answered with an "Oh, Tessa" and started to say how worried he'd been about her, she interrupted him with a "Please, not now."

"I'll be down for the party," she rushed the words. "Can we leave as soon as it's over?"

"You bet," he said.

She hung up and went into the bathroom for a quick shower. Later, the heat of the hairdryer helped soothe her nerves too long on overload. Her hair barely dry, the cell phone on the bedside table rang. She jerked it up and mumbled a hurried, "Hello."

"Honey, it's Ada. Are you all right?"

The "angel" voice caught her off guard and almost drew new tears. Her hand relaxed on the receiver. "Yes. Oh, Ada, I'm so sorry about Cede and his cousin—"

"They're fine, and they just got here for the party. Jacques' boat sprang a leak. They were stranded. That's why they couldn't get back to you."

"Oh, Ada, I'm so sorry—"

"Stop that. Can you be ready in fifteen minutes or so?"

"I'll try."

"Good girl. The party will be over in less than an hour. I'll meet you at your door and walk you up to meet Felice."

Dear Ada, the comforter. A friend from the moment they'd met, she wanted to be at her side when she met Brian's mom, the ultimate judge of how well she had fulfilled her contract. She rushed her makeup, fingers unsteady as she fumbled with a rosy lip gloss and then brushed her hair to a shiny fall around her face. Breathless, she slipped into the jade dress and, in a frenzied moment, inspected her reflection in the gilt-edged mirror. An unnatural brightness tinted her cheeks and glowed in her emerald eyes. *Felice's homecoming*, she reminded herself, *and my goodbye.*

The expected knock at the door. Rushing to answer it, she drew a deep breath for a double dose of courage.

Ada stood there in a soft camellia-pink blouse and skirt with a strand of pearls at her throat. "To look at you, honey," she said, "no one would ever guess what you've just been through."

"Oh, Ada, thank you for being here." Tessa touched her hand. "I should have told the maids where I was going or left you a note. I can never apologize enough for the worry I caused today."

"The worry *you* caused?" Ada frowned, her voice whispery as they walked toward the stairs." Darrie and Simone are to blame, honey. The Lord will deal with them."

Tessa stared at her.

"Brian was here early, of course, and asked where you were. No one had any idea." Ada caught her hand, her voice low and hurried. "When Cede finally showed up, he said you'd gone to Ardoin's and explained about the call you got about the chair. That's when Darrie arrived. Somehow Brian suspected her part in that plot about the chair right off. She didn't want you here tonight."

"I knew that," Tessa said.

"He demanded she come clean with everything she'd done," Ada went on. "She cried and confessed she'd hired an actor Kyle knew well to pretend to be Mr. Ardoin and make that call to you. She said you were just an employee and didn't belong here tonight. You were done with your work."

"And Simone—?"

"Darrie covered for her. Brian might not suspect the truth, but I do." Ada gave a vehement shake of her head. "I have no doubt Simone was right there with her, laughing and planning it all."

Tessa hesitated, her hand on the banister as they started up the stairs. Memory flashed. Hadn't Simone warned she'd be sorry she refused the latest job offer at her TV station? Like Darrie, she wanted to get her out of the house and out of Brian's sight. She should have suspected that almost from the moment they met her first night here.

"Brian was so mad at Darrie," Ada was going on, "I thought he'd have a stroke, or give her one."

"All of this in front of their mom?"

"Yes. But then, out of the blue, he said, 'Maybe the Lord used you today, Darrie.'"

"He said that?" Tessa stared at her.

"His exact words." Ada shook her head, still in apparent disbelief over Brian's remark. "Then he broke into a run for that copter before anyone could ask what he meant."

"There's so much about today I'd like to forget." Tessa straightened her shoulders, her chin going up. She wouldn't stoop to a confrontation with Darrie or Simone and spoil Felice's homecoming more than she already had. She'd make the rest of her finale here one she'd have no reason to regret.

Ada touched her arm and slowed her step. "There's something you ought to know about Felice—"

"Miss Ada!" a chirpy voice called.

They halted past mid-stairs as a petite blonde maid caught up with them. "Your potato chip cookies, they're almost gone from the table," she said. "And the pecan pralines too. I looked in the kitchen, but I can't find the extra batches Mr. Brian said you made."

"They're right there on the counter in that—" Ada began, and then waved a hand in surrender. "I'll have to show you. You go on up, Tessa. You'll see Felice right off."

Something she ought to know about Felice? The lady didn't like the way her house looked? Tessa hesitated and stared back at Ada. Did she also want to tell her Brian's mother was upset when she found out Uncle Lester's niece had been living here, and now she had also ruined her

221

homecoming?

Tessa intoned another "Dear God, please" and gripped the banister for support as she trudged slowly up the remaining stairs to accept her fate.

She approached the door to the sound of soft music and chatter. Groups sat in circles, others lingered around the serving tables, especially the one with the red velvet cake and other desserts. Here and there giggles or quiet laughter sounded in a roomful reminiscent of a Chandelle party.

And there she was, the lady who doubtless had posed for the portrait above the Steinway piano. Felice, older and a bit matronly around the waistline, wore a fashionable, off-white, two-piece outfit. Short, gray-blonde hair curled softly around her oval face. Subtle makeup accented her startlingly blue eyes. Whatever distress she'd suffered over something she didn't like about the house or the scene between Brian and Darrie earlier, Tessa thought she hid it well.

Now the lady exchanged pleasantries with a young couple.

Tessa stood aside, another silent "Dear God" plea for courage to face her when the moment came.

Brian emerged from a melee of guests.

"Tessa." The strong, warm fingers she had come to know well caught her hand.

"Brian." An up and down of emotions warred inside her.

"The night we met, you wore jade." His voice lowered, his fingers tightening a fraction on hers. "You looked stunning then, and you do now."

Startled that he should mention the night they met, she murmured, "Thank you, and you look handsome," disturbingly aware of his tall, broad-shouldered physique. Now he also wore his suit coat and had knotted his tie.

In those few seconds while waiting to meet Felice, Tessa sensed something different about him. After the compliments they'd just exchanged, he fell silent, his manner subdued. No surprise, guilt nagged again, that her escapade at Ardoin's had cooled his party mood.

Felice nodded the guests to a refreshment table and then turned to her and Brian.

"Mother, I'd like you to meet Tessa—"

Before Brian finished the introduction, his mother reached to clasp her hand.

"How do you do, Mrs. Le Moyne," Tessa said. "I'm sorry to be so late."

"Don't worry about that." Felice said. "We're just happy you're all right. It's a pleasure to meet you, Tessa." A smile accented the lines at the corners of her eyes, and she gave Tessa's hand an extra squeeze. "I can't tell you how delighted I am with everything you've done. It's one of the most wonderful surprises I've ever had."

Tessa could only look at her, each word replaying inside her like an answer to prayer. "Thank you, Mrs. Le Moyne," she said softly. "You don't know how much I've wanted to hear you say that. Your approval means everything to me."

A tall, gray-haired man in a dark suit came up, jovial brows lifted in a grin.

"Now let me introduce someone very special to me," Felice said. "Tessa Chandelle, please meet my fiancé, Lucian Patin."

Tessa's startled gaze flitted from one to the other. A smile and hand extended to meet his, she said, "Congratulations, Mr. Patin. I hope you'll both be very happy."

He lifted her hand to his lips. "*Merci beaucoup, Mademoiselle* Tessa," he said with what she thought might be a Parisian accent, "for your good wishes and for restoring my fiancée's home to her great pleasure."

Dazzled by his charm, Tessa wondered if Felice's engagement was what Ada was going to tell her when the maid interrupted them earlier on the stairs. How fortunate for this handsome couple to have found each other. And how long had Brian known about this? She looked around and saw him engaged with an animated group.

Warmed by the couple's open-arms approval, Tessa found it easy to say, "I hope you won't mind if I leave as soon as the party is over. I need to settle into my apartment in New Orleans before Monday. I'll be helping the staff at Mirbeau's with a decorating project."

"Lucky, both you and that house. You'll work well together." Felice gave her another animated smile. "I understand your time is limited. Perhaps we can meet for lunch one day?"

"I'd like that."

"By the way, Lucian and I will have a home in the city. I hope you'll find time to help me decorate it."

"A second home," Tessa applauded. "I'll be glad to work with you."

Other guests came up. Before they might have a chance to mention the episode at the Ardoins, Felice introduced Tessa as "the antiques expert and talented decorator who restored our home almost exactly like it was before the fire."

Basking in praise she had wanted to receive, Tessa gradually eased into the crowded room and bumped into Estelle and Martin. They hugged, Estelle whispering in her ear, "God love you, friend!" Then, with a giggle, "You look more beautiful than ever in that dress I picked out for you." Talk about the food, the music, and Felice's engagement followed. To Tessa's relief, not one word about her disastrous afternoon at the Ardoin's.

When Tessa apologized for not being around to help hostess the party, her friend said, "Nothing to do, really, except smile and mingle like all the guests seem to be doing. Margie and her team have everything under control. Oh," she lowered her voice and glanced sideways, "Darrie and Simone."

Tessa turned. She saw an animated cluster of guests around the two, obviously the center of attraction.

"Mother doesn't want to live in this house any more than I do," Darrie's gleeful tone rose. "I knew all along she'd want to sell," Simone added.

Tessa turned to Estelle. "Did you hear that?"

"I got in on the buzz earlier. It seems Felice did agree to sell. And, gossip says we'll hear another big announcement or two," her friend whispered, and then turned to extend a hand to an approaching guest. "How nice to see you, Catherine!"

Tessa exchanged smiles with the newcomer as she and Estelle led her to a table nearby for finger sandwiches and cold drinks. Yet her mind was locked on what she'd just heard about Le Moyne House. The apartment in New Orleans would not be a second home for Felice and her husband, but their only home? And Brian had said he wanted to please her by returning Le Moyne House to its former glory?

She drew a long, trembling breath. Simone and Darrie must have been right when they said she wasn't needed here, that Brian had offered her a job out of guilt. Wasn't that what she herself had believed from the start? Uncle Lester had caused problems for the family and so had she. Not God, but feelings for Brian had led her here. How could she have allowed that to happen, especially after she met Simone, his supposed second love?

Another look around, and she found him, his dark head inclined attentively in a circle of guests now by a refreshment table. The change she'd noticed in him tonight could be nothing more than sadness because Le Moyne House would be sold. She understood the pain of signing away a beloved ancestral home. Earlier, besides the news about Felice's engagement, had Ada also wanted to tell her the house was for sale? And what about the announcement concerning Simone, the one Estelle said folks would find out soon?

Tessa glimpsed the devoted housekeeper, seemingly unruffled as she mingled with the smile expected of a hostess. As for herself, gone was the relaxed mood she'd found before she overheard Darrie's comment. While her heart cried, *Poor Brian,* her brain answered, *None of your business, Tessa. This is a private, family decision.* She needed fresh air and eased toward an exit door.

She bumped into Gene. "Step outside a minute with me?"

Camera hanging around his neck, he wedged a path for them onto the balcony.

They walked up to the balustrade. Tessa tried to ignore the high flush that burned her cheeks. "Have you heard the news, Gene? This house is up for sale."

"I'm shocked as you are. Some think there's a buyer already."

"And is Brian okay with that?"

"So I hear."

Tessa looked out on quiet, shadowy trees and banks of flowers sprinkled with moonlit glitter. Brian loved this house. She just knew it. But maybe he had a change of heart and was relieved his mom no longer wanted to live here. Perhaps she wanted to get away from constant memories of her deceased husband in the old family home. As for Brian, had he finally accepted Maureen's death and wanted to move on with his life, with Simone? Whatever the family's motives, she'd always regret not finding the Alphonse.

"You look beautiful as ever, Tessa," Gene said, "but you must be tired. It's been quite a day for you, hasn't it? When you didn't answer your phone this afternoon—"

"I worried you, and I'm sorry. I let Darrie do a number on me."

"Who told you?"

"Ada did."

"Well, I found out Simone helped, though Darrie took all the blame to protect her."

"I heard that too." Tessa sighed and looked down to the tiled floor where she stood. "Thank God everyone survived. I pray the Ardoins can forgive me for upsetting them."

Gene glanced off toward the moonlit grounds, his manner reflective. "That quickie assignment Darrie and Simone insisted only I could do sounded fishy. But how was I to refuse? I'm only hired help."

"I'm glad I didn't involve you, after all. Except to hijack your boat. I'll pay for any damages."

"No harm done. Cede says my 'swamp yacht' survived without a scratch. Now Brian? That's a different story."

She raised a finger to her lips. "Sh! Drop it, please."

"Okay. I hear you." Gene shrugged. "Guess I'd better get back to work inside, or I'll lose my job for sure."

"I'll be there in a minute." Tessa pulled her cell from her side pocket. "I just want to check for messages."

As he walked away, she flipped open the phone. Her gaze froze on the words:

Chandelle's creditors paid in full. Donor/donors to remain anonymous. Receipt in mail. Congrats. Greg Jackson, CPA

She read the message again. There was no mistaking the news—*she and her parents were debt free.* She wanted to let out a whoop, and then stopped. Generous benefactors who knew her parents? Instead of their money going to the mission fields, they paid Uncle Lester's debts? Or, maybe Brian had compensated more times than she could count for her work?

She took a deep breath and looked off. No way would she and her parents accept donations to pay Chandelle's creditors. As soon as possible, they'd get to the bottom of this news meant to be good news for the family and return every penny to the would-be benefactors or benefactor. Right now she did know the One who always deserved their utmost gratitude. She looked up and murmured, "With all my heart, dear Lord, thank You for Your loving care."

Her last night here. From inside, sounds of music. While one burden was gone for now, another must be dealt with tonight. This one, only her heart could let it go. She slipped the phone back into her pocket. Soon the party would be over. She'd say good-bye and walk out of Brian's life forever.

Head lowered, she turned and went back inside.

At the door, Brian waited. "Tessa, we need to talk."

"Now?"

"Please."

Puzzled by the somber urgency in his tone, she let him lead her to a sparsely occupied corner of the room.

"Gene said your bags are packed." He frowned.

"Yes."

"It doesn't have to be goodbye for us." He edged closer, that mesmerizing gaze absorbing hers.

Yes, it does have to be goodbye, her heart answered. Ever the gentleman, he would give hope to the parting word. She glanced off where a couple swayed to the music.

"You're really leaving?" he asked. "When?"

"Tonight." She looked back at him and let the word fall softly, like a final curtain between them. "Why would I stay? My work is finished here. You know that. Your mother said she's pleased."

"Very pleased." He nodded and stroked his chin, as if something else was on his mind and he was trying to find words.

She shifted from one foot to the other, her eyes on his.

"Gene is a lucky guy."

"Gene?" she asked. "Why?"

"He's taking you away, isn't he?"

"Taking me away?" She tried for a smile. "He's only driving me to my apartment in New Orleans. Monday I'll start helping at Mirbeau's with a project for homeless people." *Just think of the facts,* she tried to tell herself. *Forget about this moment and him beside you.*

Martin walked up and tapped Brian's shoulder. "You're needed at the mic."

"In a minute," Brian said.

"The finale, I don't have to tell you." Martin walked off.

Brian reached for Tessa's hand, the pressure urgent. "Don't leave, please?"

"I'll be here if that's what you want."

She watched him walk off, still confused as to just what was on his mind. They had settled their business contract days ago. He wanted to give her more "thanks"? She had expected him to chew her out about the afternoon's escapade. Instead, he wanted to know if she and Gene were more than just friends? Nothing about today had made sense to her.

She watched him make his way to the podium, hand lifted toward his mother and Lucian, along with Darrie, in signal for them to join him. Gene followed, camera ready to focus on the group.

"Oh, Tessa, here you are." Estelle came up, a breathless hush in her tone. "Have you heard? Simone is moving away, flying with Rhoden to New York later tonight."

"Simone? Going off with Rhoden?" Tessa's brow went up.

"He offered her a job as vice president of his television enterprises. She starts in a couple of weeks."

"That was the mystery all along these past few days?" Tessa tried to keep her voice down. "And Brian?"

"That's all I know," Estelle went on. "He's still not talking." She turned her gaze toward the honorees with him. "Look at Felice and Lucian. What a handsome couple."

"Yes, they are." As for Brian, Tessa thought fleetingly, he'd probably join Simone later. Together they would climb higher up the corporate ladder. *As husband and wife?* For herself, she must think about a new life at Mirbeau's and look forward to what else was in God's plan for her.

Biting her lower lip, she watched Brian bent in conversation with the band leader. The music drifted off, followed by a drum roll for attention.

Facing the crowd, one hand in his side pocket, Brian picked up the microphone on the podium and flashed a smile around the room. "Darrie and I want to thank you for your presence here tonight to welcome our mother home."

The guests broke into rousing applause.

Silence again, and he went on, "This occasion marks a special milestone in her life and in the lives of the entire Le Moyne family." He gestured toward Felice and Darrie, Lucian beside them. "Tonight we celebrate the end of our mother's travels, at least for now. It also marks the beginning of another chapter in her life. How well she enjoyed her trip abroad, you can judge for yourself. Friends, it gives me great pleasure to present my mother now with her fiancé, Mr. Lucian Patin."

The couple bowed to cheers and applause from every corner of the room. "Speech! Speech!" some cried. Brian lifted a silencing hand. He stepped aside as he urged his mother forward and gave her the microphone.

"Our love and gratitude to all of you for coming tonight," Felice said, her voice vibrant in the stillness. "No one has ever been more blessed on a vacation. In time, all of you will come to know the wonderful man I met and fell in love with." Cheeks dimpling in a smile, she added, "I accepted his marriage proposal. Everyone here will receive an invitation to our wedding—soon."

Another round of applause.

"I return home to accept three gifts," Felice continued in the quiet that followed. "First, this reception with all of you, my cherished friends. Second, a beautifully redecorated home. For that gift, our gratitude goes to Tessa Chandelle, of the former magnificent Chandelle's House of Antiques, where she found many of the treasures we had lost. No one else could have done a more professional job for Le Moyne House." She looked around. "Tessa, where are you? Will you please raise your hand?"

Smile unsteady, Tessa waved to the crowd's hearty applause.

Like it used to be, her memory raced. Once more the Chandelle name was spoken with honor and respect. As the clapping died off, she whispered to Estelle, "Wait till I tell my parents about this."

Estelle smiled. "No decorator ever deserved more praise."

"The third gift we'd like to share with you is truly an answer to prayer." Felice motioned to Brian. "I'll let my son tell you about it, his gift both to himself and to us. To everyone who knows him."

Quiet settled over the room. Brian took the microphone again.

Tessa and Estelle exchanged questioning glances.

"Earlier we led you on a tour of Le Moyne House." Brian paused and looked around at the guests. "Today I became sole owner of the family home, and I want you to be the first to know my plan. In memory of my deceased wife, Maureen, it will become one of Louisiana's premier bread-and-breakfast establishments. The overseers will be our family's lifelong friends and helpers, Cede and Ada Guidry." He looked to his left. "Please stand, Mr. and Mrs. Guidry."

Tessa and Estelle craned their heads to see the couple on the far side of the room. They blew kisses toward them and then joined in fervent hand clapping, theirs the last to fade.

"So he does plan to join Simone and Rhoden —" Tessa whispered to Estelle.

She frowned. "You may be right."

"Thank you, Mr. and Mrs. Guidry," Brian continued. "All proceeds will go to spread the love of God here and abroad."

"Brian, the buyer?" Tessa raised a puzzled brow and turned to Estelle. "He wants to help *spread the love of God?*"

Estelle's eyes widened. "Talk about a night for surprises."

"My mother has already introduced the person responsible for restoring our home," Brian was going on, "and now there's something else I'd like to share with you. Actually, it's a confession I need to make."

Tessa and Estelle exchanged glances. Quiet fell on the room.

"I've come full circle today, a wiser man, I think," Brian went on. "No matter how grand, no tangible place alone can bring us happiness. My mother found that out when she met Lucian. The secret to ultimate happiness is love, and that starts in the heart. I've learned that. It's a gift from God."

Afraid she might miss a word, an inflection, Tessa scarcely breathed.

"All of you know about the events in Northern Ireland that caused the death of my wife and our unborn child. You probably know, too, the tragedy caused me to run from God and, like so many people when sorrow comes, I questioned His very existence. How could I believe His Word that all things work together for good to those who love Him? He let the innocent die, His child who loved and served Him every day of her life. And with her died the new life she carried."

Tessa didn't move, her gaze locked now with his turned her way.

"Someone asked me if, when I lost my family, I gave away everything else dear to me—just threw in my faith as well. I've been thinking about that. The truth is, now I know I just stuffed it deep inside me and pretended it didn't exist anymore. I chose to become a victim of hatred too. I became a prisoner—of bitterness."

Tessa folded her arms across her chest and rubbed at goose bumps. A tear rolled down one cheek. Another followed.

"When bad things happen to someone else, we say, 'There but for the grace of God go I,'" Brian continued. "Faced with tragedy, I became convinced God's grace did not exist. Not for those two innocent lives, and not for me. To 'Why, Lord?', no answer. I told myself Christianity is nothing but a fairy tale."

He drew a long breath, his eyes not changing their focus. Toward Tessa.

"I still don't understand why I had to lose a part of my family. But in my darkest hour, I turned *away* from God instead of *to* Him. As for how and why pain can work for good, maybe someday we'll get our questions answered if we don't here on earth. There comes a time when one has to let go," his voice faltered, "certain shadows of the past."

Not breaking eye contact with Brian, Tessa pressed her lips together to stop the tremor, her hands clasped before her.

"Maureen's last gift to me was a chair," Brian went on. "When the house fire destroyed it, I went looking to replace that symbol of her love. That search led me to you, Tessa. Not only did you give us back our home the way it was before the fire, you also helped me to realize the sin of bitterness and the joy of forgiveness. What's more, tonight when I thought I'd lost you, I knew I could no longer deny the truth, which is," he paused, his gaze never wavering toward her, "Tessa Chandelle, I love you."

Lips parted, she could neither move nor make words.

"Could it be that you—?" He held out a hand. It asked her to come forward and take it.

Tessa couldn't stop the fall of new tears. Was this a dream, or had he really called her name and said he loved her?

"Tessa," Estelle whispered, "do you?"

Tessa nodded.

"Then go on." Estelle gave her a gentle push.

She was vaguely aware that faces smiled and soft voices urged her forward. A path opened up for her.

"I love you, too, Brian." The words fell, a trembling murmur in the waiting hush. Eyes blurry and smile unsteady, she started slowly toward him, her steps measured.

When she had finally crossed over to take the hand he offered, rousing whoops and hollers filled the room. His arms suddenly around her, she forgot the audience and let her lips meet his.

A long moment, and he released her, but gently. "There's something I want to show you." He turned toward the wall behind them.

Only then did Tessa notice the tapestry that hung between the corner windows. He pulled it back. There sat the Alphonse.

Tessa stared at the elusive antique, another surprise of the evening. "Who—where—?"

"A gift from your parents. Mr. Wilby delivered it this afternoon." Brian touched her shoulder. "Will you sit, Tessa, please?"

She hesitated, her gaze shifting from him to the chair and back again to him. "Sit?"

He nodded.

She knew it then, what he had in mind. But before those faces watching them, the excited hush ready to explode as she was inside with unexpected joy? She felt color rise in her cheeks as she backed slowly onto the chair and tried for a smile that wouldn't take.

Brian knelt on one knee before her and took her hand in his, the cobalt gaze embracing hers. "Tessa, God's amazing grace sent me to your door that night at Chandelle's. I never thought I would love again. Because of you, I've found my way back to God and His purpose for my life. That purpose is to spend the rest of my days in His service and to love you if you love me too."

"I do, Brian," she said, her tone whispery.

"Will you marry me, Tessa Chandelle?"

Her lashes fluttered at the quick mist in her eyes. "Yes."

Cries of "Yea for Brian and Tessa!" filled the room. The couple embraced and then, as Gene turned his camera on them, they faced the guests.

"Be happy, Tessa." Gene winked.

"You, too," Tessa's lips framed the words.

Felice stepped up to the microphone. "The blessed homecoming of a lifetime," she declared. "Our family will never forget tonight. Thank you, everyone, for coming to help us celebrate not only three but four wondrous blessings from the Lord."

Whispers of the Past

EPILOGUE

The evening of their first wedding anniversary, Tessa and Brian were ready to leave the house and celebrate with a quiet dinner at Antoine's in New Orleans. On their way out, they stopped by the desk in Felice's old office to check their mail. They found new thank-you notes from workers in mission fields which invariably said monetary donations from MAUREEN'S BED AND BREAKFAST helped make their ministry possible.

"So, you see, Tessa," Brian said, "their contributions for your uncle's debts have been repaid several times over."

Tessa could only shake her head in wonder of how God's timing had worked for the good of the family. She turned to other personal congratulatory cards from friends and both sets of parents. Another, the handwriting a deep pink flourish, sent "Loving best wishes, from Sis Darrie and Kyle, too."

"Rehab worked a miracle on Kyle," Brian said. "I think those two will be just fine. Besides, it seems Darrie has finally accepted you into the family."

"I admit I had some growing up to do myself." Tessa caught his arm. "Just one more little peek at the babies before we leave?"

They stepped down the hall to the cribs in the nursery. Hands linked, they gazed at their sleeping three-month-old twins, Marie and Danny.

"Now don't worry. They'll be fine." Ada smiled from the doorway and then tiptoed inside. She approached the cribs and gently smoothed the pink blanket around Marie's neck with its fluff of dark hair.

"Oh, Ada," Tessa said softly, "I don't know what we'd do without you."

"Goes both ways," Ada whispered. "It's plain we need each other, isn't it?"

A couple of months ago, after trying to manage the popular bed and breakfast, Ada and Cede appealed to Brian and Tessa for help.

"We need a supervisor. Too much paperwork even with hired help," they complained.

Tessa and Brian had looked at each other and giggled like kids tearing into a rare gift on Christmas morning. In a matter of days, they packed their belongings and moved from their New Orleans apartment and into the former Le Moyne House. While Brian continued with his enterprises, Tessa was there with needed advice and support for employees.

"You didn't fool us, Madame CEO." Brian chuckled now, but softly, to avoid disturbing the sleeping babies. "We saw right through you."

"Didn't fool you?" Ada's brows lifted.

"Not for a minute. And we just loved you all the more for it," Tessa said.

"You and Cede couldn't bear to have our children grow up any place but here," Brian went on. "You want to spoil them like they were your own grandchildren."

"Like I spoiled you, Brian Le Moyne?" Ada grinned and waved them into the hallway. "Come take a look."

Tessa and Brian followed her out the door.

A couple of steps, and they stopped. A waning gleam of sunlight angled through a window and lit up the painting of Chandelle's propped against the wall.

"Adrienne sent it over. An anniversary surprise," Ada said. "Cede would like to hang it in the library above the Alphonse chair."

"Perfect place for it." Tessa stepped closer, before her the picture story of her life from childhood joys with her parents, to the pain of her uncle's betrayal, and then on to the blessing of meeting Brian at the ancestral home. Thoughts of her parents still in Ireland rushed, and she felt a childhood kind of loneliness for them. As they had taught her, she knew now without a lingering doubt that suffering can work for good to those who love the Lord. They are in His plan, and only He knows what is that plan for them here on earth.

She shifted her gaze to the flourishing jasmine in the Zuni jar on the windowsill. Her security blanket. Like herself, it had survived in the light of God's grace.

"We'd better go." Brian slipped an arm around her waist. "Tonight is our night."

THE END

Lena Roach

Lena Vidrine Roach was born and raised in Evangeline Parish, Louisiana. At an early age, inspired by her schoolteachers, she developed a love for reading and writing. After earning a Master's degree in English/Education, she became an English teacher.

Her first poem, "Success," appeared in Young People's Magazine published in Philadelphia, Pennsylvania. Other poems appeared in Kansas City Poetry Magazine and professional periodicals. She wrote a "Dear Teacher" column for several newspapers in Texas and Louisiana. Diverse articles appeared in Louisiana's New Orleans Times Picayune, Lake Charles American Press, Lagniappe Magazine, and The Voice. One of her short stories was published in Glamour Magazine, England. At present, she continues to live in Lake Charles and is devoted to a writing career in fiction, non-fiction, and poetry.